A Free Pass at
Infidelity?

A Free Pass at Infidelity?

What Science Tells Us about Human Promiscuity

YJ Chin

A Free Pass at Infidelity? What Science Tells Us about Human Promiscuity
Copyright © 2020 Chin Yi-Jiunn Dumas

ISBN: 978-981-14-8035-5

Dedication

To anyone who had loved and lost

"It is easy to see the beginnings of things, and harder to see the ends."
Joan Didion

"When you lost sight of your path, listen for the destination in your heart."
(Allen Walker, D-gray Man)
Katsura Hoshino

Contents

Nothing Stayed the Same

Her blouse would come to mind first whenever he recalled that day—bright royal blue, three-quarter sleeve, and bateau neck. Her inimitable manly-womanly voice would be next. For her, it was his ash colour hair, a little whiter on his right than the rest. It was a serendipitous encounter. A fateful one too as nothing stayed the same afterwards.

When everyone thought about that same day, fear and anger abounded. Plunging stock markets had opened up an untimely and ginormous sink hole underneath them. Later that year, America would elect her first black president. Everyone remembered that surely. Coincidence or providence? Nobody knew. Hope arose for most initially, and then faded for some gradually. Eight years later, the pendulum would swing to the other extreme, dashed all hope and portended unprecedented upheavals.

Nearer home, her memories centred on getting through medical school then. A decade later, she would run her own psychotherapy practice where he would become her client. The innocuous chance introduction would change her life forever. Six months of romantic roller coaster nearly broke her. Luckily, she survived the upheaval, thanks largely to the loyal voices in her head.

YJ Chin

Better to be Safe

"Better to be safe," she reminded themselves nonchalantly, her manly-womanly voice barely audible above the gentle breeze skimming her pale skin. His left brow twitched imperceptibly. However, he was visibly taken aback for an instant when he heard her repeated it again just now, even though it was no longer new. Her pensive gaze was steady on the misty horizon, sparsely interspersed with dark tiny Morse code-like dots and dashes: cargo ships and humongous oil tankers gliding slothfully across the open seas.

It was a cool February morning. The sun was nowhere around. Yet he could feel the slow burn around his ears. The constant breeze was much too gentle to neutralise the sensation but it helped somewhat to contain its spread to the rest of his sombre-looking face. How many repetitions are required for familiarity to breed, before a surprise is no longer a surprise?

...

He was completely stunned when she brought this up for the first time. Some months ago. Somewhere else. About three months after they had downloaded the popular WhatsApp on their individual smartphones while having coffee at a not-so-popular café in a remote part of town.

"Should have discovered this amazing tech earlier, it's so easy and so convenient, compared to SMS," she marvelled aloud to herself after a while, intending for his ears as well.

Thereafter, they became accessible to each other anytime, anywhere, unrestrained. Naturally, their individual social network on the app expanded to include others beyond themselves. By then, WhatsApp was spreading as wild fire; everyone seemed to be using it non-stop. Everywhere.

In a light-bulb moment, she became leery of their new-fangled tool. Do not lose self-control; it may not be as private, so she thought warily. Soon after, her first utterance of "better to be safe" to him.

"Familiarity cocoons us with a false security unawares, does it not?" She would ask on several occasions, without expecting an answer each time.

...

Where is this coming from this time? He reacted with dilated pupils. The question formed in his edgy mind definitely. Was he ready for an answer, any answer at that moment? He was uncertain. On the other hand, would a reply be forthcoming if he actually asked? He could not answer this either.

His faraway vision was also fixated on the blurry grey horizon. Now, a darker shade of grey. The endless series of puny iridescent waves bobbing on the turquoise sea could be quite hypnotic after a while.

"It's getting windy, a storm is approaching." Someone advised. He felt the ominous sensation around them. A massing of large and lumpy cumulonimbus clouds in the distant supported his feeling.

Her innocuous suggestion had caught him by surprise not so much by the sudden change of her posture as by its evidently obvious absurdity when juxtaposed with her bohemian personality. His idea of bohemianism anyway. Unconsciously, questions swirled at the back of his mind about her husband, her first apparently.

Will he be her last also?

What is going on?

What is she keeping from me?

Unexpectedly, some clouds parted in the gloomy sky. A shaft of slanted light instantly shot out and hit the silvery flatness of the sea before them. Both raised their hands instinctively in perfect silent synchrony: right for her and left for him. A noticeable warmth from the glare bathed their out-facing palms at the same time.

Maybe my wariness is unwarranted, he thought, hoping that this flash of glorious light might help to infuse some optimism into the sullen mood. Ominously, the gate in the clouds shut off abruptly, returning everywhere to its prior greyness.

"Of course, good to remain circumspect," he acquiesced.

"Let's wait for another time to fill in the blanks," his inner voice urged. Briefly deluded by the beguiling weather, he decided to let the earlier question in his brain slide, choosing to numb his not-so-new-yet-new surprise. Nonetheless, the suppressed unfulfilled curiosity hung inside his troubled mind. It was slowly gnawing at his heart also. He also sensed the blanks would likely remain unfilled.

He avoided looking at her, afraid she might see through his meagre attempt to mirror her nonchalant and distant demeanour. Then again, given her perceptiveness, the pained puzzlement in his glassy eyes would be transparent to her readily. He did not know, he did not think this either. His tender ears remained a little hot under his thin skin. This would have surely given him away if only she had turned to look at him then.

Meanwhile, the gust had upgraded itself, faster than they had anticipated. Picking up the big dried leaves about them, the gust carried the helpless leaves inland with fury. The air tasted saltier too. Suddenly, the grey sky electrified and blanketed the distant horizon with terror and beauty. The thunder rolled by soon after, threatening them as it passed.

"A storm has started on the horizon already. Shall we go?" She was not asking actually.

The Human Brain

For as long as she could remember, Faye had wanted to be a doctor since she was very young. Her parents (her dad was a brain surgeon and her mum was a paediatrician) discerned that in her, and had sought to help her realise her ambition as she grew into a beautiful young woman. Later, at medical school, Faye would decide to pursue psychiatry as her medical specialty. She considered the human mind to be full of mystery, which intricate workings continued to fascinate her even now as a psychotherapist.

The human brain and mind, aren't these the same? Anyhow, the brain is at the crux of the human condition and experience, Faye believed.

"Its study would span medical science and social science as well as the physical and metaphysical. Its boundless immensity would be most engaging," her inner voice gushed. The universe of knowledge—known and yet to be discovered—would pique her curiosity endlessly, and provide her with a rich experience for lifelong learning and challenge.

Wow! The endeavour before Faye overwhelmed her for a moment. With nervous anticipation, she imagined this worthy occupation to consume her utterly.

"Self-awareness, self-direction and self-pacing will be foremost if I'm to survive this arduous climb to the mountaintop. I won't want to lose my way, agree?" her inner voice counselled. The journey had just begun and she was resolute. Nothing could overwhelm her.

After graduation, Faye moved to a different city from her graduate school and her parents' home. She took up an entry-level psychiatrist position with NCDAZ Psychiatric Hospital, a social enterprise that charged patients according to their socioeconomic status and family backgrounds.

Initially, Faye had found herself a one-bedroom apartment at a rental locale within walking distance from her hospital.

"No time to waste on commute," she told herself.

Modestly furnished, it was a cosy pad, which someone starting out after years of medical school could afford. She did not need a fancy place really; she figured she would hardly have time to spend at her apartment anyway.

Work took up much of those early years. Crazy hours indeed. NCDAZ was the only specialist hospital located in a community where the demand for psychiatric services was apparently above the norm for the city and country.

Hmm...seems to have a higher concentration of older folks in this community. Reason behind NCDAZ being here? Faye wondered when this observation crossed her mind while walking home one day.

It made no difference to the hospital; out-of-town patients would travel there, adding to the already heavy load. It did not matter to Faye either. She loved her job now, occupying a front row seat at the theatre with a daily screening of the human brain: each day a different episode, each one just as interesting. Moreover, she was happy to be so absorbed all the time.

The Rendezvous

A hot breeze roused him from his afternoon torpor and woke him from his unexpected reverie. An episodic memory had sucked him back to a cool February morning. More than two years ago now but it seemed like only yesterday. It was a familiar place, reconstituted so vividly in his anxious mind.

Earlier, he had settled down at a wrought iron park bench in a corner that would afford him the most privacy in the area. Part concealed by the surrounding colonial-era terraced shop-houses. Part shaded by a large and lush Tembusu tree beside it. It was a familiar spot also. They had met here a couple of times before. Happier times! A bright smile formed on his slightly sweaty face, visible to anyone but himself. Luckily, he was alone. He had arrived early, as usual.

She should be here any minute now, he quickly assessed with the time displayed on his mobile phone. Back presently, he was now alert and mindful of his surroundings. Suddenly, a person appeared in his peripheral vision, sitting at the next bench about ten to twelve metres away. Instinctively, he stole a cautious glance at the man who seemed to be talking to himself, his hands gesturing wildly in the air.

"Could he be mental?" he asked softly, now looking a bit more intently at the man, who was too engrossed with himself to be conscious of anyone staring at him.

Kind of well-dressed isn't he? He was now doubtful of his first thought. A mental stereotype of a deranged person formed in his brain intuitively. However, he remained on guard.

"The incidence of mental illness among professionals and the white-collar workforce had jumped twofold over the last three years." His brain seemingly dredged up the statistic he had read somewhere recently.

"Better to be safe." Was that her whisper? He looked around there and then. Only two persons here: himself and the so-assumed deranged man. Thereupon, he spotted the tiny wireless pods in his ears and realised instantly that the pre-judged nut case was actually talking on his phone.

"How dumb of me," he voiced with embarrassment but the man was too far and too preoccupied to hear anything. He let out a quiet breath, becoming more relaxed at once. He then settled back to fiddle with his own phone.

No new message from her, he reconfirmed, and went back to being alert of anyone else stationary nearby or passing by ordinarily. The last few messages on their WhatsApp chat related to the arrangement of this rendezvous. After all, they had agreed to keep their chats concise, essential and to a minimum after the initial frenzy.

Meanwhile, the man he had mistaken to be mental but was actually normal got up from his bench and walked away, leaving the entire scene all to himself.

Had it been seconds only? Minutes probably but he felt as if the whole of eternity had compressed into that time. The best thoughts of her occupied his mind while he waited. Slowly, he became attentive also to the single-minded seconds ticking away on its own. The hot and humid afternoon air was now descending on his shoulders with a heavy foreboding.

Words swirled in his mind, forming and discombobulating all at once, and losing all sense on him. Words he had planned to say to her at this meeting originally. He fell back to the security of his mobile phone again, checking his WhatsApp ever so often—a superfluous gesture actually, as he had turned on the app's notification setting already. Nonetheless, a needful coping mechanism for now.

"Will she show?" Unbelievable: he found himself asking this for the very first time.

It's her volition ultimately, he supposed reluctantly, still harbouring a fading hope that she would show. Unconsciously, his intake of breath deepened then as if he was struggling with insufficient air.

The no-show would be her first ever. Her only time…and the last time. Why? He never suspected she would do such a thing. Did he miss something obvious like the case in *The Invisible Gorilla*?

YJ Chin

The Apple of My Eye

"We'll just have one child yea?" Keat proposed out of the blue, catching Mei by surprise. For some reason, they could not seem to settle on this matter despite having countless discussions.

It was a lazy Saturday afternoon. The humidity was heavy and the heat was unbearable. Nonetheless, the birds were having a whale of a time whilst taking shelter amongst the trees in the small gardens opposite their house.

Keat and Mei were taking refuge inside their master bedroom. The air-con was on full blast. Each of them in their own space with their own device. Mei was lying on the bed on her stomach with her lower legs gently flailing in mid-air, flipping through a female magazine. Keat was at his side of the two-seater sofa at the foot of their bed, engrossed in his spy novel.

By some mysterious impulse, Keat decided to put aside the remote machinations of *George Smiley* and *The Circus* crew for a while, in exchange for a personal life-impacting scene. Despite Mei's initial surprise, it was not something new: they had wanted to start a family for some time now.

"Don't think I have a problem with that, we'll have to live with either a boy or a girl then," Mei replied pragmatically, agreeing to go along finally. She turned to look at Keat but could see the near side of his face only. He was facing the windows, seemingly in a pensive mood; his pair of eyes appeared to be fixated on something outside but she could not be sure. For sure, she would love to see what was inside his thought bubbles right now.

On several occasions before, Mei had suggested the number two when they discussed this matter. However, she had always been unsure of herself and hesitant regarding this. Actually, the number was not her main concern. What really mattered was that they would have children. Mei had wanted children of their own for a long time now. Oddly, she viewed children as an undeniable proof of their union, as though this was essential to secure her marriage.

Mei also knew Keat would like to be the decision-maker for important matters like this—he had his way of going about it, and they would reach a conclusion eventually. She sensed a finality in his proposal this time while also cognizant that time was not on her side.

Another outstanding matter settled, Mei thought as she let out an inaudible sigh of relief.

"Yup, girl or boy, it doesn't matter," Keat replied whimsically, happy and surprised with the short and sharp closure. He returned his eyes to the novel, signalling that the discussion was over. He was eager to find out the outcome of another life-impacting decision. *George Smiley* had just been called back from retirement to flush out a Soviet mole, a double agent in *the Circus* after the recent death of *Control*, and *Peter Guillam*, his former protégé, would be assisting him…did he take up the assignment? In absolute secrecy of course, if he did.

Keat would move heaven and earth to have a girl if he really could. Mei knew this very well. She considered giving voice to this intuition for a while but decided to let it pass. Given the number decision, whatever would be would be. For herself, it really did not matter. But Mei had not been very honest with herself either—she would have preferred a boy. Whichever the case, one would be happier than the other would if their plan came to fruition.

In a few weeks' time, one lucky sperm, out of a quarter of a billion, would have the good fortune to marry with one of a hundred eggs in Mei's fallopian tube. Many months later, at the appointed time in the year of the Rooster, on a wet April morning in the small hours of the night, a baby girl would arrived on earth under the watchful eyes of Aries. Naturally. Keat was delighted, of course.

However, leading up to the birth, Mei was apprehensive. This was her first pregnancy, which had been difficult at times. Nonetheless, she did her utmost to educate and prepare herself for it—watching her diet and daily routine and managing her work stress well—to ensure the successful development of the amazing little life forming inside her.

As the pregnancy progressed, Mei felt more and more pressure to bring it to full term. This layered on more strain on the already tired wife as expected. However, nothing could have prepared Mei for the hellish throes she experienced during childbirth and the heavenly rapture when the slimy and fragile little body popped out of her, amidst the pungent smell of iron and hasty sounds of human activity. "Is this torture ever going to end?" Mei was unawares if she had asked this during her labour.

For Keat, the process felt smoother and shorter than he had expected.

"His perception is somewhat dubious, isn't it? He isn't the one going through the ordeal actually." Someone seemed sceptical.

"He cannot even begin to imagine what Mei has just gone through really." Someone-Else agreed.

Regardless, Keat was exceedingly glad that both mother and daughter were well at the end.

Unsurpassed, and etched deeply in the new mother's heart: the ineffable love Mei experienced with the baby rested on her bosom despite its brief and feisty protest of the doctor's gentle smack on its little buttocks a while earlier. The warm swaddle of the woollen wrap had not help either. However, the squall of the baby stopped immediately when she latched onto her mom's breast, and suckled hungrily, instinctively. A shallow dimple appeared on her pink cheek and then disappeared, and reappeared again. As long as her memory remained intact, Mei would remember this moment for the rest of her life.

She knows what to do even with her eyes closed, seems so natural. Keat thought, with wide-eyed amazement and fixation on the spectacle.

"Do newborns naturally feel hungry when they exit the womb?" He asked no one in particular, and quietly basked in the joy of this first-time experience, an once-in-a-lifetime event for both of them most probably.

The baby fell asleep shortly, flowing with the familiar rhythmic, and by now soothing pulsations of her mom's heart. Evidently, an invisible secure cord bonded mother and child still. Mei held her baby a little closer to herself, now snugged safely between her arms. She also loved Keat even more for her, and looked at him with a pair of endearing eyes, with the same love though somewhat special altogether.

For the first time: flesh of my flesh, life of our life. Can there be anything more wonderful than this? Mei sunk a little deeper into her bed with this thought, feeling extremely fulfilled at the same time. A beatific smile formed on her wan face naturally. Her pair of pretty eyes smiled too.

If Mei had been attentive to herself, she might have noticed her desire and readiness to have another child. But she was utterly intrigued by and preoccupied with her new creation—her unusual crop of warm black hair and her instantly opened and seemingly inquisitive eyes, for that infinitesimal moment before she closed them again.

Is it the bright lights in the room? Keat may have missed this part despite his attention, Mei thought fleetingly.

She will be an intelligent girl, the new mother sensed and she would be correct.

Finally! Girl or boy, it really did not matter in the end. With these happy thoughts, Mei succumbed to her exhaustion and slumbered off.

As expected, Keat would dote on his daughter ever since. Is that what 'the apple of my eye' looks like? Mei would ask herself countless times thereafter, albeit with a tinge of envy sometimes, if ever so slightly.

YJ Chin

Settling For Less

"Are you sure about this?" Faye's mentor at her medical school asked her, with deep concern in his inquisitive eyes. It is nearing graduation. Faye was consulting him about the job offers she had received: they were sufficiently numerous and encompassed a spectrum. In the mix were some highly reputable independent and university hospitals. After careful consideration, she was inclined to accept the offer from NCDAZ. Faye wanted some final feedback before doing so. In reality, she was looking for external affirmation of her decision. My mentor will be the most appropriate, he knows me best, she had thought.

"I think so," Faye replied with an assertive tone.

"I've evaluated that a specialist hospital will be best for me given my interest to specialise in psychiatry…no point practicing psychiatry in a general hospital really, the attention and focus allocated to this specialty may be variable, won't you agree?" Faye paused after sharing the first part of her reasoning.

As if uncomfortable with even a little while of silence, Faye continued without waiting for her mentor's reply.

"Among the specialist hospital options, NCDAZ has the widest range of subspecialties in practice in the field of psychiatry."

"Such exposure will be helpful to guide my decisions on further specialisation or potential areas of research should academia be an option for me down the road. May be good to keep my options open, I think. Do any of these make sense to you?" she offered up more of her thoughts readily.

More likely, Faye's excitement was getting ahead of herself. Her mouth was trying to keep up with her runaway thoughts.

Finally, she concluded with this confession, "Plus it's a social enterprise, this aligns with my cause."

"Faye seems to be defending her decision before her mentor. Is she expecting him to disagree?" Someone asked, prompted by her posture—her arms folded over each other on her chest.

Spontaneously, Faye telegraphed her mentor with her eyes: I am pausing for real this time.

Faye seems to have applied herself fully to this decision. Everything seems quite sound to me. Her mentor considered as Faye spoke but maintained his silence throughout. The black of his eyes was looking up at his prefrontal cortex every now and then as if to check that he had not missed anything.

"Sounds like you have given this matter a pretty thorough shake," Faye's mentor replied finally after a minute or so.

"If it's really what you want to do, I wish you all the best, Faye. I am confident you will do very well. You have what it takes and you seem quite determined with your choice." Her mentor acquiesced with her decision as he concluded she had made up her mind fully already.

That's it? Looks like we're done! Faye thought, quite surprised with her mentor's succinct response, with her face reflecting her feeling quite transparently. Unbeknownst to her mentor, Faye valued his opinion extremely highly. She was hoping for a substantive discussion. After all, he was one of the best professors in the faculty and Faye was fortunate to have him as her mentor. Nonetheless, his validation had bolstered her self-confidence tremendously. Her mentor made nothing of her astonished look.

Soon after, the mentor would opine to his faculty head on a separate occasion.

"Is one of our top graduates settling for less at such a young age, forgoing the more prestigious options that most of her peers will die to have?"

Intuitively, the faculty head knew his colleague was referring to Faye, she had consistently been on the dean's list after all. However, he was unsure if his own response was called for.

"Perhaps there is still some idealism in the world after all. Should be a good thing for us, you think?" Faye's mentor answered himself automatically after the briefest of pauses.

YJ Chin

Resolution of the Dilemma

"Hey baby, sorry. I've been terribly busy lately"…
"But I need 2 c u"…
"We need 2 talk ASAP"…
"Can't chat long"…
"Lots of stuff 2 settle at work"…
"Juz need 2 fix up a meet ASAP"…

The messages coursed through the internet in rapid succession around mid-afternoon the day before. Beth was home, clearing out stuff from her closet for most of the day. Then, her phone *pinged* non-stop while she was preparing dinner. Picking up her phone from the dining table nearby, she saw the WhatsApp notifications prominently displayed on its darkened screen.

"So many texts in such a short time. Why so urgent all of a sudden? He has not bothered the last couple of days. Business trip is no excuse." She grumbled as she unlocked her phone to read his messages. She was peeved with his radio silence for sure. In her displeasure, she also did not check up on him while he was away.

Reading his texts now and sensing the desperation in his tone, she relented somewhat and her petulance gave way to empathy. She replied briefly, clearly hesitant and tentative in her choice of words, yet mindful of his emotional state as much as could be perceived through unruly combinations of pseudo-words devoid of the nuances of the proper language.

England Dan and John Ford Coley were crooning in harmony through her compact music player. The sentimental lyrics of *'I'd Really Love to See You Tonight'* were wafting softly in the background. Beseechingly also. Was the universe conspiring with him? It did not matter; she was completely deaf to her surroundings. The chat had captivated her thoroughly. After some back and forth, her heart acquiesced to his persistent entreaty. However, her mind remained noncommittal. Did the airwaves coerce her reactions unconsciously?

Meanwhile, he quickly packed the details of their rendezvous into his prospective memory after he got what he wanted. She had agreed to meet him two days after his return from another upcoming business trip. He had proposed a familiar location: a small park nestled by a row of colonial-era shop-houses. Beth had brought him there first actually. One of her favourite spots: she enjoyed sitting under the huge Tembusu tree, especially during the cooler months of the year, to read and think, and people watch if the timing was right. He also proceeded to mark his calendar accordingly, on both his phone and his office app, just to be doubly sure, as if multiple recordings could banish all possibility of the non-occurrence of a future event. All the same, the office app would also inform his secretary of his unavailability during that time.

The next day, a dark cloud descended upon Beth unsurprisingly. Her reluctance to meet him from yesterday pressed upon her more and more.

"You gave in to his plea, how can you be so weak?" A voice chided her sternly, trying to be gentle to her tortured soul at the same time.

Conflicted and unsettled, she dithered for the entire day as she grieved over her dilemma. Helplessly, she left it unresolved, feeling utterly spent at the end of the day. Just as well, her day had wasted away, heaving more frustration on her.

Brooding could beget dreams, and Beth dreamt copiously that night. After her body was unshackled, her mind wandered freely to many places—some were familiar, some were strange, and the rest was random—all irrationally connected.

Like Beth appeared to have acquired a new body all of a sudden. In the next minute, she was in mid-air beside a greyish-silver glass-cladded skyscraper. A familiar place! Did she jump? Was the silvery-grey image, much greyer than silvery this time, a reflection of her own corpse-like face on the glass wall? Regardless, she was now free falling. A completely alien sensation: the terror of weightless falling alternating with a suspended stillness in an endless cycle. At the same time, a sound of rushing wind switching with an absolute silence jarringly. This dragged on for an indeterminate time.

Some while later, Beth found herself inside what appeared to be the eye of a typhoon. She was falling towards what seemed like an expansive ground below. On the other hand, could it be the ocean? She could not tell—it was too far away. Was she falling from an infinite height or towards an infinite depth? She could not figure this out either. An eerie and completely airless calm definitely surrounded her then.

The next moment, a gigantic violent and noisy whirl of indistinct objects and brushing dust clouds encircled Beth, trapping her inside. Her body was catatonic and still falling like a boulder despite the seamless change of environment from before. Absurdly, she fell into a meditative state: serene and frightful all at once. Was the eye of the typhoon not one of the safest place to be amidst such chaos? Just as suddenly, she felt a heavy *thud*. At once, a horrific squash traversed her body from head to toe, crushing all her bones completely. Surprisingly, she felt no pain at all, only a ringing darkness that overpowered all light and sound instantly. Did she just encounter Death?

At this, Beth awoke with an ice-cold shiver down her spine and with goose bumps all over. A gust of early morning breeze had squeezed through a vertical crack in her bedroom's heavy night curtains. The shielding of the slightly ajar windows was inadequate. The morning was breaking. A little of the dawning light had diffused into the room, illuminating her wan face ever so softly in the semi-darkness. She realised she was exactly where she had lain the night before. However, a sense of déjà vu held her in abeyance despite her not remembering a thing. She felt tired still as if she had not slept at all.

After a light breakfast, Beth decided to go for her regular yoga session despite her lethargy.

"A bit of exercise will help me decompress," Beth's voice reasoned.

"I'll try to keep up, if I really can't, no biggie…the yoga will definitely occupy my mind, especially when I have to focus to get into the poses properly and keep up with the teacher and the class." Beth felt competitive somewhat at the last thought. Nevertheless, a sense of dread rolled in her stomach as she approached the studio.

What an extremely taxing session! Beth had to muster every iota of mental and physical energy to keep up. However, she broke away from the group's practice a couple of times, adopting the *Balasana* pose briefly just to recover from her erratic breathing and fatigue-induced vertigo. At one point, she nearly wanted to give up and walked out of the class altogether.

"C'mon, just a bit more, you've come so far, don't give up just yet," a womanly voice encouraged Beth mindfully and she overcame that momentary lapse of will power. She was extremely relieved when the teacher guided the class to take up the final pose—the *Savasana*—shortly after. She was physically exhausted by then but her mind was off her woes for the time being. When she left the studio soon after, there was lightness in her steps. The yoga had filled her with happy hormones.

However, the light-heartedness did not last very long. Back home, after Beth had started on her routine, she automatically became conscious of her indecision from the previous day again. Her thoughts scattered and seemed unable to coalesce around some vague idea in her mind. This despite her sensing some clarity of purpose behind her actions, and visioning some nebulous outline of her life ahead.

It was surreal: her mind, thoroughly preoccupied with matters of the heart, was detached from her body, which carried on with her quotidian life on its own. Watching her went about her humdrum; it was hard to imagine her predicament. Or her mental disturbance. Or her physical exhaustion even. Amazing how she could hold the contradictions in her mind and for the most part remained a high functioning individual. Perhaps her plastic brain was adapting to her circumstances and struggles. With a timetable of its own.

"Yes, I would not meet him," her mind somehow meandered to this conclusion by mid-afternoon, after she had consumed a late lunch which was not much given her state of mind. Did Beth dust up some missing pieces of the jigsaw puzzle from her robotic-like humming and drumming earlier? Consciously, those pieces of mental stuff seemed to have snapped into position, clarifying the situation in her mind and spontaneously painting a holistic picture in her brain.

"An awesome marvel: watching everything clicking together so neatly and so suddenly!" Someone exclaimed.

"You know, lots of stuff has been slow cooking in the background for quite some time already." Someone-Else pointed out plainly.

The rational mind map evolving in her brain emboldened her intuitively, she was most sure of herself this time.

I will share *none* of these with him, Beth thought. Her mind made up with as much resolve also. Then, a mixed pang of remorse and anguish sought to weaken her, if only briefly. The resolution of the dilemma had allowed her to reclaim control over her life, overriding all else. Paradoxically, a disturbing comfort flooded her cold mind thereafter.

What came next? The sketchy outline of her life slowly filled in with details as the cloudiness faded.

"Things will shape up eventually," Someone-New informed knowingly.

Over the next couple of days, a meticulous plan slowly came into view. A stony numbness would permeate her heart surreptitiously as this happened. However, she would not feel this for quite some while yet.

It's Not Going to Happen to You

"Hey Kimmy, how's your day today?" Mei asked Kim as she stepped into the open concept kitchen. Mei was back from work earlier than usual and right on time. Mother and daughter had agreed to have dinner together that day. Keat was away on business travel. Kim had offered to prepare a simple meal for both of them, wanting to put some of what she had learnt at home economics class into practice.

"Hi mom...not great actually," Kim replied meekly, a little despondent. The kitchen smelled of garlic and ginger and steamed fish. Kim had laid out what she had cooked and set the table all ready for her mom, just short of scooping the rice into the bowls. Mei eyed a plate of boiled kai-lan drizzled with fermented bean sauce as she went round the dining table. Kim sat herself at the table after filling two white porcelain bowls to the brim with white rice. Her mom settled down opposite her, after she had put aside her work stuff on the dining console nearby.

"Oh, I am so sorry to hear that baby," Mei sympathised with Kim though she had absolutely no idea what could be troubling her usually cheerful child, "tell me what happened." Looking at Kim with solicitous eyes, Mei extended her hand to cuddle Kim's arms gently, giving her a soft massage, and feeling for the warmth of her fifteen-year-old girl at the same time.

Mei was grateful for Kim. She felt fortunate that her daughter did not seem to exhibit any teenage angst at all unlike her personal experience when she was at Kim's age. That was almost thirty-three years ago now. They were a close-knit family and she felt vindicated to have invested her life with Kim and Keat instead of her own career.

"Nat's parents are getting a divorce…you remember Natalie? She slept over a couple of weeks back," Kim disclosed solemnly as if something had just died, her voice catching a bit, as she spoke.

"Nat was so inconsolable after school when she broke the news to me," she continued, now looking sullen and a little pink around her eyes, as if Natalie's familial tragedy had befallen on her personally.

Natalie's tragedy was not the first Kim had come across in school—there was another schoolmate in a similar state. She heard from her other classmates about three months back. That girl whom she did not know personally was from another class. However, Natalie was her best friend and it had become personal for Kim. Moreover, her helplessness with Natalie's situation had compounded her misery. All she could do was to hug Natalie closely and allowed her to cry on her shoulder until her chauffeur arrived to fetch her home.

Kim called Natalie from her room after she got back from school. They talked intermittently. When Natasha Bedingfield started to sing 'Pocketful of Sunshine' from Kim's compact audio system, Natalie heard the same coming off her own B&O compact. They paused simultaneously, as if cued by an invisible nudge. Thereupon, they listened as Natasha sang and silently imagined holding each other in a kind of comforting embrace.

Natasha's refrain—*take me away, a secret place, a sweet escape…*— spoke so poignantly to Natalie's heart. All the same, Natalie felt safe in the metaphysical warmth of her best friend, the physical distance notwithstanding. They were on the phone for almost two hours. Despite that, they were not talking very much. Kim just wanted to be there for her grief-stricken friend who was feeling very lost. She did not really know what to say either—it was her first time dealing with such matters. Kim was matured for her age but this was a very adult matter, was this not? Finally, they hung up, as Kim needed to prepare dinner as promised to her mom.

"I remember Nat; she strikes me as a strong and intelligent girl. Don't worry Kimmy, Nat will be strong and you need to be strong for her too." The unexpected news had unhinged Mei as well. She was clueless on how to console her own daughter also. It was the first time she had to contend with such adult matters with Kim. She had not even embarked on the-birds-and-the bees stuff with her yet. Instinctively, she moved her chair and herself closer to Kim to give her a hug. Kim leant in spontaneously to rest in her mom's bosom.

Suddenly, a reverie pulled Mei back to a familiar single-bed room in a maternity ward. The scene began to play itself. In vivid colours. In a bit of a slow motion. So familiar. The nurse had just placed Kim on her bosom, under the watchful eyes of Keat and Aries the ram. So evocative, Mei's eyes welled up a bit. Were these tears of endearment? Tears of intuitive foreboding? Mei did not know, neither did she think this. Kim could not know for sure, her episodic memory was undeveloped at birth then. However, just as instinctual, Kim found solace in her mom's familiar heartbeat now. She felt safe in her mom's physical embrace.

"Let's finish up dinner and we can chat in your room after that, how's that?" Mei suggested; her gentle breath, audible to just the two of them, wafted over Kim's hair. Concurrently, she dried her eyes discreetly in order not to alarm Kim at all. Kim hugged her mom a little tighter now as though she needed more reassurance still.

What's going to happen to us, mom? Kim asked silently, the question remained a bubble in her head. Oddly, what was she asking actually? Why the sudden uncertainty? Did she sense something that she could not articulate, not having the words to do so effectively?

"Don't worry baby, it's not going to happen to you. You know that, don't you?" Mei offered intuitively.

Where did this come from? Maybe Mei perceived her daughter's worry and sensed that this was the assurance she needed now. Did she say it out of self-confidence in her relationship with Keat? Perhaps she had avoided Kim's difficult question, one she was unwilling to contemplate even, and substituted it with one she subconsciously was able to provide an assurance for, right now.

"Don't overthink Nat's situation. She seems like she can bounce back somehow. Just stand by her, okay?" Mei urged cautiously, hoping to settle her daughter further.

"Is Mei correct to assume that children are a resilient bunch generally?" Someone-New asked.

"Maybe doing so is easier on her conscience, to assuage herself of possible lapses in their duty of care as parents towards their children," Someone said, clearly understanding of parenting challenges at the same time.

Even so, Mei hoped that the love Keat and she had showered on their daughter and the attachment Kim felt towards them could help build up her spirit to handle life's adversities, which would surely come. Natalie's situation—removed yet personal for Kim—was just a simple test. A helpful one nonetheless.

Luckily, Kim perked up at her mom's words. Briefly, she was back to her ebullient self, "Okay mommy. Now, let's eat. I hope you like my cooking. Just tell me if the food tastes funny yeah."

For a while, mother and daughter looked like humanoids feeding themselves in a slow motion silent movie. Kim did not eat much; Natalie was still very much on her mind. However, her perception of her mom's words had settled her: her parents would not divorce, come what might. She felt so fortunate to be born into such a lovely family.

Mei did not eat much either; she was displaced by Natalie's situation also.

"It's not your cooking, baby. It is perfect really. Mom just had a rough day at work and it's affected my appetite," Mei lied instinctively. With Kim's already disturbed state, she could not bear burdening Kim further with the truth. Did she lie about Kim's cooking also?

"Maybe we just love everything our children do for us regardless. We want to protect the people we love as much as it is within our power to do so. Agree?" Someone asked rhetorically.

That night, Mei was jolted to assess the state of her relationship with Keat—something she had not done so for quite a while. They were not a symbiotic couple really—no need to do everything together, quite independent in fact. Nevertheless, they had a tacit loyalty to each other and a comfortable companionship with one another. Over the last fifteen years, Mei had invested herself in Kim (and Keat as well, naturally) for the most part. However, for the last two years or so, she had re-invested her time back into her career.

Can I hold on to Keat? Can we hold together for Kim as promised? Mei contemplated, a little unsure initially.

"Do we need to be concerned here?" Someone asked.

As Mei introspected further, a well of tenderness rose up within her: she was missing Keat intensely all of a sudden.

"Whew, that's more like it." Everyone heaved a collective sigh of relief.

That weekend, Mei initiated their lovemaking, which caught Keat by surprise. It had been quite a while actually. Keat's business trips had escalated in frequency since his scope of work expanded to encompass the whole of the Asia-Pacific region, with the addition of China and Japan. This was slightly over a year ago now. Equally, work had consumed Mei also; her role too had expanded quite considerably after her recent promotion.

Nonetheless, they took pleasure in the intimacy. Keat had always enjoyed sex. Thereafter, they snuggled in bed, feeling safe beneath their duvet. Mei could feel his warm breath flitting over her sweaty nape and shoulders, and the gentle rise and fall of his chest. What a beautiful sound. Her heart pulsates calmly, falling in tandem with his unconsciously. Unawares, each had escaped down their own rabbit hole.

Keat did not suspect anything unusual, he was only glad to follow Mei's lead. Did something stir in Mei? Was her initiative the impulse of an intuition that had yet to form fully?

Intriguing Web of Chemicals and Electricity

How long had it been? Ten years? Fifteen maybe. He winced wistfully—no words, just thoughts. The memory had flashed across his mind just now, as vivid as a noonday sun on a cloudless day, as if everything happened yesterday. Sometimes it occurred this way as he recalled the episode. For other episodes, some had gotten hazier with each passing recollection, with some frames disappearing and reappearing at different times, until they went missing altogether. Was it forgetfulness? Worse, his memory starting to fail?

"Sean, what's on your mind?" He sensed the question quivering vaguely in the air. Strangely, the vocal tones resonated with fuzzy familiarity but somewhat distant like a faraway echo.

"Where are you? Please come back," Faye begged, interrupting gently. At the same time, she leant forward slightly, searching for contact with his charcoal black eyes.

"Oh…where am I? What am I doing here?" Sean asked uncertainly, looking displaced and worried, his mind caught between two places, maybe more. He looked around the room for visual cues…for something to anchor his mental frame.

The room was handsomely fitted with understated modern furnishings, his vision less blurry now. Yet, it exuded a warm and homely ambiance allowing almost anyone to settle in quite easily and quickly. Everything seemed neat and efficient and in its proper place. The room felt comfortably bright and unobtrusively spacious. Natural light from the morning sun poured in from floor-to-ceiling windows on one side of the room. Its glare thwarted by day blinds, half drawn from the ceiling. Looking out, he chanced upon a couple of swifts flitting pass. The jolly chirpings of other birds and faint street traffic could be heard streaming in from outside.

An ambulance was approaching the office building. The screeching of its siren intensified and hit a crescendo as the ambulance sped by. At that same exact moment, a magical wormhole opened in Sean's mind, and forcefully pulled his wandering consciousness back from his past to the here and now. Sean did not hear the siren receded as the ambulance pulled away. He was working on reclaiming the present and weaving it seamlessly with the momentary past held in his short-term memory—not in his metaphysical mind but one grounded in physical temporal reality.

"We need a sense of continuity of time and space to give life some meaning, agree?" Someone asked softly.

"Take in the present environment and situation, and mesh in our understanding of the past and the structure of our world constructed therewith to inform our expectations of the immediate future and our plans for the not-so-immediate future—this is the foundational memory system that underpins our mental soundness and stability, correct?" Someone-New chimed in also.

"Including our identity and grounding in reality too." Someone concurred.

"What happens when this system fails?" Everyone seemed to ask the psychotherapist at the same time.

"You are in my office, Sean," Faye reassured him, "we are here for our regular chat, remember?"

"You can recall who I am, can't you?" Faye's vantablack eyes implored, while she seized on the opportunity to check the status and test the workings of his memory.

Sean looked at Faye with unclear curiosity. Behind his probing eyes and dilated pupils, the synapses in his fusiform gyrus, straddling parts of the temporal and occipital lobes in his brain, were firing frenetically to recognise the face before him.

Involuntarily, Sean's brain was hard at work, flashing through complex mental tasks, racing towards an answer to Faye's question. It was relentlessly accessing the vast repository of his semantic memory, searching through the gamut of characters and words collected over time, sieving out a special class of words: names. Specifically, names of people he had known and memorised to associate with the tender face and gentle voice: what is the precise name of the now-so-familiar woman sitting in front of me?

Automatically, the psychotherapist's brain was hard at work also. Face blindness is an uncommon condition, a hereditary disorder mostly.

"Sean definitely did not have this condition from birth, nor was he ever traumatised into developing one thereafter," Faye spoke softly unawares.

However, difficulty with remembering names is normal; most people experience this to some degree. Nevertheless, having trouble with putting a name to someone who is supposedly part of one's quotidian existence is a warning of potential trouble ahead.

"If so, this is definitely a cause for worry," Faye concluded.

Faye peered at Sean. Her warm black cat-eye spectacles framed her soft expectant eyes, yet giving her a sterner countenance than intended. There was an informality between them, cultivated over fortnightly therapy sessions held over the last four months. However, Faye hesitated to put her hand over Sean's to assure him again. Her knowledge that a sensory impulse from a familiar source could prompt his cognitive processes and expedite the retrieval of a specific memory in his brain tugged at her nonetheless.

"Better to be safe," Someone whispered.

"Appropriate behaviour and professional reputation are paramount," Someone-Else decided for Faye prudently.

Consequently, she kept her hands where they were—the left holding a pen over her writing pad, which her right held firmly, both items on her lap, over her solemn-looking pencil skirt that grazed her knees.

"Careful now, be patient, let him take his time," Someone repeated its advice. Anxiously, Faye waited with full attention on Sean.

Had it been minutes only? *Whatever!* It felt like a lifetime. Strangely, our sense of time fluctuates with the contents of our emotional reservoir that really suspends amorphously inside our brain, which in turn is a complex and intriguing web of chemicals and electricity actually.

It's Very Private

"**D**amned it! I'm going to be late," he swore beneath his breath. She was already there when he finally showed up at the apartment.

The apartment was at a condominium on the fringe of the city. Its name evoked an indistinct visual in his mind. He had likely driven through the district itself. Once or twice when he was trying to get to a commercial-cum-industrial hub northeast of the city from his office. Nonetheless, no specific navigational map to the condo formed in his mind when he considered the destination, despite the intense electrical impulses in his hippocampus and the surrounding medial temporal lobes of his brain. Instantly, he proceeded to google for directions using the exact address she had provided him during their phone conversation last week.

...

"It's very private," her snappy voice rattled in his head, "memorise the access sequence and passcode to get into the development, or write it down. If you forget, just call my mobile."

He heard a faint incomprehensible voice in the background and the call terminated abruptly. He was peeved. A while later, she called back to apologise, blaming the mobile network for the dropped call earlier. He left it be, giving her the benefit of the doubt; they settled on the rendezvous.

"Please WhatsApp just to be doubly sure," he requested. Nonetheless, he packed the details into his prospective memory after the call.

…

He was done for the day. Google had provided an estimate of thirty minutes to get to his destination when he just checked. Being a stickler for punctuality, he padded in an extra ten minutes to cover for want of familiarity.

She was there early, as she wanted to prepare the place for him. She wanted it to be perfect: clean, tidy and at the right temperature for him, especially on such a humid day. With absolute certainty, she knew: first impressions form in the blink of an eye—a tenth of a second. She recalled reading this somewhere but could not remember where exactly.

"Is this for a face or a place?" She asked. Her pupils dilated as she tried to recall the article she had read either in a magazine or on some web site. However, she gave up after some meagre effort.

Thereafter, longer exposures will not significantly alter first impressions—she continued with her earlier recollection. Best to avoid being wrong-footed, it would take a lot of work to recover his favour, she thought.

She wore her favourite bateau neck blouse for luck. At least she felt lucky on those occasions when she had worn it though she was not exactly superstitious, or so she thought. She had applied some light make-up too. Just a touch of warm peach blush on her youthful cheeks to give them a fresh and healthy tinge, black eyeliner to accentuate her eyes a little, and transparent gloss to her pink pouty lips to give them a luscious sheen. She also knew that facial impressions were an essential part, if not the leading part, of the overall package. Instinctively, she liked to look attractive.

"All women want to look attractive, do they not? Moreover, attractive people tend to get what they want," she believed. "Tall, handsome men benefit from this all the time," she believed this also. However, her limited anecdotal observations informed this belief instead of sound understanding backed by empirical data and statistical analyses.

She is not alone. In general, humans do not think in numbers naturally. Even if we do, we tend to pay more attention to the arguments and conclusions than consider the reliability of the information that underpins them.

"Okay, okay, got it! No need for all this mumbo-jumbo. This is not going to help with the situation right here," Someone was obviously getting impatient now.

"He is late, that should put him in a delicate and defensive posture," she hoped, and smirked with a mix of nervousness and gladness as she tried to restrain her latent irritability. Her face was becoming transparent but she could not see herself.

"I'm sorry I'm late but just a bit I think," he said self-consciously as he stepped hastily into the apartment. A studio actually.

Hmm…nice blouse. This first impression bubbled up inside his brain and stayed there.

Salt-and-pepper hair (ash colour to some) was what she visually registered at first, as he bent down towards her, to remove the pair of black leather loafers on his feet.

He is sorry. *Really?* She wondered with disquiet.

Is fifteen minutes a bit? Her thoughts continued as she trained her black eye-lined eyes on him intensely.

A bit is how long? Three minutes? Five minutes? How can fifteen minutes be a bit? She protested further as she tried very hard not to let her irascible thoughts got the better of her.

"You're being petty now, drop it! And be polite." Someone-Else instructed.

"Hi, you must be Sean. I'm Nyx, we spoke last week?" Nyx gave Sean a stilted smile and extended her hand confidently towards him. She half expected him to grab it as soon as he had removed his loafers, and half worried that he might exert excessive force on her, which then might cause her to stumble as he crutched on her to steady himself.

"So sorry, Nyx…yes, I'm Sean…nice to meet you finally. Sorry again to keep you waiting," Sean replied amiably, shaking her hand briefly and firmly without causing her to lose any balance and dispelling her nervousness all at once.

He is pink with blush. Is it because he is late and rushing? Am I the cause? Nyx's mind sure was buzzing with distractions.

Nyx was wishing for some compliments, was she not? Of course, she was. As a gauge for Sean's *first* impression?

"Did she forget that she is here to show him the studio?" Someone asked.

"Has she sidetracked from her determination to secure a client for the rental studio by the end of the week?" Someone-Else shared its concern too.

Indeed, Sean could be a distraction. After all, he was a prepossessing sight with his youthful-looking features: well-placed almond-shaped eyes and thick brows, a barely visible cleft on his slightly pointed chin set against a strong jawline. Only the crow's feet around his eyes and his full head of salt-and-pepper hair betrayed his middle age.

If he wanted to, Sean could easily disarm people with his charisma and wit still. Regarding this, he was self-aware and was careful about his ways with people, as his mother had taught him. She had perceived this in her son since he was much younger. When he was mature enough to understand the ways of the world, she inculcated in him the value of truthfulness in his conduct and of treating others with kindness and respect, the former especially towards children and the latter especially towards women. Strangely, in delicate situations, he would sense the gentle and firm voice of his mother nudging him along those lines.

"He looks cool and credible, not what I expected," Nyx held that thought also when Sean stepped into the studio earlier, not that she had any knowledge of Sean's credentials or any yardstick to measure these by even if she knew.

Nyx had not expected how uncannily familiar Sean appeared to her also. Unbeknownst to Sean, his facial features had triggered a flashback in Nyx's mind. When did that happen? Maybe when she was gazing at Sean with such intensity? Nyx was unconscious of this—somehow the mind seemed divorced from real time.

Actually, Nyx flashed back to a time when she was fifteen years younger, to a place where her first love first kissed her. The vision in her mind was so evocative that it embodied her. Her heart flitted and her muscles tensed unusually when the most memorable episode—reconstituted on the fly and retained in her working memory—replayed in her mind automatically. Was this the cause of her distraction?

"Shall we get on with the viewing?" Sean asked, his baritone voice instantly dispersing the buzzing bees in Nyx's head.

Am I the client, or what? Sean frowned as he thought.

"Sorry…that's why we are here, are we not?" Nyx apologised reflexively.

In many ways, the studio was similar to a super deluxe suite in the seaside resorts in Bali or Phuket where Sean had vacationed, albeit with a decent size open counter kitchen and a small dining area that could seat two persons comfortably.

Sufficiently generous for a king-size bed and a workspace, Sean check-marked mentally.

There was also a petite balcony flanking the living area, deeper than a French balcony and suitable for a quick drag—nothing to shout about really. Nonetheless, Sean caught sight of the setting sun and took a moment to appreciate the awesome view, and feel the warm irradiation on his face. Did the ebullient rays anoint him with a yellowish-white halo just? Nyx thought so when she chanced a glance of Sean in the moment.

"High enough," he remarked casually, referring to the studio's level in its block but Nyx heard nothing.

Can tuck a compact two-seater sofa neatly into the corner just by the balcony—he envisioned as he moved along.

Sean liked that the shower in the bathroom was a wide rectangular shape with the footprint of a bathtub sans the tub (mental check). Unlike the rest of the prospective units he had viewed so far, he figured he would definitely have an agreeable shower here. Sean was very particular about the length and quality of his shower. This was one activity he found most enjoyable and relaxing at home (or was it sex, or both…he could not decide). It was an expeditious and easily accessible escape from the day's stress and disturbance.

Most essential: Sean could linger in the shower in absolute privacy and enjoy his stark nakedness unbounded for as long as he wanted. He could stand motionless under the rain-shower and let the heavy pelting of hot water massage his head and body. The temperature sufficiently high to melt away the day's woes. The flow volume sufficiently strong to wash his troubles off him and down the plughole. For minutes on end, sufficiently long to infuse a light-heartedness to last him at least for the night. After that, a good read or some good sex, whichever he had the mood for and conditioned on another's availability and eagerness if it was the latter.

Back at the viewing, Nyx expressly pointed out the installation of a rain-shower (definitely a man's thing, Nyx knew from experience) and a hand-shower.

"Excellent!" Sean remarked, mental-checking this too after running the water briefly to ensure the pressure was satisfactory.

"It's also *very* private," Nyx reminded him one more time, betting her gut that this might be the deal clincher.

Sean had made a mental note of this important point from their call last week. He wanted to confirm this detail for himself. His sensing during the viewing concurred with Nyx's assertion during their call. Sean was elated, another one of his criteria had checked out: an overriding one his biased mind had dictated.

Earlier in the day, Sean had revisited the online ad for the asking rent, and noticed that the property had been on the market for coming to four months now. He had missed this detail the first time round when he came across the ad last week.

"This locality appears to be at the farthest edge of the areas I'm looking at." Sean commented to himself when he screenshot the property on his phone then. He also annotated the picture with a number: the output of his invisible neural network to prioritise the places on his shortlist according to a feature set residing somewhere in his unreadable mind.

Not long after, Sean called the mobile number listed in the 'Contact Me for a Viewing' section of the ad to find Nyx at the other end of the line.

Major Neurocognitive Disorder

"It's coming to a year already. Am I right, Faye?" Her colleague asked over lunch one day.

"Think so…thanks…time flies indeed…" Faye replied as if her mind was somewhere else.

"Congratulations! You made it," Faye's colleague added, conscious of this crucial milestone for a young adult starting out in the workforce.

Actually, her regular lunch companion's question had thrown Faye into contemplation. It prompted her to self-appraise her first year at NCDAZ. During that time, Faye had discovered herself gravitating towards medical conditions that involved the older segment of the population, and in particular, the impairment of cognitive acuity with the aging process caused naturally or by illnesses.

Sometimes, Faye wondered if her parents getting on with age had unconsciously primed her specialty inclinations, despite them being healthy and well still. She especially felt such impulses after each visit back home, which she did regularly despite the long drives. These cross-country drives were her catharsis. They provided her the opportunity to think about things too. The flexible pit stops enroute gave her an inexplicable sense of control and freedom all at once.

When Faye dealt with dementia patients at NCDAZ, she invariably imagined her parents to end up like them in some form and shape sometime in the future. Though an unpleasant subject, maybe ungrateful even (as if to think unkindly of her parents it seemed), she would rather think ahead, be aware and 'hope for the best, plan for the worst'.

Is this from *Killing Floor*? Faye remembered reading this in a novel but could not recall which one specifically.

Did *Jack Reacher* say that or was it Lee Child? Nonetheless, good advice, she nodded approvingly.

Moreover, if it really came to that, Faye would be of help to her parents then. It was one way she could repay her parents for giving her the life she now enjoyed.

Faye avoided the accident or trauma departments as much as she was able. Her preference was to attend to patients with conditions where treatment or early intervention could have a higher chance of positive impact or better still, where proactivity (which aligned with her approach to life) could help prevent those conditions from developing in the first place.

Almost at the same time, Faye also discovered she had the empathy and the temperament for dealing with difficult situations and disturbed minds. Clearly an area of strength for her.

(Did I get this from mum? Faye wondered. She had observed her mum at work previously: she was wonderful with children and especially patient with them and their parents. Some could be extremely onerous indeed.)

Faye had a genuine interest in people's lives and their stories. This shone through during her psychotherapy sessions with the patients assigned to her. Definitely an asset for the hospital, and a gift to her patients.

Sometime after, NCDAZ decided to set up a unit of psychotherapists to deal with neurocognitive disorders especially.

This included major neurocognitive disorder—the more technical sounding term for the commonly known condition called dementia.

"Learning a profession includes learning its language. Medicine is no exception. However, keeping up with its evolving and growing vocabulary at an accelerated pace can be daunting." Someone reminded Faye of something she had known all along.

"She has tackled the challenge very well so far," Someone-Else noted with satisfaction.

"Hey Faye, remember the new dementia unit the CEO announced last week? There are a couple of open positions published on the intranet. You may want to check this out," her regular lunch companion informed her.

Naturally, Faye put in an application that same evening immediately after her work for the day was done. The application ended up in Dr Lee's email, the deputy director of medical services who was supposed to start up this practice within the hospital. Aware of Faye's performance, talent and passion, Dr Lee arranged for an interview immediately after perusing her application. Just as well, he was under pressure to get the unit up and running as soon as possible.

"It's going to be very hard work dealing with dementia patients, not to mention the toil on your emotional and social lives. You are a little young to be doing this right now, yes? You sure you want to do this?" Dr Lee started after some formalities, half advising and half enquiring.

"The position is yours if you want, I just need to be sure it's what you *really* want," Dr Lee followed up after the briefest of pauses. His presumptive offer of sorts put Faye completely at ease instantly.

"Plus the conditions are mostly incurable for now. Not your typical doctor profession: our training geared us towards ridding our patients of their illnesses or diseases. Can be quite depressing down the road if not managed well." Dr Lee added just to make sure Faye was conscious of the reality she would be dealing with on a daily basis. He also wanted to dispel any romantic idea her unconscious mind might have lulled her into.

Actually, Dr Lee did not have many in-house applicants to begin with and would gladly have Faye on his team. However, he believed it was important to provide his recruits with all the information essential to their decision-making process. He was keenly aware that people function largely based on all that they could see at the time when they were making those decisions. Just as crucial, he believed appropriate motivations were important also to keep one going when the going got tough.

"Oh, on the depressing part: I am referring to ourselves— doctors, therapists, caregivers, and the like—and not the patients," Dr Lee clarified just to be doubly sure there was no misinterpreting his words.

"Can even morph us mentally and physically over time. Not sure if you have read *Thinking, Fast and Slow* by Daniel Kahneman. Pretty good stuff, some parts quite damning on us humans unfortunately, if you ask me," Dr Lee continued, smirking in a fatherly sort of way. However, no one else was present. Faye did not ask any question for sure. She did not look puzzled either.

The interview is a two-way process, correct? While I am certain I will like the job, I need to be certain Dr Lee and I can get along as well— Faye thought while Dr Lee was talking, studying him quietly at the same time. After all, he was going to be her new boss now that he had more or less offered her the job and she would expect the working hours to be hard and long. His ridiculous work regime informed her.

"We are not as smart and rational and in control as we think we are," Dr Lee laughed at this point, clearly in a philosophical mood now. Then he realised he had been dominating the conversation.

"It is more of a monologue than an interview if you ask me," Someone said in a whisper.

Now where is that coming from? Unconsciously, Faye was frowning as Dr Lee was talking about daft, irrational and out-of-control humans.

At this point, Dr Lee paused to give Faye an opportunity to consider his words as he brought his hands together to form what looked like the Eiffel Tower with its top touching his relaxed lips. Faye could tell that it was her turn at the conversation from his questioning eyes and holding posture.

Faye pondered for a while and replied with her usual confidence, "Yes, Dr Lee, I am absolutely sure. I understand your concerns and appreciate your advice. I've decided to specialise in this area."

"You are an old soul, aren't you? All right then. We are set. Don't say I didn't warn you," Dr Lee grinned with parental pride and satisfaction, as if welcoming his own child home. He was convinced that Faye would be an excellent addition to his team.

Huh! We're done? This isn't much of an interview, is it? Faye thought, surprised with its brevity.

Well, closure can be swift if everyone is clear and on the same page, no need for superfluous talk that enervates. Dr Lee and Faye grasped this naturally, and seemed to connect telepathically too.

"Oh, I may need to start including you in some meetings and activities soon. I'll keep you posted. We'll start as soon as we start…the unit that is," Dr Lee forewarned Faye.

From this, Faye gathered there would be more work: help set up the new unit, and her current load. Likely, she would have to hold on to her extant duties until she transferred to the new setup fully. There was no one to share her workload given the labour crunch at the hospital.

Dr Lee's warning on the toll on my social life seems to have taken effect almost immediately, Faye supposed with some ambivalence.

"Certainly. Appreciate you giving me this opportunity. Thanks Dr Lee," Faye replied with a deferential smile nonetheless, and shook his hand firmly as she rose automatically to leave his room.

By this time, Faye had invested a little over three years of her medical career with NCDAZ.

"I am fast approaching thirty already," she ruminated aloud that night over late dinner, "Time to double down on a specialty and grow from there." She concluded with satisfaction that her career had worked out for her so far. Faye normally knew what she wanted quite quickly.

"She seems focused on her mission and in a hurry as well," Someone remarked matter-of-factly.

A couple of weeks later, she would procure *Thinking, Fast and Slow* by Daniel Kahneman, chancing on it while browsing at her regular bookshop in her neighbourhood on a lackadaisical Sunday. She would read it slowly over many months—contemplating the deep insights and observing the people around her more keenly as if to validate her new knowledge and discovery. She would also apply what she deemed relevant in her psychotherapy practice. *Yes*, she would agree with Dr Lee's takeaways from the book as well.

Dr Lee would go on to recommend Faye many books being an erudite and voracious reader himself. All the same, he would share things that would pique her curiosity or add to her universe of knowledge.

He is a most interesting person to engage with, Faye would think every now and then.

Faye and her new boss got along just fine. She enjoyed her stint under Dr Lee's leadership immensely, and counted it her good fortune to have benefited from his experience and grown under his guidance, professionally and philosophically.

Five Hundred Dollars

"What's the asking rent again?" Sean queried Nyx without looking at her. He had finished his viewing and was ready to proceed further, whatever that meant. Thinking to secure a better bargaining position with detachment, he had kept relatively quiet throughout except for the occasional nods to indicate he was following Nyx's commentary.

"Three thousand eight per month, it is on the ad, including the condo conservancy charges only, and furnished as you see it. Everything else will be incidentals and will need to be borne by you, assuming you are happy to take up this unit of course. Rental period term is 2+1 years. Minimum 2 years non-negotiable. You can ignore the +1 if you want. It is available now as you can see." Nyx rattled off automatically but was unsure in her tone. Her black eye-lined eyes were fixated on Sean again, with the same intensity as before.

Nyx was unaware that Sean might possibly misconstrue her gaze as rudeness. However, she was fuzzily conscious of who he had reminded her of. Just a much older version with his stylishly cropped ash colour hair—this thought crossed her mind as well. The vexing bees had returned.

Regardless, Sean felt uncomfortable with Nyx's long, lingering stare. He deftly averted her gaze to deflect the pressure to commit to anything. Innocently, he had misread the cue behind Nyx's gaze.

The studio had been on the rental market for almost four months now. Sean knew this already. The property owner had wanted to engage another agent in addition to Nyx, after the initial three-month exclusive agency period lapsed. She requested for more time, and the owner agreed to extend the exclusivity period by another month. This would terminate by the end of this week. Sean would be her best and final chance. No more viewings for the rest of the week even though there was still four more days to go.

The rental market had been in the doldrums for quite some time now. Yet, property owners continued with their unrealistic expectations. *Sigh!* Nyx needed to close the transaction with Sean, otherwise, she would be facing competition next week—more pressure and work for the same or less return. One of the vicissitudes of life that the universe throws at us sometimes.

"Lady Luck, where the hell are you? Why don't you bloody show up when I need you most?" Nyx swore angrily. This was yesterday.

Had it been seconds only? Minutes probably but it felt like eternity to Nyx. Her chest tightened a little and she oscillated faintly as her anxiety welled up inside her. The uninvited and unexpected flashback had messed with her emotional state as well. Then, as quickly as she thought them, she blurted out.

"How do you feel about the location?"

"Do you like what you see?"

"What is your budget actually?"

"When do you need an apartment?"

"Shit! Are you losing control?" Someone chided Nyx for her unusual behaviour. Nyx ignored it totally. The psychological pressure valve was released instantly there and then. She needed this to regain her lucidity. It is better to let things boil over sometimes.

What's his story? There's always a story behind these things. Why does he need a rental apartment? Her brows furrowed a little but Nyx found the restraint to stop her tongue from giving voice to her curiosity this time.

"Careful now, be patient. Let him take his time. He doesn't seem to be in a hurry to go anywhere," Someone-New pointed out. Nyx was calmer now. She bit her lower lip self-consciously, which made her lips looked poutier than usual.

"The unit is fine but the location is a little further away from where I prefer. Nevertheless, a good location, and very private as you said" Sean conceded.

"Negotiable? My budget is closer to three thousand," Sean disclosed after a while, becoming more transparent than he would have liked. Was someone else doing the talking now?

Instantly, Nyx experienced a huge welcomed relief when Sean proffered what seemed like an offer. The deal had not closed yet but there was now a number to work with and a definite gap that she could attempt to close, she figured instinctively.

"Three is a little way off. How about three five? If you are prepared to go with this, I can work on the owner to lower his expectation," Nyx countered without batting an eye.

Was her intuition in control? Nyx had been a property agent for the past ten years. She would be an expert in her field by now. Oftentimes, her hunch would be accurate. Like now, a set of automatic reflexes had taken over the negotiation process, which would be normal. She was responding on cue to all the situations that were within her realm of familiarity. The exchange was conforming to predictable sequences. Even the number she threw out just now might have been predetermined in her (unconscious) mind when she was preparing the place earlier for Sean's viewing. Her mind, programmed over time, recognised what was ordinary. Unless there was a surprise, Nyx was contented to let her intuition run the show. Nothing appeared out of the ordinary so far, or so her brain deemed. Then, where was Nyx's attention if she was conducting this preliminary negotiation with robotic-like predictability?

"Three five? Let me think about this and come back to you. Meanwhile, may I take some pictures of this place?" Sean made eye contact with Nyx with apparent eagerness now, expecting her to yield without hesitation.

"Sure. Please don't take too long to consider…one other viewer is serious about this unit as well, and I have another viewing tomorrow morning," Nyx lied naturally, hoping to bait Sean with her unsophisticated ruse. Her eyes caught her lies, the tip of her nose itched and her voice softened a little towards the end of her sentences. Spontaneously, she looked away from Sean to avoid him catching her lie.

However, Sean did not notice, his focus shifted immediately after he got her permission. Automatically, he started snapping away with his jet-black iPhone, immersed in the activity in no time.

The so-called other (serious) viewer visited the studio three weeks ago, just before the first expiry of Nyx's exclusive agency arrangement. Nyx was hopeful, as the viewer appeared quite interested then. She asked many questions.

"This condo doesn't engage human security guards at all?" "What happens if there's a security breach?" "2 years rental period is the minimum?" "Do you know the occupants of the unit opposite?" "Are they renting also?" "Do you know what they do for a living?" "Are they noisy (or nosy)?"

She repeated the same questions for the units above. *And* below also. Nyx was hard-pressed to provide the answers; she found some of the questions absurd and vexing actually.

"How would I know? I don't stay here!" She defended herself then (in her mind, of course). Nyx gave up after some follow-up when the viewer stopped replying to her texts.

There were no more viewings since and no viewing scheduled for tomorrow morning either. Sean was still her best and final bet before the expiry of her exclusive arrangement with the owner at the end of the week.

"Sean, can you revert with your decision by tomorrow night?" Nyx raised her voice despite him being just metres away from her. She wanted to ensure her request would lodge firmly in his prospective memory while trying for a presumptive close of sorts at the same time. Clearly, the exigency of her situation had reasserted itself in Nyx's mind.

Suddenly, she felt the frailty of her own heart again. For a moment, she considered to use the now fictitious viewer as a ploy to instil a sense of urgency in Sean. Then, as quickly as the thought appeared, she banished it completely so there would be no chance of it transmuting into words. She felt a gentle wave of penitent pleasure instantly that erased the imprints of her guilt from before. Nyx was pleased with her self-control this time, which went some ways to ease her anxiety.

"I'll do my best," Sean acknowledged, no hint of any ignored or unregistered bait.

"Thanks," Nyx replied out of courtesy, but clearly wearing her disappointment on her face. Her shoulders sagged ever so slightly. She had succeeded in getting his attention; she had failed in getting a firm commitment from him. Her heart raced a little, her breathing became somewhat asthmatic too. Slowly, her simmering desperation was coming to a boil again.

Sean would not have bothered even if he had known Nyx's predicament; he was in a quagmire of his own with its quandaries to resolve. At the top of his short-term memory stack was the pressing need to find a rental apartment as soon as possible.

For the past six months or so, he had been wondering, "who is in a direr situation than I am?" When we are in trouble, life-shattering kind of trouble, our circumstances always appear to be the only ones that are huge enough to warrant any attention in this world.

"Most likely has to do with distance and vision—how to see clearly, wholly and objectively when the problem is up so close and personal?" Someone asked with a mix of sarcasm and pity.

Well, one item was definitely on its way to settlement. After toiling at it for the last few weeks, Sean had made up his mind to take up the rental when he left the studio earlier. Did he already decide after the 'It's also very private' was check-marked on his mental list? Was someone else in his driving seat?

The proclivities of the unconscious mind lead the conscious part to act. The former foreordain the ending while the rationalisation of the latter merely provides the script and props for the plot. Still, our intelligence demands the indiscernible rigmarole behind the drama that provides the context and background for our intentions and actions.

Sean decided to follow Nyx's proposed deadline. "Why not be kind to her and do it now?" Someone-Else asked. "Maybe his conscious mind needed more time to chat with his unconscious counterpart." Someone-New guessed. Naturally, the voices were conversing quietly. Consciously, Sean had other bothers. The universe did not give a damn either; it merely followed its own unyielding rhythm and pulled everything else forward in synchrony. Nonetheless, things appeared terribly chaotic some times.

Lucky Nyx, she did not know it yet: she would be celebrating with delight tomorrow. Now, another night of torturous uncertainty seemed inevitable. "Sigh! Need to destress, time for a nice hot soak." She tried to be good to herself whenever she could afford it. After putting on her music player, she proceeded to run the tap for her bath. Adele's sultry soulful voice wafted in her apartment, the lyrics of *When We Were Young*' cuddled Nyx's heart as she recalled again the bitter-sweetness of her very first love. Unconsciously, the tip of her tongue skimmed and moistened her pouty lips.

Not-so-lucky Sean, he would have to fork out an extra five hundred dollars each month. That was a small worry: what money could address was no problem at all. What money could not solve? Now, that would be a *real* problem indeed!

"Fuck! ...Fuck me! ...I'm so fucked!" Sean swore helplessly, pounding his clenched fists on the steering wheel at the same time. For five minutes now, maybe ten, he had been sitting inside his car, parked in the car porch of his house, feeling extremely trapped and stumped all at once.

The Best Psychotherapist

Who does not like to be normal? Normal life flows easier. Daily social interactions are freer and spontaneous, and require less effort. Where mental illness is associated, a sense of normalcy avoids unwanted stress and stigma. So Faye thought as she assessed the image of her two and a half year old psychotherapy practice.

"*Client* is a friendlier term and gives the practice an air of regularity, like a *client* of a legal firm or a business consultancy. How can you call him a patient? He is not suffering from dementia. At least not yet…if ever." Her voice reasoned further.

Effectively, her conscious mind was endorsing her unconscious impression and bias. Consequently, she made a judgement call about the terminology to apply to people like Sean who might be at risk of but not diagnosed with dementia at all.

When Faye first set up her own practice, her clientele were patients only, a handful of early-stage dementia sufferers. They had followed her into private practice from her prior appointment at NCDAZ Psychiatric Hospital where she had distinguished herself as a psychotherapist. Her clientele grew steadily by word of mouth through the family members of her patients mostly. This held special significance for Faye. It was an acknowledgement that she had positively affected the lives of her patients, and maybe their families as well. She was pleased with what her inner voice was telling her.

"Why would someone recommend me?" Faye asked but the voice was quiet now. "I have to be excellent in ministration, temperamentally fit for the profession, and have effective treatment programs for anyone to refer me, do I not?" She continued with her rhetoric, feeling quiet contentment and utmost pride as the thought lingered in her mind.

"How can one continue to be good at a craft that exacts so much of one's intellectual capacity, emotional energy and social sensibilities if not for the passion and belief in the goodness of one's work?"

"She's becoming self-indulgent now," Someone-Else said disapprovingly.

Without a shadow of doubt, Faye derived tremendous satisfaction and fulfilment when she considered the success of her practice after such a relatively short time. She was purposeful, her work was meaningful and she was exceedingly glad at this point in her life.

It was Friday evening. Faye was contemplating this from the comfort of her home, cavernous for a two-bedroom apartment. It was located in an exclusive suburb outside the city—sufficiently near so she could get to her office quickly if required, sufficiently far so she could disconnect from the bright lights and enervating noise of the city. The city had become far too boisterous for her liking, even during the small hours of the morning. On weekdays too. She much preferred restful sleep that would keep her mind and body sharp and attractive. She was vain after all.

Her apartment afforded her lots of privacy: one of two on the top floor of a single block condominium, with its own elevator that went from her parking lot in the basement to her unit and opened directly into a foyer prior to the living room.

"They are a very private family," Faye's agent commented on the Caucasian family occupying the one other unit opposite hers while she was property hunting. Faye valued her personal privacy immensely and her agent knew that.

Shortly after Faye moved here, she chanced upon the couple with their toddler at the swimming pool. They were Germans and had been renting for a little over two years by then. The husband was on a transnational posting with his company, his first outside of Europe. Faye liked it that they were a very private family indeed.

Faye's apartment came with a good-size balcony that opened to the unshielded expanse above and a picturesque view of the city. Beautiful at night when the city was all lighted up like sparkling gems in the distant. Beguiling and magical when the night was cool and the cloudless sky was sufficiently dark for the universe to flaunt its sublime constellations. Her apartment was white-painted throughout and tastefully furnished: modern with zen-like simplicity. Very charming. Very Faye.

"Now, time for a nice hot soak." Faye's eyes sparkled as she looked forward to her bath. She could afford to be good to herself; she had earned it after all.

"Think I should move upstream, take up cases of people who may be at-risk but not diagnosed with dementia (yet)," Faye pondered aloud. The temperature of the hot bathwater cocooning her still winsome body did its wonders to relax her muscles and calm her nerves after a long and hard day. The soothing beautiful music of Enya's *'Only Time'* emanated from her bedroom, hauntingly echoing throughout her apartment, and mystically adding cogency to her thoughts at the same time.

"Most logical to work on early intervention and prevention rather than post-diagnostic treatment. I've always preferred proactivity anyway. Can help me be a better diagnostician, expand my repertoire and keep me on the cutting edge of my practice." The voice rejoined, adding to Faye's pleasure.

On top of that, if the person eventually develops dementia, I will have all the history I need for a proper prognosis and be in a better position to prescribe a treatment program. More effective and seamless too. She rationalised further.

"All right then, strategy done and dusted, straightforward enough. Now onto execution—I will start sending word out to affect this next week," Faye summed up her decision quite easily.

"What has just happened? Is that how she decides?" Someone-Else asked. Did Faye intuitively decide based on some heuristics? Obviously, she was confident that those were the right decisions although the process appeared short-circuited somewhat.

"Why the sudden need to expand the profile of her clientele?" Someone-Else asked further. "She is probably getting bored; maybe she needs some excitement in her life," the voice proffered. "May not be sudden at all, just seemed so." Someone added.

Faye was doing very well surely. However, she was settling into a holding pattern unconsciously as her practice became more effortless with time.

("Easier is a good thing, isn't it?" Her mum would say, almost every time, whenever she asked about her daughter's well-being during her visits, which Faye still felt very at home in.

"There is more to life than work, baby," her mum would nudge Faye along some tacit path.

"You sure about the path you are suggesting? Your marriage is not exactly panning out the way you had wanted, has it?" Someone asked her mum during her daughter's most recent visit.

"My work is my life," Faye would retort, but she knew work was losing its shine, she feared her mind would become spent. All the same, her parents' recent separation had disheartened her.

Her mum would look at her daughter with a rueful smile.

"She's a big girl now, it's her life after all," Someone advised and her mum left Faye be.)

Faye had a revolting disdain for the quotidian. Behind her empathetic façade, she was an intellectual snob really. (Did she get this from her dad?)

Settling into some form of routine and becoming more efficient was fine; flowing in autopilot tedium, becoming brain-dead in status quo ennui was not okay with Faye in the least bit.

"Automation is most applicable to a predictable and repeatable process," the technologist informed Faye (from some recollection).

This will fuel more talk of artificial intelligence taking over human professionals, how can I allow robots to destroy my life's work? The pugnacious thought crossed Faye's mind.

Psychotherapy is both science and art; it is not as straightforward as what some uninformed technologists may think. There are algorithms. There are heuristics. Then there is the infinite-faceted, multi-layered and unpredictable human nature. Just ask robots to handle humans and you'll know what I mean. Faye was incensed at this point. She seemed to be growling at the imaginary technologist in her mind.

Faye's practice had become her identity. She was also missing the exhilaration of achievement-centred affirmation—the rush of dopamine and endorphin—that would give her a mountaintop feeling. "The most recent one was quite some while ago already," Faye reminisced wistfully. When recalled, she seemed to value the memory at the time of her achievement over her arduous experience enroute to it. Surprisingly, she even neglected the time duration of that experience in her memory.

"As illogical or unexpected as this might seem, Faye is quintessentially human after all. We do the same all the time, unconsciously." Someone-New explained.

Definitely settled, then. The reasons Faye articulated in her mind a while ago were the afterthoughts to satisfy herself that she had given her decision due process. *Whatever!* She was not one to indulge in overthinking or superfluous self-examination anyhow.

"And her antagonistic tirade on robots?" Someone-Else asked.

"Just an emotional outburst, don't bother," Someone answered.

"Robots cannot do what I do, not in my lifetime surely," Faye was acutely aware and thoroughly convinced of her belief.

"Don't be so certain," Someone-New cautioned nonetheless.

With her professional reputation and a small but significant network, Faye started taking on new clients not long after.

Concurrently, she also initiated a review of her current clientele. For a couple of them, their conditions had progressed beyond the early or mild stage of dementia. The skills and treatment required for advanced stage dementia were quite different from her extant equipping and equipment. Most likely, an increase in the frequency of the therapy sessions with these patients would be required, which Faye was not prepared to do. She wanted to live life on her own terms now. In fact, her ideal would be a fortnightly arrangement, and most definitely not more than once a week.

I will forward refer them to other specialists better suited to handle their condition, she decided after some consideration.

Some of them may need to move to assisted living facilities even, which will be better for their well-being and safety, she justified further.

Once I do that, I will have more time for *new* clients. Faye perked up on that last thought.

"There you go another conscious decision and action motivated by unconscious inclinations and desires," Someone-Else remarked cynically. Faye was really trying to re-profile her client base. Briefly, she flashed back to her interview with Dr Lee at NCDAZ Psychiatric Hospital.

"It's going to be very hard work dealing with dementia patients, not to mention the toil on your emotional and social lives." "Can even morph us mentally and physically over time."

How prescient his advice then! How uncanny her reflection now!

Faye's gait seemed affected as if she was carrying more than just the weight of her head on her shoulders. Her instinctual body knew that she needed a rejuvenation.

Faye always did her utmost to prime her own destiny. "I *still* want to be the best psychotherapist I can be." Faye informed everyone unequivocally.

"She just needs to know what she's giving up in exchange for all this ambition." Someone-New offered up for everyone's consideration.

The Emotional Fast Thinking Brain

Everyone was out and Ming was alone in his study. He sat himself in the armchair by the corner facing the full-length windows and wall-high bookshelves. Now in control, he stopped feeling harried. The shower had delivered on its promise as usual.

"Hey" …Ming WhatsApped Beth when he was certain it was safe for him to do so. It was night already, and it might not be convenient for Beth to respond.

He got up to insert a CD into the Meridian audio system, a special edition unit released in collaboration with Alfred Dunhill. It sat alone and centrally at an eye-level, on a shelf allocated fully to it, commanding reverential attention like a little emperor on his throne.

When Ming first bought the Meridian and brought it home, he had taken pains to ensure its positioning was optimal, and would not compromise the quality of the sound produced by the audio system. He was exceedingly pleased when he first used the system thereafter. The sound was so immersive like none other than he had experienced before.

An impeccable addition to the study, he thought then.

As the CD played, Ming settled back into his armchair, and quietly appreciated the deep, slow gravelly whispering-talking-voice of Leonard Cohen, which flowed from the system with absolute high fidelity. While he waited for Beth's reply, he tried to occupy himself with the magazine he had purchased yesterday.

Incidentally, Ming had come across the magazine while browsing in a bookshop near his office, and waiting for his colleague to pay for his stuff at the cashier. The magazine contained a review of Beth's latest novel—*The Debauched Sepulchre in Wat Khemathaya*—of her *Therasudorsa* series. What intrigued Ming initially was that critics were still reviewing her novel though six months had passed since its launch. This was quite unusual.

Moreover, the title of the review article baffled him—*Beth Neo has done it again: produced a home run of a novel*. Why a local literary critic would use the baseball game as an analogy was beyond him. This was the first time he had come across a sports analogy deployed to review a piece of literary work. Secondly, baseball was not even a popular sport locally. Perhaps the review was in a sports magazine. Brawn trying to be brainy? Regardless, he was curious to read the lengthy article but he could not apply himself fully there and then at the bookshop.

Back at his study, the words of the article failed to connect with Ming. His mind kept circling back to his predicament. His situation had continued to evolve and taken a dramatic shift about six months ago. Actually, the tremors could have started with invisible cracks months or even years before, and built up to what happened eventually.

For Beth, her grand unravelling of sorts occurred a year ago. Her situation had stabilised somewhat after some initial unrests. That was what she had been telling him all this while.

At the very beginning of their relationship, they had agreed on some ground rules and time windows during the day (and night) where they could communicate with each other privately and not expose themselves to undue risks. Ming had more flexibility and control during the day; he was working for a transnational corporation and quite senior in the company's hierarchy. Beth worked from home mostly, sometimes wherever she could find inspiration for her writing regime. She worked from the libraries also if she was conducting her research and collating stuff for her writing. Home would be more constraining naturally, especially when her husband worked from home occasionally but with no specific routine. Sometimes, he would be home earlier than usual without prior notice. This unpredictability strained Beth greatly, even after her grand unravelling.

They would talk on the phone whenever possible or just text otherwise. Their chats would last about fifteen minutes mostly, sometimes longer but rarely going over half an hour. The shorter duration ones tended to concentrate on scheduling for meets (some might call these trysts though they much rather keep to meets, and not for reasons of social respectability or personal probity). Then, they could spend substantial time together, abandoned to each other without a care in the world.

If they could not talk at all, "No worries, it's not the end of the world yea" would be Ming's crisp text on some occasions. He would try to sound cheerful and light-hearted to hide his disappointment.

At other times, Beth would sound her usual refrain, "better to be safe" (especially before her situation unravelled with her husband).

"There would always be another opportunity," she would add, to keep their flickering hope alive.

Complacency would set in after some time; they did not plan this. Their brains found it tiring and boring to maintain constant vigilance.

"Quite a common human behaviour actually, it happens naturally most times." Someone said matter-of-factly.

However, exercising self-control was not always easy. Impulses and emotions could suddenly seize control, and the primitive brain would demand to have its needs met instantly. Having zero control, the chemicals in their brains would inflame their situation further. Under such circumstances, Ming and Beth would try their utmost to exercise self-control, judge their situations against a larger context and make choices that favour future benefits over short-term gratifications. However, the future benefits for them, with the concomitant unrests, might be just as troublesome, so the trade-offs were not always apparent or straightforward for them. They could find no weighing scale that could accurately compare a certain short-term and an uncertain long-term.

"The emotional roller-coaster and self-control exercises are really taxing our brains, plus the hormonal rush, all keeping us young and fit," Ming quipped, trying for light-heartedness during one of their meets.

"But it's really draining, don't you find it?" Beth replied in a defeated tone, as if giving in to the stubborn heaviness that refused to go away. What they experienced was axiomatic: denying the *fast* thinking instincts what they want was hard, exhausting brainwork.

They did wonder if there was any future at all—sometimes aloud in their conversations, most times quietly during their own contemplation. The latter were quite trying: there were no one to check his or her isolated thinking and intuitions.

"This is my first time; it's hard to figure things out. Between us, whatever we see is all there is. There is no one else to help us see what we are missing. That's problematic, isn't it?" Beth shared this sentiment one day when they were *slowly* thinking through their situation. Ming concurred immediately; the same thought had crossed his mind as well.

Strangely, Ming sometimes wondered if this was truly the case for Beth, her first time that is. Her bohemian personality hung like a perennial question mark over her head.

Then again, given the complexity and spectrum of human relationships, this could well be the first of its kind for her. Ming defended Beth in his mind.

"That seems like stretching the truth; you are giving excuses on her behalf now?" A voice questioned Ming at the same time.

However, he kept this doubt to himself; in fact, he chose to give Beth the benefit of the doubt.

"Innocent until proven guilty," and so he repeated every time to shut the voice up.

Beth did not like to talk about her past. However, some vignettes slipped out from time to time, on rare occasions when she was in an introspective and talkative mood or when she was exhausted and her guard was down. Ming did not feel compelled to dig into her past, not at the beginning.

Alluring and interesting—this enigma about Beth, Ming thought instead. Was he lost in enchantment?

When it came to chatting, at night would be especially sensitive for both of them. However, they had allocated a window for *emergency* as they originally intended, which seemed ridiculous considering what actually happened. They would chat during that night window when the circumstances were hardly dire, dangerous or at a crisis-level going by the common understanding of *emergency*.

Initially, they would utilise the night window for days and weeks on end, seemingly in a continual hurry to share some memories and their day. So much to say, so little time to say them. Overwhelmed, they just wanted to get the words out of their brains before they all disappeared, unsaid. However, the memories were part of them. They were not going anywhere. Recallable anytime as long as both brains stayed intact and death did not steal anyone away prematurely. Still, they gave in to this hard-to-control impulse most times.

Love is possessive of time, is it not? It wants to fill every minute of the present with its fullness, every bit of the past with its memories and every hope of the future with its dreams.

Is this limerence: the love potion (an addictive and some say a dangerous cocktail of hormones—dopamine, oxytocin, vasopressin, testosterone, oestrogen and norepinephrine) floods the physiological brain impulsively and holds the psychological mind hostage to the concomitant obsessive-compulsive disorder-like thoughts, emotions and behaviours? Can this be *real* love? Beth and Ming could not differentiate but they were not thinking this consciously (or *slowly*) either.

"We didn't actually define what *emergency* meant," Ming would justify later on when they were having afternoon coffee at their usual not-so-popular café in the familiar remote part of town.

"Stop kidding yourself, as if it would have made a difference," a voice yawped sarcastically at him. Ming was affronted.

"Fuck off! There's no need to be so blunt!" He bellowed back to shut the voice up immediately. However, his eyes betrayed his guilt.

Beth would interject in her calm manly-womanly voice whenever she was lucid and restrained, and remind themselves again, "Self-control and circumspection will be essential and vital if we want to protect what we have."

They were lucky…until their luck ran out, or their complacency set in. Then the distinct worlds each had sought to partition up started to collide and unravel—first for Beth, then for Ming.

Habitually, they continued with the ground rules set at the beginning even after the unravelling. "A habit starts to form when the sequence of activities and the rules and innuendoes that associate these activities together are stored as procedural memory in the malleable brain. With sufficient repetitions, the habit takes over unconsciously." Someone-New reminded everyone. It had dredged up some technical stuff from an article in a psychology review that Ming had shared with Beth some while back. "During formation, we may even register some emotions with the habit. Later on, these associated emotions may prompt us into automatic actions. The same goes for changing habits."

"Why the sudden lecture?" Someone asked.

"Well…habits have gotten them into their current quagmire, do you not think so? As in driving, it is crucial to stay focused on the road conditions, otherwise subconscious habits can lead us to miss life-impacting traffic and warning signs." Someone-New answered.

"Most prudent to be watchful of the emotional *fast* thinking brain," all voices chorused, which seemed to harmonise Beth and Ming's thinking around their shared predicament at this point.

I'm Happy if You Are Happy

"Hi"…Beth replied ten minutes later. Her text woke Ming's iPhone up. *'In My Secret Life'* (by Leonard Cohen) was now playing in the background but Beth could not hear any bit of it. *Duh!*

"How's ur day?"
"Guess what"
"Found the place I want to rent"
"Think u'll like it"

Ming texted away in rapid succession without giving Beth a chance to reply.

"That's gr8"
"Is it one of those I sent u?"

Beth ignored his first question. (With WhatsApp, she had also become sloppy with her spelling.) Her day was not good at all; she felt out of control and had not done much but she thought not to burden Ming with her frustration. But she felt a flurry of excitement when she saw his text, which lifted her spirit visibly.

Stay focused on his rental apartment search, Beth's inner voice directed. Shortly after Ming had informed her of his decision to move out of his matrimonial home, she had forwarded him some suggestions that matched his selection criteria and budget.

"No. Found this myself"
"U wanna view?"

"Is it avail oredi?"
"May not be safe 4 me"

"Sure safe"
"Arrange 2 view like a customer"
"Yes avail now"
"Plan to cfm with Nyx 2molo night"
"Ard 8pm"

"Let me think". Beth was not inclined to Ming's suggestion at all. Her gut was telling her something but she could not quite make out what it was. Was the stress of their predicament getting to her?

"Btw Nyx is the agent"
"And guess what"
"She has the same type of blouse as you"…
"Your bright royal blue one"
"Hers a snow-white one"
"Btw pls view b4 that"
"Sending over the contact now"
"N the details of the unit"
Ming paused his WhatsApp after this torrent of messages, pulled out Nyx's name-card from his contact app and shared it over their chat-line.

"Do I really need 2 view?" Beth remained reluctant, and highly sceptical of its necessity. Intuitively, she wanted to distant herself from his decision.

"What about the others?"

"Have u viewed those I sent u?"

Beth was clearly disappointed that none of her referrals seemed to have interested Ming at all.

Ming called up his photo app, searched for the screenshot of the property, the one with his annotation in it, and shared it over the chat-line, followed by another salvo of messages.

"Good if u can. I like u 2 like it 2"

"It's really private"

"Runway getting short"

"Really need to bed down on one soon"

"This is the best of the lot"

"Including some of those u sent me"

"Time running out"

"No need 2 c anymore"

Time was also running out now as they had been chatting for slightly over fifteen minutes already. Despite this, Beth was extremely curious about the rental unit. She skipped Nyx's name-card, ignored his texts about Nyx's blouse (not interested at all, who cared what she was wearing!) but immediately opened up the picture of the rental unit when it appeared on her phone. Then, she went on to search the property portal directly for the same listing.

Just as Beth had suspected when she saw the picture a while ago. She had come across the same studio in her own searches about a month back but on a different property portal. Quickly, she consulted google maps just to confirm the location. In a flash, Nyx's face flickered in her mind; it corroborated with her earlier hunch instantly!

"Hey I need to go"

"Kim back soon"

"Like anytime now"

"Give me a min" Beth texted back after a long pause…
"Viewing the stuff u sent over"

"K"
"Pls b quick"
Ming replied and did his best to be patient.

Slightly over three weeks ago, Beth had viewed exactly the same studio. Around a month before that, she had started her own rental apartment search for herself. She had decided to keep her plan from Ming right from the start. Hence, she did not inform him after she had viewed the studio. For some reason, she did not forward this listing to him either. Ming did not suspect that Beth was evaluating rental apartments herself; he had assumed she was helping him cope with his situation.

Finally, Beth broke the suspense.
"Ok. No need 2 view"
"Studio looks gr8"…
"If u think it's good, go ahead n commit"…
"Don't worry about me"
"U r the 1 moving in"

Ming went quiet instantly when he read the last few messages from Beth. His brows twitched spontaneously. His study sounded speciously quiet too despite the CD now playing *Dance Me to the End of Love*' (also by Leonard Cohen, it was a CD of his songs, was it not?) at a relaxed volume Ming would normally set at when he was alone in the study.

Are there new developments at Beth's end? He wondered automatically though not immediately conscious of the thought. There was something in the tone of her texts. Such certainty. So final! His body reacted too; his jaw muscles tightened and he felt some indistinct physical discomfort on his shoulders.

"Hey, u still there?"
Beth texted again, sensing something was behind Ming's lengthy pause. Was Kim back already?

Then Ming texted back, "Here"
"All right, if u think so"
"I'm cool 2"
"Let me know if u change ur mind yea"
"Anyway will send over some pics of the place"
He decided to go along, as it was time to close their chat soon.

"It's very private, u said" Beth queried again as if she needed further assurance of what was clearly still retrievable from his texts just a while ago.

"Yes n I plan 2 cfm the rental 2molo"

"Ok, I'm happy if u r happy"
"The pics shud be good enuf"
"Let me know once u hav sealed it"
"U gotta go? Kim back?"
"I gotta go 2"

"Ok. U go. We chat again 2molo"

"Ok. Night. I luv u" Beth said, and waited for a while to see if there would be a reply.

"Nite luv u 2"
"Sleep tight xoxo"

Ming texted back almost immediately. He then put his phone into screen-saver mode and laid it on the table beside him, with its face down. All part of a habit.

What is Honesty, Honestly?

Beth's eyes remained glued to her WhatsApp. She considered whether to delete the messages.

"Better to be safe." She heard a soft and subdued voice whispering between her ears but decided to ignore it and left the messages where they were.

No difference, it is an open secret among the few of us already anyway, she concluded with ambivalence.

Next, Beth went through her chat with Ming again, downloaded his screenshot of the rental unit and saved it in her photo album. She remembered making a similar screenshot a while back but Ming's picture had his annotation, and she wanted to keep this detail as well as the property portal where Ming had found it. Whatever for? She did not know exactly. Irrationally, she thought some need for it might present itself at some future time.

Then, Beth created a new album—Ming's studio—in her photo app, downloaded all the pictures Ming had sent her, and stored them there. She noticed the warm light and beautiful sunset in one of them and smiled delightfully, unawares. Beth had viewed the studio in the morning. Naturally, she would not have witness any sunset at that time since the studio was west facing.

Beth ignored Nyx's name-card altogether. She had deleted all of Nyx's SMSes as well as her contact in her phonebook after Nyx could not convince the property owner to let out the unit for a year only. This was some weeks ago now.

Unknowingly, Beth's thoughts switched to Kim suddenly. Until now, Ming had shared very little of his daughter with her, not even a picture of Kim. Yet Beth felt a certain affinity for Kim. Her fusiform gyrus could form an image of a face even, which vaguely associated with the familiar sounding name. Amongst the countless autographs her fans had requested, Beth could recall a Kim Tang as one of the addressees in her signings, albeit indistinctly. Nonetheless, an uncommon combination of names that seemed to have stuck with her. Was this memory reliable? Otherwise, her impression of Kim a mirage? She did not bring this up with Ming at all. A quid pro quo intuition to shut out his curiosity about her husband?

"Why are you keeping Ming in the dark regarding your rental apartment search?" the voice pushed Kim out of Beth's thought pattern and reasserted the rental apartment subject abruptly. Its tone appeared interrogative this time. Beth felt a sharp pang in her heart. Was that a flash of guilt? Or for what was about to happen? She could not distinguish one from the other.

"*He didn't ask!*" Beth riposted feistily.

"Do you think it will occur to him to ask? Do you not think he would want to know? Given what he's done for you, don't you think you have a moral obligation to tell him?" the voice barraged on, poking at her selfish heart and trying to drum up some guilt in Beth concurrently.

"How dare you put it all on me? I went through goddamned hell too…you jolly well know what happened…way before his own bloody shit broke through his god-forsaken fence." Beth bit back with the reflexive ferocity of a cornered dog. Her distressed heart was pounding her ears with no mercy by now. The voice had struck an extremely raw nerve, delivering what felt like a mild attack to her heart. Or a stab on her back? Regardless, her stress hormones shot right through the roof then.

"I thought you are on my side," Beth whispered meekly after a while, feeling thoroughly betrayed. However, silence resounded. She thought she knew the reason for what she did and did not do. Now, she was not so sure anymore. Nonetheless, her psychosomatic episode appeared ominous.

Beth knew that she was a worrier. Her natural disposition? Ming opined that her craft shaped her into one, and would drone on with his thoughts on the artiste class.

"Most writers are empathetic: they sense things, are curious and attentive."

"They see details that most others miss."

"They feel stuff, more deeply than may be helpful sometimes."

"Imagine possibilities."

"Develop creative solutions quite easily, naturally even."

"The questions they ask, different to say the least."

"Unusual most times. Absurd sometimes."

"Or borderline crazy at times."

"It helps them surely, needful even—inventing stories and fabricating fictional characters for a living."

Actually, Beth was quite successful in her craft. Some others would consider her an expert in her art. She could lay claim to a small oeuvre—the *Therasudorsa* universe she created, which was critically acclaimed by her peers. There now existed a significant fan base for her novels that was still growing, among the junior college-graduating teen and undergraduate youth segments. She presumed their parents would also be readers of her works. The stereotypical parent would want to know what their kids were actually reading. (These parents surely excluded Ming, as he had never come across the *Therasudorsa* universe until he met Beth.)

"The total readership is probably larger than the sales volume of my books." Beth shared her suspicion with her publisher at one point.

In the last five to six years or thereabouts, the readership of Beth's books had grown to include the young adults starting out in the workforce also. Seemingly, this occurred after the publication of her third novel—*The Deadly Mace of Barabudur*. Beth greeted this happenstance with smug satisfaction: she had always sensed this segment would be interested in the themes expounded in her *Therasudorsa* universe, her sublime storytelling aside.

"You are unconventional surely, your problem may be in overthinking things," Ming told her a couple of times before, at different junctures and with absolute confidence each time.

"You are seeing shadows and ghosts where there aren't any, and it's making you more edgy and mercurial." Ming would add each time.

Beth had considered his opinion and discarded it the second time onwards. It was her nature; she was confident of her own self-awareness.

Beth also knew Ming to be opinionated and cocky at times. It would rile her up badly if he persisted in his views despite her informing him otherwise.

"Too sure of himself, talks out of his depth sometimes. *He is not listening to what I am saying!* If he continues like this, he's going to miss stuff." She became disheartened at this point.

"Nature or nurture? That is an age-old question." Someone commented.

"Both really, the latest scientific understanding apparently." Someone-New shared.

"What about the mix between nature and nurture?" Someone-Else asked.

"It depends on whom you ask." "This is the foremost question now compared to the earlier one." *Whatever!* Everyone found this quite bothersome after a while.

Quietly, Someone-New sensed that Beth had begun to share lesser and lesser with Ming unconsciously.

"Remember the law of least effort?" her brain seemed to urge innocuously, "Why bother? He's not interested in sharing your shadows and ghosts anyway, however real they are to you."

Circling back to her own rental apartment search, Beth knew she had stonewalled the voice. Why was she harbouring secrets from Ming? Did they not agree to be honest with each other?

"Ming did not seem to care, *he did not ask*," Beth repeated her excuse softly, quite defensively this time.

"What is honesty, honestly?" Beth was spinning in her own mind now.

"Is it only acts of commission—I did not lie?"

"What about acts of omission—wilful withholding of information that may be relevant, important even, to the person concerned?"

"Is honesty the same as transparency?"

The maelstrom of voices in her head was tearing at her in earnest now.

Surreptitiously, a deep tenderness for Ming overwhelmed Beth; she was missing him intensely all of a sudden. Just as well, she felt mentally drained by this time.

Inexplicable: how all of our emotions can swing so wildly and extremely and suddenly all at once. What does all this punishing stress do to our fragile hearts?

"*Enough!* Time for some wine," Beth surrendered; her depleted brain needed some sugar replenishment.

Mental exhaustion has a way of unleashing our primal appetites—good food (and wine), sublime music, agreeable fuck, or sleep when combined with extreme physical fatigue—and forging the path of least resistance towards fulfilment.

Beth had no energy left for self-control, let alone honesty.

Ever so slowly, the climate of their relationship was a-changing: like incoming waves, the seas of the spoken would wash over the sandy shores of the unspoken, leaving no imprints on the sands when the tides go out, and changing the shoreline ever so subtly with each in-coming wave and each out-going tide.

All the same, Beth would become economical with her words over time.

"*He is not listening to what I am saying!* Better left unsaid," Beth would justify sometimes when she was conscious on her part. A cop-out?

"*He didn't ask!*" Maybe she expected Ming to read her mind instead. A greater folly then?

Unfortunately, some secrets would gather among the unspoken stuff, festering an environment for misunderstanding, delusion and distrust eventually.

Better Not To Know

Back in his study, Ming tried to read his magazine again but his mind quickly became noisy and distracted.

After a while, he picked up his phone and went back to reread his chat with Beth. Words and thoughts comingled in his mind as he scrolled the chat bubbles back and forth.

"She didn't want to view."

"Unusual! Given her natural curiosity?"

"She seemed so certain and final about it also"

"Is this all there is?"

No answers associated in his mind. As much as Ming could remember, he did not think he had missed anything. Then again, as in *The Invisible Gorilla*, he might have missed what was obviously in front of him, and still believed he had not missed a single thing.

Ming knew Beth to be enigmatic, especially with respect to her past. She wanted her space: be free and accountable to no one. *And* for nothing. In this regard, talking about her past seemed to impute a responsibility on her that she resented deeply. If only Beth was just complicated: given enough time, Ming would have figured her out; but she was utterly complex: no amount of time could clear up the murkiness surrounding her life.

"The past is passed, we can't do anything about it, no point talking," Beth's manly-womanly voice drifted into Ming's consciousness.

"This posture might have been all right at the beginning when things were tentative. However, he has a right to be curious about Beth at this stage." Someone said, giving voice to Ming's sentiment.

"She should feel safe to share her past with me after what I have gone through for her. After all, I share with her *everything*, anything, when she asks." Ming justified to himself consciously now, in a mumbled jumbled sort of way.

"Then again, sometimes it is better not to know some things," Someone-New counselled knowingly.

Ming's mind wavered as thoughts buffeted him from all sides.

We prefer our loved ones to lie to us sometimes, do we not? Suppose we like it best when we cannot tell the lie from the truth—a lie we want to believe in, a truth we are not *yet* ready to accept.

Ming felt heavy-hearted and discordant at this point.

Suddenly, Kim knocked on the door. Did his spirit just jump out of his body? Regardless, Kim entered his study—without asking for permission nor waiting to receive one—crashing his train of thought instantly.

"Dad, regarding my uni, you were priming me to research into the US colleges, all the stuff you forwarded me while I was still in Zurich? When can we dive into these?" Kim asked enthusiastically, impervious to the bewildered look on her dad's face.

"Let's try this weekend," Kim's father replied impulsively, albeit a little robotically akin to a voice answering machine.

Then, Keat woke up to his daughter's presence, "Listen Kimmy, dad needs to get some stuff settled. Can we rain-check again this weekend?" correcting himself almost immediately after.

"Sure." A little disappointed with his wishy-washy reply but Kim sensed that her father wished to be alone.

Looking at his furrowed brows, Kim speculated on the matter on her father's mind. She suspected something was going on between her parents, as things had been quite weird after her return from Zurich two weeks ago. On a few mornings, Kim caught her dad entering his bedroom while hugging his pillows. She was going to wash up then. Flagrante delicto. She thought her dad was unaware.

"Is dad sleeping in the guest room downstairs? Hmm...seems bizarre." Kim wondered to herself after the second sighting.

"First time may be an accident, second time may be a co-incidence, but the third time may be the start of something real, a pattern of sorts, and time to be watchful." Her dad's utterance resounded in her mind.

"Better not to intrude right now, they will tell me if it's something I need to know," she self-advised deferentially.

Unexpectedly, a dinner scene flickered like a feeble candle flame for an infinitesimal moment. Familiar visuals formed in her brain. She was safe and secure in her mom's bosom. Her mom's reassuring words replayed in her mind. Ominously, it disappeared as suddenly as it had appeared a moment ago, as if a thumb with its forefinger had appeared out of nowhere to snuff the flame out completely.

"Don't stay up too late. See you in the morning." Kim advised her father in a singsong way, squeezing him lightly on his arm a couple of times as if to massage his brain knowingly. (Did parent and child just switch roles?) She then trotted off as casually as she had let herself in earlier, leaving Ming to wallow in his own quagmire. A pig in its swill? Definitely not a happy pig.

'Boogie Street' wafted from the Meridian: a ghost was serenading in his study. Leonard Cohen's deep, slow gravelly whispering-talking-voice seeped in to fill the void that had opened up quietly inside Ming.

It was almost mid-night now; the air was still and thick with nostalgia. He reminisced as he listened wistfully: his serendipitous meeting with Beth. Unwittingly, he had escaped to somewhere familiar and safe, pausing the rigmarole in his brain for the time being.

Contact Me for a Therapy

Two years after Faye started taking on clients, she bumped into a friend (well, not exactly one most would call a friend) at the supermarket. The only supermarket in her neighbourhood that stocked everything organic and only organic. It was a Saturday morning; Faye was on her weekly grocery run when the serendipitous meeting happened.

"Hey Faye, it's been a while. How have you been?" Tess called out from the end of an aisle. Faye was in the middle of the same aisle, looking to replenish her usual oatmeal at home. There was a new brand on the shelf and she was studying the label while evaluating if she should try it.

"Oh hi, Tess. I'm good. How about you? How's your mum doing?" Faye replied enthusiastically as though she was in a dire need of some social connectivity. Simultaneously, Faye was trying very hard to refresh her mind of their last encounter. She remembered Tess's mum very well—one of those patients from NCDAZ whom followed her into private practice.

However, Faye had forward referred Tess's mum to another specialist more than a year ago now as the patient's condition had advanced beyond her practice's capability to handle. Subsequently, after some joint diagnosis with her specialist friend, they had recommended to Tess for her mother to relocate to an assisted living facility for dementia patients.

"It would be for the best," they had advised Tess, "you mum's condition has advanced quite dramatically in the last three months. At this rate, she will most certainly need round-the-clock full-time care quite soon. Currently, her ability to manage the daily living activities, like personal hygiene and meal taking, on her own has become challenging. For a start, keeping to her daily medication is crucial; you know that, don't you?" …"Plus you will need to think about her safety as well." It was a lot to process but Tess knew there was no avoiding this predicament. Already her mum's recognition of Tess's face and her name recall were becoming difficult and uncertain.

Tess held a regional marketing position with a transnational corporation in the information technology industry. Her job required her to travel half the time throughout the Asia-Pacific region. Even when she was not travelling, she kept ridiculous hours at work.

Could this explain why she was still single, her mum's condition notwithstanding? Faye wondered but it would be impolite and inappropriate to probe. After all, Faye valued her own privacy very much; she assumed Tess would want that for herself too.

"Anyway, Faye should be more concerned about her own social life. Is she not in a similar category as Tess?" Someone asked.

"Age wise, you are both probably a year apart, two max?" The voice queried too.

No idea, we have never gotten around to comparing our ages. Faye seemed to answer. She herself being single had not bothered her. Perhaps until recently.

Back to her mother's condition, Tess took a while to come around to the specialist's recommendation. There was no one else actually—her father had died in a fatal car accident shortly after she graduated and started work—she was her mum's only child. Tess knew her mum would loathe living in a place other than her own home. Her mum had made known her sentiment while she was still lucid. Tess thought the stress of staying at an assisted living facility might compound the problem and even caused her mum's condition to deteriorate faster than if she continued with the familiarity of home.

For some time, Tess experimented with home nursing care but found the service provider wanting in every way. She gave them three months, thinking there was always a run-in period for everything, more so in a difficult area like dementia care. However, their ministrations were inadequate really. Tess did not have peace of mind when she was at work. She felt guilty when on business travel, as she would be somewhere else when emergencies occurred at home. These emergencies were becoming more frequent. The situation became untenable for Tess and came to a head eventually.

Tess finally terminated the home nursing care service after four or five months.

"About time!" Everyone breathed a sigh of relief.

Tess also agreed that the assisted living facility would be the best option for her mum and her own sanity. Subsequently, Faye helped Tess with her evaluation of the various facilities she was considering for her mum, ever mindful to let Tess own the final call.

Back at the supermarket, Tess replied light-heartedly, "I'm still quite harassed actually. However, my situation has definitely improved from six months ago. Thanks for helping me with the transition. On hindsight, should have done so earlier." Tess chattered gladly and easily as if Faye was a long lost friend.

Ah, this was when we last met, Faye recalled quietly.

"Are you travelling as much still? Maybe we can catch up sometimes," Faye offered, also settling into an easy conversation with Tess, mirroring her sanguine demeanour and aided by her own happy hormones.

"Yeah, still punishing myself with the crazy hours and mindless travelling. So glad I can do so with peace of mind, more or less," Tess rejoined.

"Hey, I've been waiting to ask you." ..."You still have time to take on another client?" she asked warily as if she was afraid of what the question might provoke.

"Absolutely," Faye answered eagerly, putting Tess at ease immediately. "There's definitely space for a couple more," she volunteered this information without Tess asking.

"Great, I'll let him know though I'm not sure if he has engaged one already. We chatted last week. I had you in mind when I learnt that he is in need of a psychotherapist. I offered to help and then I had to make a business trip at the last minute. So sorry," Tess gave Faye a guilty look, at the same time giving Faye's forearm a gentle rub, in a sisterly lovey kind-of-way.

"What are you sorry for? You are just helping. Who is he anyway?" Faye queried curiously and watchful of her tone at the same time so as not to sound imposing or interrogative in her queries.

"Oh, how forgetful of me ...he used to be my boss some while back in my current company. However, he is somewhat semi-retired now, in some kind of an advisory role to the regional president of the company. Took care of me and mentored me for the second half of my career with the company while he was still running the business. Terribly understanding of my situation regarding my mum." Tess confessed pensively, and realised that she actually missed having him as her boss.

"So what happened? How did he become mental?" Faye flushed pink with embarrassment instantly, fully aware that she had jumped to conclusions prematurely. Her intuition had seized control of her words and tongue.

"I mean why does he need a psychotherapist?" Faye tried to recover from her boo-boo just now, and consciously reclaimed control of her vocal faculty in case it tried to escape her grasp again.

Tess noticed her blushed cheeks but thought nothing of it. From dealing with Faye when her mum was still under her care, she found Faye to be kind and empathetic.

(Faye seems to have the right temperament for the role. Probably the best psychotherapist around, Tess had thought of Faye then.)

"He's gone through quite a bit of turbulence and turmoil in his life…maybe better I leave him to share the rest with you if he becomes your client. Don't think I should be gossiping behind his back," Tess checked herself there and then. With a slight regret, she realised she might have divulged some personal details shared with her in confidence.

"Hey, I really need to run. Tell you what: I will pass him your contact if it is all right with you. It'll be best for him to make the connection should he decide to seek your counsel, game?" Tess suggested to Faye, hoping to put paid to her questions. Her own gut also figured this to be the best way to extricate Tess from an awkward situation.

"On! You can ask him to contact me for a therapy anytime, I trust you will not refer psychos to me," Faye winked her right eye at Tess hoping to put her at ease again. She sensed Tess's discomfort with her probing.

Should have been more sensitive, Faye chided herself.

"Let's catch up for coffee when you can," Faye tried to keep the connection alive. She reckoned that if she did take on Tess's referral as a client, she might need to corroborate information on her new client as part of the diagnosis down the road. Tess would be an excellent source based on what she had just divulged. Instantly, she felt ashamed for being so self-serving.

"Good idea, chat again then. Meanwhile, be good and take care yeah. Bye," Tess's tongue nearly could not keep up with the words her brain was pushing out. As she spoke, she turned to make a dash for the shortest line at the cashier counters at the other end of the aisle, dissolving into the supermarket crowd in no time.

"Thanks. You too. See you," Faye replied and raised her hand for a short wave concurrently but saw Tess's back only and then none of her almost immediately.

That night, while having a nice hot soak, Faye said to herself, "In any case, Tess could be a good friend."

No one around disputed that. Faye realised she needed a life beyond work as well. Her mum was right all along, she finally admitted reluctantly. At this age, she might well be running out of time.

Tess and I may just hit it off. *Who knows?* Faye thought hopefully.

"Tess is in a different industry, may be interesting to widen your social circle beyond your professional network. Your life is getting too monotonous and uni-dimensional, don't you think?" The voice advised objectively.

Faye agreed wholeheartedly as she took in Celine Dion's powerful rendition of *The Power of The Dream*.

On a Friday morning, almost a fortnight after her chance encounter with Tess at the supermarket that sold everything organic and only organic, Sue would buzz on Faye's office phone, "Dr Wang, your new client, Mr Sean Tang Ming Keat, is here for his first session. May I show him in?"

"Yes please," Faye replied. Then, she got up from her desk and moved herself unhurriedly towards a set of sofas, offset a little from the centre of her spacious office.

She felt lucky to be acquiring another client.

Success was never certain for Faye despite its seductive plausibility, especially with hindsight. She recalled coming across this formula for success (was it from the first book that Dr Lee mentioned to her?):

$Success = Talent + Luck$

It is axiomatic, Faye had thought then. However, some years later, she would add her own experience to the calculation:

$Success = (Talent + Ambition + Hard\ Work) + Luck;\ and$

$Luck \Leftrightarrow Hard\ Work$

"You must want it bad enough, and fully motivated to go through the hard slog and the whole nine yards. I just cannot imagine how success can happen for anyone without ambition or who is lazy," Faye thought with deep conviction.

Equally, she was totally convinced that the harder she worked, the luckier she would become. Her investment of time and effort in her own preparedness would position her well to capture any opportunity that might come her way. While hard work could not guarantee success by any means, it could improve her chance of success all else being equal, she believed.

All the same, she was also conscious of the crucial role luck played in her life. She was ever grateful to Lady Luck who had provided her with worthwhile opportunities at providential junctures—the serendipity of life.

Finally, Faye would work on her social life. There is more to life than work, baby—her mum's prescient words would echo in her mind every now and then.

"Lady Luck, please help me." If Faye muttered these words, she was not aware at all.

He Looked Normal

Time seemed to slow at the exact moment as Faye's heartbeat sped up.

"He's not coming back anytime soon," Someone speculated.

"Why not focus on what you can? Now is not the time for a workout." Someone-New advised further.

Automatically, the psychotherapist took refuge in the safety of her experience as if triggered by a survival instinct.

The first and most obvious possibility came to Faye's mind: Sean produces my name intuitively, correctly and confidently. This will be best for him surely, and quotidian stuff and life can resume as usual.

Failing which, Sean will be ruminating through a shortlist of probable names, according to some obscure algorithm or some equally mysterious heuristics that only Sean knows. (*Really?*) An infinitesimal instant later, he will proffer them one by one to me while seeking an acknowledgment of a right answer from my eyes, like a child trying to decipher its mother's non-verbal cues from her face. At this point, it did not really matter whether my name is in the shortlist that made Sean's cut. Succinctly, Sean thinks he has an answer but he is not sure, his gut leads him to hazard a guess.

"But we still don't know what's actually going on in his brain. The quality of the invisible cognitive effort applied in his guesswork was indeterminable. The unknowable adds to the worry," Faye lamented, the metronome inside her chest upped its tempo involuntarily at the same time.

Regardless, Faye came up with an initial diagnosis in her mind.

"His memory may have deteriorated from the last session. Is this a transitory lapse or the beginning of short-term memory loss?"

"The former is a common glitch as one gets older and its frequency usually increases with age; normally, the brain recovers the desired information after a while, sometimes when prompted by some sensory stimuli."

"The latter, however, may be symptomatic of a more serious condition"

"It will be alarming if Sean has no recollection of this entire memory exercise at all afterwards."

Faye's brain continued its feverish synapsing frenzy: in this situation, I'll have to order some post-mortem tests for Sean to determine the nature and significance of this episode; what comes next will depend on the test results. At this thought, Faye's heart palpitated perceptibly. Spontaneously, she gave her constricted chest a gentle *thump* as if her heart was in need of defibrillation.

Meanwhile, following the sunlight from the windows in Faye's office, Sean cast his pair of cataract-corrected eyes onto a wall full of bookshelves on the far side of the room. He was still feeling for the ground: he guessed the shelves were made of cherry wood at the back of his mind.

Yes, it was cherry wood, Sean remembered the bookshelves vividly, fully attentive now. His head warmed as the memories crystallised in his brain: how the books on the shelves held his gaze when he walked into this room for the first time.

"What an awesome and eclectic collection!" The excitement he felt then now electrifying his brain with colours.

"From the diversity of subject matters and the genres of fiction on display, its owner must be erudite and a voracious reader, a most interesting person to engage with," Someone-New had informed him then.

"Yes, Faye, I remember! Your office looks very familiar now…exactly like the first time I stepped inside here," Sean interjected, gushing with passion, and rousing Faye from her own transient state of abstraction. Instinctively, his eyes were looking beyond her cat-eye framed spectacles, trying to make contact with Faye's absent eyes.

"Good grief!" Faye reacted instantly, jolted by Sean's abrupt awakening. "So glad to have you here. I thought I lost you back there. Where have you been?" Her words poured out on reflex, her relief was clearly discernible from her face.

"His fusiform gyrus seemed to be functioning fine, he just needed a little more time with the name recall task or maybe he was really lost somewhere else," Someone informed Faye.

Still, her brain considered the worst possibility automatically, despite its dreadfulness: Sean cannot identify you at all; he has blanked out completely. Your name may no longer reside in his memory or still there but somehow irretrievable by his cognitive processes; part of the immaterial, airy mess encased inside his head is dysfunctional or destroyed. Your personality erased from his mind completely and forever, which can happen gradually, or quite quickly and suddenly also.

"Sean seems to have averted the worst this time," her brain concluded after speeding through this analysis in unfathomable brain-time.

Involuntarily, Faye let out an audible sigh at once, as if an unmeasurable weight had just suddenly disappeared from her shoulders.

"Looks like we're both here now," Sean responded spontaneously, heaving a sigh of relief too, as if he too felt the lifting of Faye's stress off her shoulders.

"Just as well, what a precise and confident answer and with language fluency too," Someone-Else observed.

Faye felt jubilant as though Sean had picked the winning card at some imaginary game of chance.

"Dementia, get lost!" She spoke defiantly to the invisible disease as if it had taken on personhood in front of her.

I will do my best to make sure you do not come anywhere close to Sean, she vowed resolutely while staring down the unwelcomed stranger unawares.

"You want to continue, and talk about the rendezvous?" Faye followed up eagerly; curious to know what happened after Sean's speech disconnected from his thought process earlier. Then, his voice had gone soft as if the volume knob of a talking machine turned lower slowly and then switched off completely. With his unblinking bottomless eyes also informed his doctor that he had checked out and gone elsewhere already.

"Or do you want to leave this to our next session since our time is almost up?" Faye offered reluctantly after a while when she sensed his hesitancy. She was half hoping that Sean would choose to continue with the session, albeit verbalising this time what went on in his mind earlier so she could participate in his story and scrutinise his mental state together.

(Actually, Faye did not care to keep to the prescribed hour. In fact, after the last session, she had instructed Sue to block out two hours of her time when scheduling Sean's sessions.

"I can decide to let the sessions overrun if there's a need without any pressure from waiting patients; other pressing matters can wait also."

The entire rigmarole was associated intuitively and composited for coherency in Faye's mind then.

"Why do this for Sean only?" a voice interrogated Faye at that time but it quickly disappeared when she tried to listen for it again. None of this infinitesimally swift exchange was conscious to her at all; she was aware of the outcome only, which sounded like an instruction of sorts to her.)

He is still so invested in them after all these years, and he narrates them with such soulfulness and charisma; stands out quite differently from all my other patients and clients, Faye beamed with satisfaction at the thought of her clientele, which went unnoticed, as Sean was not exactly attentive to her.

He has such an interesting past, so different from my life so far, Faye romanticised in her mind. Sean's stories had grown on her. He seemed to have awaken something that was asleep inside her. Besides, his baritone voice was such a delightful sensation in her inner ears, gently massaging and pulling the right chords. So calming and pleasurable.

"Are you becoming invested in Sean more than appropriate," the same voice was back, making its presence felt this time, "genuine interest in your patients' lives notwithstanding?" Feeling testy, Faye dismissed the thought instantly, against her professional judgement.

"I'm feeling tired, not sure if I can carry on anymore. Let's continue at our next session if it's alright with you," Sean answered finally, expecting Faye to yield.

Great, he has registered my query. Very lucid responses, fabulous indeed. The psychotherapist remarked silently.

"Of course, why would it not be alright with me," Faye replied, a little stilted, forcing a smile on her face to conceal her disappointment. Nonetheless, her unusual pitch and the stiff contraction of her facial muscles might have given her away.

None of these mattered to Sean: part of him had wandered off again to another place. Despite this, the remaining part of him prepared to leave Faye's office with the pleasantries uttered automatically.

"Bye, Sue. See you next time," Sean waved habitually as he passed Faye's assistant, seated at her desk just outside Faye's office, concurrently aiming for the elevator.

He looked normal altogether. Memory intact apparently. For now.

Leap Before You Look

"It's coming to a year already, am I right?" Ming was fully alert to what Beth just said even though the surroundings were full of activities vying for his attention.

The bright lights around them was overpowering with the moon seemingly taking cover behind the clouds in what appeared to be an overcast sky. Ming just got off work and they were having a very late supper at a makeshift alfresco hawker centre set up next to a temporary carnival. Then a gust-like breeze whizzed by, its swirl swept up the big dried leaves on the ground around them and caught a small piece of tissue paper at Beth's fit-flops, lifted it off the ground and carried it away from where they sat.

Storming soon, probably later in the wee hours of the morning. Ming thought quietly. Thunderstorms were common across the country during this time of the year.

The carnival was in a neighbourhood that was not-too-near and not-too-far from Beth's residence. These itinerant carnivals would pop up everywhere whenever the National Day approached. They were not particularly enamoured with the food there but this was about the most convenient locale to grab a quick bite at this time of the evening. There were fast food restaurants, of course, which both of them completely eschewed no matter what; they would rather go hungry. Besides, a sea of unfamiliar faces obscuring their presence seemed like an excellent cover for their furtive rendezvous. The place was still teeming with life despite the late hour.

"Seriously, we'll have to decide where this will go, you know," Beth continued, as Ming picked on the green-and-white odd-size cucumber slices and purple-and-white crescent-like onion leaves among the chicken satay sticks. Ming practically consumed all of the bite-sized chicken pieces that came skewered on the skinny bamboo sticks originally.

"You may want to lighten up on the peanut sauce," Beth said disquietly, somewhat irritated now by his distracted look. Strangely, she had a puzzling bias against peanuts. This never failed to come up whenever they ate satay together.

Ming's wary eyes darted around in a seemingly haphazard fashion as he chewed on his food. His forehead furrowed occasionally. Was it the chicken, cucumber, or onion? Maybe he spotted someone familiar. Regardless, Ming was clearly not relaxed at all. However, his working memory was attentive to Beth, having registered her every word distinctly despite her voice being barely audible above the din. Equally, he liked the intonation of Beth's manly-womanly voice. Such a calming and pleasurable sensation in his inner ears, shielding him against the cacophonous onslaught of the carnival. He enjoyed her presence very much also despite the tension.

Just then, Ming got a whiff of Beth's sweaty aura as a breeze, now gentler, skimmed pass them. Briefly, he became distracted as a hard-on built up involuntarily. The perfect combination of Beth's voice and her sharp after-sex-like sweaty scent plus the tension-fuelled hormonal flush seemed like a sure-fire way to turn Ming on. It had happened before but never in places with so many busy bodies like this.

Ming looked at Beth with lustful eyes, wishing he could whisk her off to a very private place, a secret hideaway just for two. Nevertheless, they were not going anyway and he was not about to propose anything to this end either. Unlike a teenager, his prefrontal cortex was fully developed. Beth mistook his lingering longing stare and extended her hand to find his. A tender squeeze from her. A full erection for him. Ming was now battling the stiff awkwardness in his pants and an unwelcomed blush on his face. Fortunately, the bright lights were inadequate and they remained seated. He felt protected; there would be time for his discomfort to subside.

Beth was completely ignorant and did not notice Ming's reddish-pink face against the backdrop of bright lights and shadows. She ate very little also. No appetite at all. Not for food, not for sex either. She just needed to unburden to Ming right now. There was no one else really—both were in a peculiar universe of two only. Questions surrounding the future of their relationship had been plaguing her for quite some time now.

Not that Ming was not troubled either. He just seemed to be avoiding them somewhat—questions with no ready answers did not rhyme with him currently. While he could be very at home with complex problem solving, this was one tough pickle actually. Maybe he was hoping that things would sort themselves out somehow.

Just need to give them time. The universe has its way of working things out. Whatever will be will be. He would think so sometimes. Was he being fatalistic or feckless?

"It's going to cost us both a lot if we want this relationship, you know that don't you?" Ming said finally after his discomfort had subsided. He was replying Beth's question obliquely with another of his own, albeit a rhetorical one. Actually, he did not have any answer to begin with, he was still figuring out stuff for himself, for his beloved daughter, for his marriage and for them. Was this the priority of his subconscious thought process? All the same, this seemed like one needle he just could not thread at all.

At his non-answer question, Beth felt the invisible gravity of society upon her instantly despite it not being a new sentiment. Their individual success and accomplishment would most definitely bring unwanted attention if their secret got out.

In the beginning, they had shared with each other some of their favourite things. Among these, a common favourite they both shared was the 1940 poem *Leap before You Look* by W. H. Auden.

The sense of danger must not disappear:
The way is certainly both short and steep,
However gradual it looks from here;
Look if you like, but you will have to leap.

Such a strong action-oriented push. They had both taken inspiration from the poem for the audacious endeavours in their individual lives. Auden's urge towards courageous risk-taking— trusting oneself and entrusting one's fate to the universe both at once, it seemed—was pivotal to their success at significant junctures of their careers, they believed.

For Beth, she had somehow found a way for this to blend with her worrier nature and her proclivity towards safety. We are all complex and seemingly full of contradictions, are we not? Some more than others, and everyone in their own distinct ways.

Was this how it happened for them? They had leapt across a threshold, almost a year ago, after sliding into the relationship bit by bit. Now, they were looking! Asking each other, and wondering in silence all at once.

Regarding Beth's question, was she beckoning them to leap again, albeit to also look clearly this time? About Ming's question, was he thinking of the by-laws of their society? They were unconventional and non-conforming on their own surely. Societal norms never held them back in the past. However, this time was different!

Now, Auden seemed to have resurrected from his grave to speak directly to them yet again. From his last stanza, one lover was exhorting the other.

A solitude ten thousand fathoms deep
Sustains the bed on which we lie, my dear:
Although I love you, you will have to leap;
Our dream of safety has to disappear.

They would be challenging a different space and concomitant set of norms where their relationship was concerned. While others before them might have taken somewhat similar paths and some others after them might decide to follow suit, there was just no living another's life really. This decision would definitely be the first for each of them still; and the path they would take finally, should they decide so, would be theirs and theirs alone. They would be up against the judgement and biases of their own tribe, betraying people who loved and had been loyal to them. Most distressingly, they would be heaping burning coals of unrests on everyone. Unmeasurable no doubt.

Meanwhile, the breeze had picked up speed and intensity and become a gust. Without warning, a superheated web of lightning discharged far away, overpowering the bright lights now and silhouetting the lenticular clouds in the distant sky. Seconds later, a deafening thunderclap jolted Beth and Ming from their preoccupation; still the seething crowd seemed unperturbed by the menacing display of the heavens. The inclement weather had unleashed itself somewhere else but the sensation on their skin and the smell of distant air confirmed the certainty of its imminent approach.

Beth and Ming decided to head for the safe shelter of home, still separate for now. They had substituted the difficult questions about their future with an easier response to the foreboding weather. Both were cognizant in their gut that the onerous questions dangling in their heads would be in limbo for a while longer. How much longer? No one knew.

In a few weeks' time, they would celebrate their first anniversary of sorts though they would each pinpoint a different date when each had leapt in the first place—earlier for Ming, later for Beth. In a year's time, give and take a few weeks, things would start to unravel—first for Beth, then for Ming.

Session No.5

"What do you call this—psychological discovery, intelligent gossip or voyeurism with permission?" Faye asked no one. Maybe a bit of everything, she supposed.

No point over-analysing, to what end and whose benefit anyway. Faye resigned, treating the random thought flashing across her mind as an interesting, but nonetheless inconsequential curiosity. As soon as she allowed her attention to slip from the mentally sapping question, she felt totally spent—mentally and emotionally, and extremely hungry.

Sean had just left after his session, which had overrun the usual prescribed hour. He appeared to be in some kind of a flow and could have gone on for hours. Faye considered the likelihood of their session going beyond, and decided to let him continue with his ramble, motivated by an unconscious impulse. Sean was covering new territory near the end of the hour. She was curious to discover more: first-hand gossips that were just too fresh to pass up.

Really, it was like watching an intimate exposé of his life from a front row seat of the theatre in his brain. An unfettered access to truly private stuff. Activities conducted behind closed doors. Altercations known only to couples involved. Windows to secret thoughts, and intentions conceived but not consummated.

"There is a voyeuristic streak in all of us. Some are simply more honest with ourselves than others are in this regard." Someone pointed out.

"Moreover, it need not be sexual in nature either." Someone-Else added knowingly.

"Our penchant for gossip attests to this, does it not? As does our curiosity with the lives of friends and strangers alike on social media." Someone rounded up the short discourse.

Good thing it was my last session, no pressure, Faye recalled, visibly relaxed as she took a big gulp of the soda on her desk instinctively. Almost immediately, she perked up a bit and felt replenished. Sean's sessions were usually in the morning; however, Faye's calendar was full for all mornings this week.

("Important to keep to the cadence for the first six months for any new engagement." Someone reminded Faye. This was standard procedure when she started with her private patients, which carried over from her experience at NCDAZ. She continued with this habit when she started taking on clients as well.

"Dr Wang's calendar is full for the mornings that week. Is it alright if we schedule your next session on an afternoon, Mr Tang?" Faye randomly recalled Sue asking Sean after the previous session, within earshot as the door was closing after another one of her patients had entered her office. "Will 4pm…" The door cut out Sue's voice abruptly when it finally shut.)

Robotically, Faye packed some stuff into her briefcase, including Sean's dossier, powered off her desktop computer and prepared to lock up her office.

"Remember to ask Sue tomorrow to allocate two hours for Sean from the next session onwards," her mind instructed as she was making her way out of the office. Where did this come from? Faye had no idea. Was she compos mentis? She was not sure—two voices had transpired in her head apparently, albeit extremely briefly—she was aware of the outcome only.

Has it always been like this after her sessions with clients and patients? Faye wondered as she picked at the plate of salad in front of her. She was not eating very much. Either the Caesar's salad was not agreeable with her tonight or she already had her fill after the delicious bowl of lobster bisque at the start. She had consumed it totally with sweeping gusto, even polishing her bowl with a piece of the complimentary home-baked bread. She had always liked artisan bread.

Faye tended to eat fast when her mind was preoccupied. ("Slow down," her mum chided gently—if it was possible to chide gently at all—when she was much younger. "You are going to choke yourself to death at some point if you continue this way," she said with disapproval then.) Her mind was back to Session No.5 with Sean just a couple of hours ago. She put down her cutlery and took a small sip of the red wine.

Then an epiphany, if you could call it that: it's definitely not like this with the others, this only happens with Sean. Immediately, memories of Faye's previous sessions with Sean, starting with the first one, crowded her mind. Her episodic memory was hard at work now despite it having been a long and hard day for her. Faye had exceptional memory. Her study group mates in medical school would envy her for that—elephant memory, they called it then.

"I am so thoroughly exhausted after each session with him," Faye voiced her realisation softly, out of earshot of people around her. Her memory was all she could count on. There were no notes in Sean's dossier that could corroborate with the evidence of her experience, as her brain had recorded. The notes in the dossier were about Sean only: what he said, how he felt and what he remembered. It contained specific details and observations by herself and some general ones too. Records of his follow-through of non-therapy related activities and intentions, and follow-up questions for her to think about or ask him at the next session were in the dossier as well. For Sean, drugs were unnecessary. Most crucially, the dossier summarised her assessment of his mental condition, specifically to answer this question: is Sean likely to develop early-onset dementia.

Of course, Faye had trained to deal with depression as a mental and medical condition as well. Mostly, she had dealt with depression as a corollary to dementia. For referred patients or clients whom she subsequently diagnosed as having just depression and unlikely to develop dementia anytime soon, she would forward refer them to one of a few specialists in her network who focused on clinical depression. Normally, she would need two or three, at most four sessions to ascertain this.

In Sean's case, depression-related symptoms might have prompted him to seek professional help. Depression is also a known risk factor for Alzheimer's disease and other related forms of dementia later on in life. Sean knew this already, which might have led him to seek treatment early as a precaution. For sure, he was unambiguously mildly depressive, a condition certainly treatable without any need for medication. After five sessions of therapy, Faye had determined that Sean was highly unlikely to develop dementia, if ever. Definitely not anytime soon. Yet, Faye was holding onto Sean as a client, contrary to her usual practice. To what end and whose benefit? Only Faye knew. *Really?*

Faye did not record her own emotions or experiences encountered during therapy sessions in the official documents; such was not expected nor desired in her profession. As she was thinking this, a familiar voice interposed.

"The practice of psychotherapy is supposed to be objective. You need to be very compos mentis, be in full control of your faculties and be extremely mindful during your practice. It is not about how you feel. It's all about what you think your patient is feeling, and thinking, and whatever else that's going on between their ears." The voice of her professor at medical school resounded in her head. She said this during her course on *'The Art and Science of Psychotherapy'*.

"Check yourself every now and then. Whether you are just starting out or after you have been practicing for a while. Again, watch out for cognitive illusions. I cannot overemphasis this enough. Do not be tripped off! Constant practice tends toward automatic responses in our brains. These may intermix with our intuitions. Our sensory stimulations, emotions, and beliefs and biases are all informing our intuitions non-stop. Objective judgement may become coloured if we are not careful. Be extremely self-aware. Best to get your peers to check on you every now and then." The voice continued reminding with heavy foreboding. Unconsciously, the psychotherapist just had a refresher of sorts.

Back at her apartment, Faye plonked herself on the plush comfortable sofa in the living room after her shower. She was feverishly rubbing her damp hair with the already damp towel, but her unthoughtful attempt at drying her brownish-black hair appeared futile.

Perhaps I can check my journal—a random thought distracted her. Actually, the earlier puzzle during dinner was still on her mind.

Faye developed the habit of keeping a personal journal at medical school. She picked up this habit from one of her study group mates. (Oddly, her dad kept diaries too but it did not rub off on her. Curiously, how do we decide to pick up a habit?) Nothing extensive really, Faye would record some unusual or absurd observations, intelligent or insightful quotes or jokes, which usefulness would present themselves at some opportune time in the future. In addition, emotions: hers mostly and other people who were significant in her lives at those times. Except for some periods, her journals were mostly light on emotions. Not that she had not felt them, as she was clearly empathetic in nature, more because she wanted to be economical with paper.

"Absurd, is this not—to value dead trees over lively emotions?" Someone-New asked rhetorically.

On the issue of long-term physical storage of these journals, she had evaluated digital alternatives but these had their trouble as well. What with technology obsolescence obliterating her stuff. They could become irretrievable because of incompatible hardware and software also. Moreover, the idea of paying a subscription fee to someone to store her stuff somewhere and nowhere put her off totally.

"Some things are best done the old-fashioned way," she romanticised, "and there is a charm about them, like paperbacks compared to e-books."

Consequently, she would store her hard backed journals in her home safe, which she considered as the best physical protection. Her journals would became an extension of her memory, albeit a more precise and reliable one.

Come and Go as You Wish

"Here, you can come and go as you wish," Ming pressed a set of keys into her right palm and wrapped her hand around them. He had minted an extra set for Beth a week after he had moved in but only managed to pass them to her now. They just had lunch at a new café that Ming came across on his Instagram feed. As they walked into the twenty-seat café earlier, a steady stream of people started to leave, which afforded them an ample choice of seats.

"Now, this feels like a good thing, thanks baby," Beth accepted with light-hearted gladness, and reached out to give him a quick thank-you peck on his lips, picking up the sour-bitter aftertaste of remnant espresso. They were seated in some sort of a private zone in the café (that had mostly become devoid of people by now), surrounded by the easy melodious background music.

"Look at them. What a happy couple. They are in a really good place." Someone murmured softly to no one, swooning carelessly. Ming's hands were still cupping Beth's lightly fisted hands with the keys safe inside.

Now, Beth had another place to take refuge in when she needed to write in solitude or a safe space to meditate and imagine. The studio afforded her that on weekdays when Ming was at work. Some months later, she would go over on some weekends when he would be away on business travel. She liked it very much that she had complete unfettered and autonomous access to his studio. Beth found it more relaxing than her home, away from the stress that emanated from the unpredictable work patterns of her husband. This was before they separated.

Truthfully, she preferred her old home still. She had decorated it herself from the start, about seven to eight years ago now. It had assimilated her essence and reflected that back in the colours of the interiors, the furnishings and the curtains. There were also carefully selected pieces of furniture and curated paintings of South-East Asian and Chinese artists—watercolour and Chinese ink mostly— collected over time. The pristine paintings seemed to liven up specific walls most appropriately. Ming had not been there actually, he had seen pictures only. Beth had shown him photos from the album on her mobile: only the public spaces, and all devoid of humans.

"Of course! They have *never* shown each other any picture of their family members actually." Someone ensured everyone was fully across this fact.

Beth had gone to the studio with Ming a couple of times before. The first time was a day after he had moved in as if to inspect his new living conditions for herself. Then she noted all the stuff that was in the kitchen.

"Amazing how women can remember every detail when it comes to the kitchen," Witnessing Beth in a domestic setting for the first time left a permanent imprint in Sean's mind.

On Beth's next trip there, they brought some stuff back— procured at Ikea just before—things that were absent that Beth thought he would need to get by, and things she would need if they were to prepare simple meals at the studio.

"You don't want to be eating out all the time, do you?" Beth said, a few days after her first visit to the studio. They were having dinner at a Thai restaurant somewhere between Ming's office and his studio. It was a weekday and nearing closing hours, they were the last couple in the restaurant and the workers were waiting impatiently for them to leave. An eager beaver was needlessly wiping down a table next to theirs.

"Think they are telling us it's time to leave. Shall we?" Ming asked sheepishly, directing Beth to the restless waiter with his eyes. He sensed that Beth was about to enter her motherly mode with him, and this could be a good segue to divert her attention away from whatever she was about to start on.

Ming held a very senior position in his company responsible for a huge business and a sizeable organisation. Did Beth not know that?

Why is she mothering me as if I am her little boy? Ming thought these intuitively but the thoughts stayed in his bubble.

Beth could not imagine Ming in his corporate role. She did not get to see this side of him; she was also not bothered that she did not seem to get it. It was immaterial to her; it was not what attracted her to him. She mostly knew the management of one—herself, and she was quite contented as it was.

"Career wise, they were from quite different worlds actually." Someone-New remarked astutely.

Regardless, Ming liked it when Beth did what she did; he just loathed admitting it. He considered it weakness to do so. *Really?*

"But it's still twenty minutes to closing, and I'm not done yet," Beth rejoined testily, and took a sip of water in her glass just to proof it. Then she caught the eyes of the buzzing waiter and batted her eyes at him (not the kind that she flirted with), something Beth was quite good at doing if she wanted to intimidate with her eyes only. Immediately, the waiter hurried off, a little flustered. Now that the pest was off their backs, she returned her attention to Ming and continued.

"Hawker food is affordable but it can be quite unhealthy. They are salty and oily, and the oil they use isn't good at all. It's the cheapest kind of vegetable oil mostly. What's the difference between food cooked with palm oil or in lard? Why not have *char kuay teow* every day then?"

"You'll tire of café and restaurant food like this pretty soon. It is hard to eat alone at such places anyway. Given the portions they serve nowadays, you cannot have much variety. Anyhow, you end up packing back the leftovers and then throw them away a week later when clearing out the fridge. What a waste! Besides, you can't get the mix of nutrition that's good for you," Beth pushed on. It might not be obvious from her tone but Beth was concerned for Ming's well-being. *Really!*

How to disagree with Beth? However, Ming was just not into cooking. He really had no patience if the food preparation took more than fifteen minutes. By then he would have lost his appetite. He definitely did not see the need to apply his creativity to this area. Where food was concerned, he was purely a consumer.

"And you shouldn't be eating instant noodles or processed food on a regular basis," Beth rounded up her points with this last directive of sorts.

Once, or twice, a month might be regular but it was hardly frequent enough to be harmful, Ming retorted, in his mind of course. He was wise to hold his tongue.

"Ok, we can go grab some stuff if you want, whatever you think is needed," Ming acquiesced, feeling disappointed at the same time.

Did Beth not know me by now? I believe in healthy eating, an essential for quality of life. Moreover, there can be no out-exercising an unhealthy diet. She ought to know that I will do my utmost to practice my beliefs.

As well, Ming experienced a déjà vu when Beth was talking earlier. He had a flashback: the first day of his university at his dorm room. He had just checked in. His mum was there too, and he vaguely recalled the familiar words vocalised. Well, more or less. When he went back the following weekend, his mum had bought some stuff that she considered was needful and insisted he brought them back with him when he returned to the dorm after the weekend. *Really?* Was his recollection reliable?

Some men never grow up; need someone to take care of them. Most men actually. Beth had stopped talking but she had not stopped thinking or reacting.

Now he's on his own mostly, just needs to make sure he keeps well. At this thought, Beth softened and felt a tenderness for Ming. Then she stretched out her hand to squeeze him endearingly on his arm. With a puzzled look, Ming put his hand over hers and caressed the back of her hand gently, which inspired a noticeable tingle between her shoulders.

About three months after Ming shifted his life to the studio, Beth would visit him on some weekends. Since they started meeting regularly, their meets were on weekdays, rarely on weekends. The most recent weekend was when they bought stuff from Ikea. Now, she brought along her work as well whenever she went over. However, she never stayed over at his studio. She always drove herself home no matter how late the night was.

Strangely, Ming never asked her to stay over as well. Beth never broached this subject either. If she ever sensed the subject bubbling up, she would pre-empt and deftly steer the direction of their conversation away or simply change the subject altogether. Given her mastery of her craft, Beth was quite adept with segues and non-sequiturs.

Perverse Discrimination

"Get out! I want you out of my bedroom," Mei screamed at Keat the moment he stepped into the master bedroom, with a loudness that seemed appropriate considering the gulf between their hearts. She was trying very hard to hold herself together at the same time. She had wanted to tell him that for the past two weeks already. Her heart was pounding so hard she could feel it throbbing in her inner ears.

Keat stayed where he was but his breathing quickened that instant. A deadly silence: the sudden wintry environment in the room seemed to have frozen the medium for transmitting sound, even the sound of time. Did the floor quake and open up the chasm between them in that split-second?

"Excuse me! It's my bedroom also, in case it slipped your mind," Keat broke the ice in a slightly heated and evidently unashamed tone, but at a calmer volume (and not because he felt any closer to Mei then). Instinctively, he was trying to de-escalate the situation and keep the altercation from descending into a shouting match.

Too late! Most likely, their neighbours would be aware of Mei's hysterical demand by this time—a first since they moved here almost a decade ago.

Oh, shit! What are our neighbours thinking now? Keat thought unconsciously. His face displayed fully his loathing that they had attracted unwanted attention at this late hour. Keat could be all mind and cold logic if he needed to be, an automatic behaviour honed from decades of management experience in the ruthless dog-eat-dog world of corporate life. Undoubtedly, he was concerned about the public broadcast of their private affairs in the neighbourhood and its impact on his standing in the local corporate scene, especially in the technology industry.

Trouble in personal life, especially martial and family life, was frown upon in their largely conservative society. Such trouble invited unwelcomed and embellished gossips at the workplace and in social circles, which usually conveyed exaggerated information. Regular people believed that character failures led to these troubles but they were likely to be wrong more often than not. Regardless, corporate honchos must have impeccable character, and be role models in every sphere of their lives—such was the unfair expectation still.

"Why do we expect perfection, even the perception of perfection, since it's truly impossible to find?" "We're human after all. Even Zeus and Odin are fallible." Someone-Else read out Keat's thought bubble to everyone.

No one cared.

All the same, relationships do fail in real life, all the time. Keat rationalised. He had become more forgiving since his personal transgression actually.

"Forgiving, certainly. Repentant, not sure," Someone-Else remarked again.

"Tough luck. Such is the lay of the land, and his survival and safety depends on playing by its rules, adhering to its norms and navigating its inconsistent and contentious environment." Someone remarked stoically.

Alas, pragmatism demands a reckoning with the reality of the moment: the inability of, or perhaps the lack of enlightenment and sophistication in, the corporate world to view and judge professional and personal lives separately. The former a company's entitlement, and for the latter: protect every individual's privacy and dignity.

"Say what you want, Keat most definitely faces a reputational risk if his marital crisis spirals out of orbit and ends up as a public circus." Someone-New warned ominously.

While the norm seemingly applies to both men and women in positions of power, women, like Mei, seem to suffer a perverse discrimination.

"Between an unfaithful man and a faithful woman with an unfaithful husband, the latter appears more terrible." "If she cannot hold on to her husband, how she can hold on to the business—such is the unspoken but common perspective." Someone observed with understandable apprehension.

Sophistry betraying one's judgemental bias? Maybe an old boys club's Pavlovian reflex to protect and entrench male privilege and patriarchy?

"With such deep-seated biases, how will this pan out for Mei?" Someone-Else also empathised with Mei's struggles.

If Keat was gravely concerned, his nonchalance masked it thoroughly. His lowered but unyielding tone was a spontaneous attempt to revert to normalcy, a survival response that kicked in instinctively. He was not worried about Kim at this point. She left for a six-week student exchange programme in Zurich yesterday. Regardless, the anger Keat was working hard to conceal was amply on display in his defiant eyes. His heart pressure rose, his jaws tightened and his shoulders tensed up: he was getting ready for a fight.

"His insensitivity and ferocity is so revolting, you think?" Someone asked Someone-Else, clearly disgusted. "Obviously! Mr Hyde has come out to play." Someone-Else lamented with a sorry sigh.

YJ Chin

Get the Fuck Out

"Where is this coming from, Mei?" Keat asked after taking in a few deep breaths, and softening his eyes just a bit; his tone more conciliatory this time. Mei could tell from his clenched fists that he was trying very hard to control himself still.

This was completely unexpected, Keat had a long and awful day at work and was looking forward to destress when he returned home. From his perspective, now was a terrible time for such an outburst.

"*Seriously?* Who is the one that started this mayhem?" Apparently, there were other voices in the room adding to the brouhaha and confusion as well. Was Mei or Keat paying attention to any of them?

"You jolly well know where this is coming from! Stop acting blur. Your bloody charm doesn't work on me," Mei retaliated sharply, torching Keat with the orangey-red tongues of her flaming voice. However, her volume now more measured as if she had morphed to mirror Keat's demeanour instinctively. She had every intention still to maintain her sombre disposition and keep up with the tension. If necessary, she was even prepared to ratchet up the acrimony sufficiently to coerce his compliance.

Why now? Why not two weeks ago when the affair became known? They did have a couple of intensely fervid and soul-gutting exchanges after the unravelling but Mei did not drive him out of the master bedroom each time. Was she holding out until Kim had flown off? Coincidentally, the earlier skirmishes took place in Kim's absence as well. Was Mei shielding her daughter from the truth until she had worked out what would be best for their well-being? Naturally prioritising safety for herself and her tribe as much as she was able to provide under the extant situation. Was Keat an outcast of the tribe now?

Keat did not think all these of course. However, he had considered Kim's well-being before everything unravelled; he had tried to envisage how things might possibly play out if his affair became known—intentional or otherwise. Since the unravelling, Keat and Mei had not discussed about Kim actually. Mei's emotional state made any meaningful dialogue almost impossible. So far, nothing had happened according to any set playbook, if ever there was one.

It's a good thing the unravelling took place after Kim's final examinations. Keat consoled himself silently.

"Are such upheavals ever a good thing?" Someone sniped cynically.

Meanwhile, Keat totally overlooked the turmoil Mei was going through. His attempt at conviviality was purely self-serving. Mei's face was a transparent display of outrage, torment, confusion and fear. However, his egotism had numbed him to her anguish completely.

"Can't you feel the considerable heart-wrenching pain Mei is experiencing right now? Do you not even have an iota of compassion for her? Her state has been engendered by the heart-breaking blow of your treachery, you heartless prick!" Someone-Else berated, hoping to resuscitate his cold heart to life. Alas, his stolid expression said it plainly: all was vanity.

Is this heartlessness: a cruel impenetrable hardness, a sharp hurtful meanness, a psychopathic inability to empathise and feel pain, shame or guilt? Is emotional barrenness inevitable as one approaches the extinction of love, the abyss at the end of a shared journey where henceforth, what one can inflict on the other is only hurt and pain in ever-greater intensity?

Unawares, Keat's alert brain was registering Mei's emotional MRI-of-sorts. His sound memory was videotaping the drama as it unfolded actually. Later, he would discover that his brain had recorded and packed away this and other traumatic episodes in his mind. They could play back when recalled. Sometimes involuntarily by indeterminate triggers, and at the most difficult or inconvenient junctures too. Much later, he would discover also that some of these memories would become inaccessible where playbacks would be vague or incoherent as if some parts were snipped off altogether and the rest rejoined awkwardly. Another survival instinct to protect our fragile identity? To enable quotidian sanity?

Regardless, Keat wondered to himself, consciously this time, "It's Friday today, she could have done this last night as Kim flew off in the morning …is this a good thing?" Keat was an eternal optimist: he had faith in his own indomitable spirit whenever he was in trouble. What about a trouble of his own making?

"Selfish bastard! Think this guy cannot make it." Someone said to Someone-Else, relinquishing whatever hope there was.

"Can it be self-preservation for Keat?" "All along, he has sought to keep his affair a secret. Unexpectedly, the China-wall he has erected to separate his family and affair fell apart, crushing the familiar order all of a sudden. Now, there is danger lurking on every side." Someone-New started rationalising Keat's situation before everyone.

"Naturally, he reacts to insulate himself from Mei's distraught state. How else can he continue to function at work? The flux entrapping him is multi-faceted and multi-layered with multiple centres of gravity."

"Everything is so volatile and he's navigating new discoveries along the way."

"Moreover, the unravelling has run its course for two weeks only, surely, it is impossible to reclaim control and re-establish a new order in such a short time."

"Surely anyone in his shoes will find his situation to be extremely disorienting and taxing."

Everyone just kept quiet after Someone-New paused for anyone's reaction.

"I'm just covering the grounds in case we miss something, you know. Need to guard against the emotional fast thinking brain a bit."

"Better to cover all angles, agree? We may be forced to pick sides, you know what I mean?" Someone-New added in a flurry, feeling a little defensive now given everyone's reticence.

What a bloody mess. Whose situation can be direr than mine right now? Keat swore in frustration without verbalising a word. He felt lost, and desperately in need of some solace now.

Was it seconds only? Minutes most probably, but it felt timeless. Was the universe suspending time?

"Sean Tang Ming Keat, you know it's not my character to say this. Just so you really get what I am TELLING you—GET THE FUCK OUT of my FUCKING room right NOW!" Mei essentially repeated her demand, this time in a chillingly steady yet acerbic tone. She was fully compos mentis. Her intractable, now drier but still reddened eyes were staring Keat down. Did the intensity just burn through him?

Keat was briefly stunned and completely dumbstruck by her lucid assertiveness and self-control. Something peculiar happens when one's full name is called. It usually commands our full attention to the exclusion of everything else. Equally, her fluent and effectively intoned and embellished articulation of her uncompromising demand had floored him. He might have taken a step or two back. Right now, with every thought arrested, he knew only one appropriate response remained, yield and let this go.

There would be many firsts. Like the unthinkable amalgamation of crystal-clear iciness and red-hot fury in Mei's eyes. Like the inconceivable question until now—could Mei ever harbour a hatred for Keat? Like her language: was Mei breaking out of her conservative mould?

For Keat, a new distinct fear: a gripping shiver down his spine with his feet tethered to the floor rigidly. This inexplicable fear—like a millstone now shackling him—had definitely displaced the numbness in his heart.

"Fear is good if it does not paralyse—floods our system with adrenalin and pumps our hearts hard. We feel alive." Someone-New started again, this time dispassionately.

"The same happens with extreme emotions like love and anger."

"Instantly, we sense acutely what is threatening our livelihood, what is essential to our survival."

Right now, Keat's family essence—its safety and familiarity—was being threatened for the first time.

"Did you not think carefully before you open the Pandora's Box, you idiot?" Someone jumped in with a censure, refusing to give Keat a free pass for his fecklessness.

Another first: their tragic situation, they were in completely uncharted territory now.

"It is not any less of a struggle for me actually," Keat implored quietly to no one in particular.

"Why did he subject everyone to such turmoil? Did he consider this necessary?" Someone-Else rebuffed too, seeming to have sided with Mei now.

"There's enough rooms, take your pick. You're lucky, you don't have to sleep in the street," Mei added compromisingly, her voice still as emphatic as before.

Mei was not passive; neither did Keat think this at any point in their relationship. At home, Keat could be a little bossy (a behaviour carried over from his work place) but in a nice sort of way. Mei would be happy to play along most of the time. At those times when she did not feel like it, she would let him know her position in a gentle manner to protect his ego. However, her readiness to accommodate Keat was never a sign of weakness. It would take self-assurance and confidence to do as she did. Mei was no doormat at all.

Keat finally acquiesced, so informed his sensibility. He then took two of his usual pillows from the familiar-but-now-forbidden king-sized bed.

As he was about to leave the bedroom, Mei remarked, "You may want to think of what to say to Kim when she comes back."

"I will not be your long-suffering supportive wife anymore and I surely am not putting up with this absurdity any longer." Mei's voice betrayed her broken heart despite her attempt at distancing.

"Meanwhile, I strongly suggest you consider moving out of this house. It will be the best for everyone." Her final amicable yet confident tone left no room for negotiation or misinterpretation. Her mind was very clear, at least for now. Visibly, the acrimonious row had exhausted her; she was done with the enervating drama for the time being.

Even as Mei heard her own words, she was uncertain of her own preparedness if the eventuality occurred. The perception (by their relatives and friends) of them as a relatively ideal and successful family unit shattered. The loss of familiarity and safety cultivated over twenty years of marriage. A new status as a divorcee, a single parent to Kim (she was confident she would win any custody battle if it came to this). A new co-parenting arrangement between Kim and her father. What did she really want? What could she live with? What was she prepared to give in exchange?

Did she just propose the D word implicitly? The thought bubbled in Keat's brain spontaneously. His eyes gave away his puzzlement. However, Mei had taken her eyes off Keat now. Despite the buzz in his head, which was dying to be resolved, Keat decided to let the matter rest and live with the ambiguity for now. A smart choice indeed, considering the situation.

Someone said jadedly, "Are we not living in a *VUCA* world now? Get used to it everyone!"

"What's that?" Someone-Else asked.

"Volatility. Uncertainty. Complexity. Ambiguity." Someone-New answered quickly to quieten everyone down, and return their focus to ending the feud in the room.

Keat felt utterly exhausted now—mentally and physically. His day was now longer and more awful than he had expected when he first got home. As to his desperate need of a nice hot shower, Kim's bathroom would have to do for now, she had no need of it for the next six weeks. This was his woeful consolation: a hot shower would be a certainty, not so sure about the nice part though.

"Let's find another time to talk when we are calmer and less unhinged. Good thing we have the weekend ahead of us." Keat said while making his way out, his back now facing Mei. He then uttered a hollow "Goodnight" and shut the door gently yet firmly behind him, not expecting any response from Mei.

"Damn you! How can this be a good night?" Mei fingered at the closed door. For a moment, she considered throwing a pillow at him but abandoned the idea altogether, convinced of its futility—the pillow was too light, the distance was too far, and the target was out of sight already. Though worn out, she was still in control and mindful that her heart really needed a break. Her blood pressure remained elevated but her breathing quickly normalised as all the oxygen in the room belonged to her now. She also realised that her vocabulary just then had embraced words she already knew but had found no vocal use for them until now.

"I need a fucking hot shower right now," Mei let out finally. She felt good thinking it. Her voicing of it? Fucking liberating!

What does trauma do to us? What did the unravelling of Keat's secret do to Mei? Whom was Keat referring to as unhinged at the end of their brief and decidedly one-way exchange? Paradoxically, the unpacking of the secret had boxed one in and unboxed the other altogether.

Salmon or Cod?

A month after receiving the keys, Beth went to the studio on her own for the first time. They planned to have dinner together and Beth had offered to cook.

"Just simple stuff" Beth texted Ming at 11-ish.
"Grill some fish"
"Make a simple salad"
"U have roasted sesame?"
"I'll bring a bottle of wine"

"Yes" It was 12.34pm when Ming finally replied.
"I'll be back ard 7"
"Customer lunch. Gotta go"…
"C u later"…
"Luv u, xoxo"

"U good with salmon?" …"Or cod?" Beth texted around 2pm when she was at the supermarket. After fifteen minutes, a little peeved when Ming still had not replied, she went ahead with her choice of fish.

Beth arrived at the studio around 3.30pm. She let herself in and quickly transferred her minor haul from the supermarket to the fridge. After popping a thin square of 99% as-good-as-completely-dark chocolate into her mouth, she started to inspect its contents meticulously. The milk coffee had expired which she removed promptly and discarded it in the bin nearby. Beth also cleared out the stale stuff—leftovers of takeaway food—which was starting to give out a putrid smell. She then scribbled on a piece of blue square paper that she retrieved from a box full of these on the kitchen counter.

Milk
Roasted sesame ("There'll be none left after today's dinner")
Eggs
Blueberries…

Stuff Ming needs to replenish, Beth thought as she wrote. Then she pinned it to the corkboard beside the fridge.

"Think I better do this myself," Beth said beneath her breath. There was no one else around to approve or object.

"He'll likely forget." ("She's giving excuses on his behalf," Someone whispered disapprovingly. Beth knew him very well: he was generally careless with domestic stuff.) Whereupon, she unpinned the blue square paper and put it into her simple yet stylish grey tote bag.

Then, she put the radio on the Meridian—one of their favourite channels was rolling off the system, playing a mix of oldies and contemporary hits. After that, she removed a small bouquet of white tiger lilies with a spray of baby's breath from its paper wrapping, and arranged them in the transparent crystal vase sitting on the kitchen top after filling it with sufficient water.

Beth brought the vase out and placed it on Ming's worktable, and walked further to draw the curtains, flooding the living space instantly with the afternoon sunlight. A breath of cool, fresh air gushed into the studio when she slid open the balcony doors. There was a heavy tropical thunderstorm—typical during this time of the year—as she drove here earlier. However, the storm stopped completely as she was about to get into the basement parking at the condo. Quite unpredictable sometimes, the ways of nature though Someone wondered if Jupiter had her back.

"There, a bit more life. The timing of the rain was perfect," Beth purred. A beatific smile formed on her cheerful face, which exuded a healthy pale under the warm sunlight. 'Marry Me' by Train came on the airwaves easily. Caught up with domestic familiarity, she was not paying attention to anything in particular. The music from the radio station simply became part of the ambient soundscape presently.

Beth recalled her memory of the studio when she first viewed it on her own eons ago. The imprint in her mind matched with her current vision.

"It's just a little more lived in now." "And the privacy, it's simply terrific." Beth whispered on reflection. The property owner had insisted on a minimum lease of two years, otherwise she would have been the one putting up here. Now, it had the aura of a bachelor's pad. Regardless, she was glad that Ming had rented the studio and given her unfettered access to the place.

For house warming, Beth had gifted Ming a painting—a reprint of a Chinese ink painting of some hutongs in Beijing by a dead Chinese artist, fitted with a silvery metallic frame. She had bought this piece on a whim some time ago. Somehow, she could not find a place for it amongst the other pieces in her house. Consequently, it had been in her storeroom since, carefully wrapped of course. The painting hung on a white wall in the living area of Ming's studio now.

"Hmm…it has found a proper pride of place. Ming has a good sense of space and positioning too," Beth remarked smugly when she admired the pristine painting again. A perfect addition to the studio, she considered approvingly. Beth had a good eye for things, especially beautiful things. Slowly and subtly, she was personalising the place, infusing her essence into its ambiance.

The books Beth had borrowed from the library were all over the coffee table and sofa—they were research materials for her final project for a publication. She had brought them over when she was here previously. The environment was becoming effortlessly familiar—yet different—and surreptitiously safe for Beth. As it gained familiarity in her brain, her body loosed the edginess she felt during her first couple of visits here. The physiological was embodying the psychological gradually.

Domesticity would set in after some time. Beth and Ming did not plan this actually. It happened spontaneously after some random spawning, like their chance encounter.

"Keeping separate lives and secrets can be punishing work for the brain and the body. Familiarity is more effortless, and we incline towards safety naturally. All the same, domestic life breeds familiarity and safety." Someone-New hoped to highlight Beth and Ming's very human struggle.

"Such is the natural flow of their entwined lives." Someone suggested the inevitable, seemingly.

Oddly, domesticity was a kind of familiarity that sat extremely well with Beth. Odd considering the stereotypical view of artists— writers, painters, actors, and the like—as bohemians who are audacious, flighty, edgy and experimental, unconventional and non-conforming. Domesticity with its implicit tedium and invisible anchor appears incongruous with this group.

Yet, Beth could be in perfect bliss when she was flowing with her quotidian humdrum. She seemed compelled to return to this whenever she drifted from it somehow, especially when she needed an escape from something. The rhythmic routines were her catharsis. Here, her undefined dreaminess could find expression in definite activities. An incubation process for her creativity perhaps, commingling the metaphysical and the physical.

"Ok with salmon"…"Think cod is better"…Ming texted back finally. Too late of course.

Why even bother now, Beth thought peevishly. She just ignored his texts totally. "*Whatever!*" she remarked aloud to no one in particular, and returned to her comforting humming and drumming.

I Am Leaving You

Now was the wee hour of the morning. Despite her extreme tiredness, sleep eluded Mei. For the past hour, she had been alternating between staring at the ceiling fan diligently going about its single-minded job of cooling the already cooled room, and tossing back and forth across the entire breadth of the bed. Her body was still reacting despite having her demand met almost three hours ago now. The hot shower was helpful, she felt a little drowsy after that. However, the blower, which she used to dry her hair with after her shower, was of no help at all. She would not sleep with her hair damped, it would create a dishevelled mess of her after she woke, and this would irritate her tremendously.

Sleep was becoming torturous. The tossing and turning was causing indistinct aches all over Mei's body. For the last twenty years, she had shared the king-sized bed with Keat. Now, she felt strange having it all to herself. She tried thinking of the last time this happened. None that she could recall. Those times when Keat was away on business travel, which was quite frequent in the last five years, did not figure. Physically, it was the same space actually. Now, it felt more expansive metaphysically, loneliness had taken up the side where Keat used to lay instead.

The aloneness seeped into Mei's empty heart too. Unable to control herself, she wept—the extreme emotions inside needed to bleed out of her. She hugged her pillow a little tighter, it hugged her back warmly—no arms, no heartbeat, just a semi-firm, semi-soft mass of down feathers—consoling her with its docile quietness.

Drained but sleep-frustrated still, Mei got up after a while. She turned on the radio as she relocated herself to her side of the two-seater sofa at the foot of the bed. The soft music from the radio felt a little shrill at this time of the morning. She switched on a small standing lamp by the sofa, and picked up a half-read novel lying on the sofa—*The Handmaid's Tale*. She had started on this before the unravelling but had become too distracted and distraught to return to it since.

Mei opened the book and proceeded to read. However, the words blurred and disconnected quickly after, and the logic linking the sentences appeared nonsensical. Her attention was not on *Offred* nor *June's* tragic tale in the dystopian *Republic of Gilead*. In her mind, she was parsing her own life story, zoning between the present and the past in a sleepwalking kind of wakefulness.

Ten minutes later, she collapsed on the sofa out of sheer weariness. The lyrics of *Breakeven* (by The Script) gently massaged her subconscious as she dozed off, easing her transition from drowsiness into otherworldliness seamlessly. Was the universe identifying with her pain? Mei would not know and she was not in any position to care anyhow.

After an indeterminate while, Mei found herself walking along an unfamiliar road alone. Suddenly, she lost sensation and agency of her limbs. Still in motion, she was gliding over the solid concrete path that was slowly acquiring a watery texture now. She reached a familiar place at the end: a reservoir. Keat had brought her here before.

The yellowish-almost-white gibbous moon was hanging from its usual place but she could see no shadow about her. The moonlight though was sufficiently luminescent to help her make out the dark swathe of forest at the other side of the reservoir. Then something fluffy carried her towards the forest despite no contraption beneath her feet. She was flying across like a ghost now. The water surface was glassy, completely still without a ripple, yet there was no reflection of the moon anywhere. Staring through, she could not make out the depth of the bottomless darkness underneath. The surreal surroundings were utterly eerie and awful. Quietly, the fine hair all over her body stood on salute, goose bumps had popped up everywhere.

Where was she going?

What was transporting her body now semi paralysed waist down?

As Mei approached the far shore, she heard a faint voice calling her name and some other indistinct moans. The moans were human-like—a very weak human, a very tortured soul, she suspected. A damp staleness of putrid flesh grew stronger in the air as the shore of the reservoir drew nearer—the smell of Death. Was that his scythe she just saw?

The moans became clearer now. She could make out a soft groan—Mei, say something, I AM GIVING UP ON YOU. They seemed to emanate from somewhere deep inside the forest.

The moon was on the wrong side. It was completely dark when Mei made landfall. After adjusting to the surrounding darkness, she figured out the forest to be not trees but giant mushrooms of varying sizes, and other kinds of out-sized fungi of seemingly three colour compositions—sepia with white speckles or darker shades of grey with blood red spots or completely brownish-black.

As if on cue, the refrain stopped instantly the moment Mei landed on the shore.

"Hello?" Mei called out. An unfamiliar haunting voice gave her a fright—it was her own actually. The forest swallowed her cry instantly and then resounding silence again.

Whatever was transporting Mei continued to move her down a path that presented itself on the swampy shore. The foliage automatically parted as she moved towards the mushroom forest. Then she melted into it smoothly like a fluid penetrating some invisible membrane.

At that moment, Mei imagined putting her hands to her chest, supposing whatever to be underneath there was still pounding. Instead, she felt nothing. This could not be real—Mei was petrified. What was keeping her alive? She continued moving inwards, feeling a frigid airlessness about her now.

What was *really* going on?

After some indeterminate distance into the forest, Mei came up against Keat suddenly—face only, puffy and punched up, in the body of a mushroom stalk. The stalk was as wide as the trunks of a Banyan tree. His eyes were the size of fists, completely dark with no whites, and they focused intensely on Mei as if he had been expecting her all along.

How could she tell, there was no distinct pupils or irises to guide her? Was everything just an imagination?

At this thought, Mei's back stiffened. She reckoned the refrain must have come from him. He was sobbing, squid-ink tears streaming down his cheeks, and clearly tormented. She sensed he was trying to reach out to her but could not—he had no hands, no legs, without a body in fact.

"Please say something, I AM LEAVING YOU," he pleaded. She wanted to say something but no word formed in her parched mouth, and her throat was sore. She was heaving with her uncontrollable breath now shallow and arrhythmic.

At once, sensation returned to her body. Something was crawling up her legs now. Huge tendrils (or were these the roots of the Banyan tree?) grew out of the ground like mangroves and were wriggling up her body, growing sharp ancillary thorns at the same time. Mei wanted to run but her legs were utterly rooted to the ground. The tendrils were compressing her and the thorns were piercing her skin everywhere they reached. A claret-coloured viscous fluid was oozing out from where the thorns had penetrated. The fluid congealed about her feet, gradually turned burgundy red, and finally overlaid onto the blue-black gelatine-like ground around her.

A tsunami of pain flooded her completely. Then she became numb after a while.

All of a sudden, she felt the tendrils constricting her so forcefully, cracking her bones like twigs. Simultaneously, the mushroom stalk was dissolving Keat into itself. Finally, he vanished and darkness ensued, swallowing up everything around at the same time.

Mei could not make any sense of what was happening. She could only sense herself transfused into another medium: her body diffusing into complete darkness and melding with the ether.

Continuous moping could beget dreams. Mei was dreaming copiously now. Completely untethered, she traversed multiverses endlessly the whole nightlong.

YJ Chin

The Innermost Sanctum

"I'll clean up later." It was Saturday night and Beth was just done with dinner at her rental apartment. Remnant smells of sambal-grilled fish and garlic from the sautéed broccoli lingered in the open concept kitchen. She poured herself another glass of her favourite Pinot Noir, and swayed leisurely to the living area.

Since moving here a little over two months ago now, Beth had been dining alone every weekend with only her compact audio system for company. Initially, she considered to adopt a dog but changed her mind before she could act on her impulse.

"Don't think I can be responsible for another being at this time. It'll be selfish of me to do that," Beth concluded. A wise decision indeed.

After resting the wineglass on the coffee table, Beth picked up a fashion magazine next to it, and plonked herself onto the two-seater sofa, overlaid with a thick aquamarine Indian cotton cover. Lazily, she flipped through its pages, intending to read an article when she came to it. Actually, the article had prompted her to purchase the magazine, which was quite unlike one in her regular staple.

"Research material for my current project. Good to have a latest feel of the public pulse on the subject of infidelity," Beth had thought when she came across the magazine on the shelf two days ago while browsing at her usual bookshop. She had a commission to write an essay on Genetics and Infidelity. That was just the current working title. Usually, she would revise it once the essay was complete and ready for publication.

The subject matter came about when Beth chanced upon some scientific journal that contained a publication with an interesting title—Genetics and Infidelity. *Duh!* It was based on a ground breaking study conducted by some researchers from a reputable American university, and had suggested a possibility that infidelity in humans could be genetically linked. However, the coverage of the study was quite limited, mostly lacking in depth and appearing in niche publications only. The combined reportage was rather disappointing in her opinion. Perhaps there was inadequate peer reviews prior to its technical publication. *Who knows?*

Beth became interested in the subject nonetheless and conceived the idea of publishing a researched essay in one of the media publications that had retained her services for editorial or columnist work. She thought she could delve deeper into adjacent domains and give some time for relevant works to come to the fore for inclusion in her research repository to give the subject matter a more substantial and holistic treatment. She also figured that this topic would have widespread interest as it had the seductive ingredients of relationships, sex and the hint of secrets and lies. It will tug at the voyeuristic string in all of us, she sensed. Additionally, the scientific underpinnings would give the subject an air of respectability and appeal to the intellect of the readership.

"Including interviews with eminent local scientists and medical practitioners will lend more weight to the matter," she conspired with her voices. "Need to draw up an appropriate list of these people," she informed finally.

"Nice to have something to blame for our extra-marital pursuits or promiscuous urges, do you not think so?" Beth asked aloud. Being adult about our behaviour and taking responsibility for everything that we do are hard and tiresome sometimes. Is there not some degree of childish fecklessness in each of us? We need some fun and excitement sometimes to escape from the harsh realities of life, do we not?

Everyone simply listened only.

Unsurprisingly, the first publisher Beth broached her idea with promptly snapped up her special project proposal. It was over lunch at one of his favourite Japanese restaurants. He loved everything Japanese, having spent about seven years in Japan, split unevenly between Tokyo and Osaka. Then, he was on a transnational posting with another international publication before the current one recruited him to head its operations here five years ago.

He had done extremely well for his current company (and himself of course)—its three publications (separately in the journalistic, fashion and teen categories) each had the highest circulation metrics, commanding an unassailable lead over the nearest competitor in its own category.

He rejuvenated his company's digital platform also, which now boasted the highest number of paid subscribers among its peers, one of a few platforms that were currently profitable in the industry. The last detail was private information but he was proud of his achievement enough to share it with Beth.

"So pretentious! I'm sure he shares this with others too," Someone echoed Beth's suspicion.

"Beth, what a sensational idea! No need to talk further, I am sold. We will do both print and digital yeah. Shall we target to have your reportage-cum-essay included in the November issue, or the annual special edition in December at the latest?" Her publisher proposed, clearly excited.

December special sounds perfect, Beth decided in her mind but kept this to herself. She sensed her publisher would come to this conclusion eventually. After all, that would be a better platform for her essay rather than the regular run, she sensed also. Besides, she would need the longest possible runway she could get.

Expecting Beth to yield, her publisher continued after the briefest of pauses, "Nearing end of year, people may be in the mood for such stuff. Something substantial but not too heavy at the same time. Interesting mind-food and talk at Christmas and New Year's parties, you think?"

Beth knew where all this was leading to in his mind: how much would this help drive up the circulation of his pub. She did not bother with an answer. Presently, she was happy with the pretty and enticing array of sashimi in front of her—a welcomed distraction from the boring business chat now that he had agreed to underwrite the project.

(This restaurant is *really* one of the best in town for sashimi and sushi. Beth recalled Ming's vouch the night before at the same time.)

"That'll be about eight more months, should be long enough runway for your research, interviews and everything else? We certainly don't want to take too long, you agree?" Her publisher concluded in a polite but authoritative tone. He definitely was not asking. Beth knew that, she was familiar with his style and had gotten used to his usual drone by now.

Corporate honchos like him loved the sound of their own voice. Thinking aloud, they would say. They loved to be in charge and ensured everyone knew it too. Beth believed and experienced so. (Did she consider Ming similarly?)

"And if that edition hits all the circulation metrics, I may just consider giving you an award or a bonus for exceptional contribution," her publisher added as an afterthought, again not expecting Beth to react.

"There you go. I can read him like an open book!" Beth thought instantly and a thin smile formed on her delicate face, beautifully complementing her smug-looking eyes.

Actually, award works for me. Medals too. Beth thought, blending in her recollection: the string of awards and medals she had collected during her younger days. Spontaneously, her smile broadened a little which her publisher mistook to be her tacit approval of what he had said so far.

Nonetheless, she considered his proposal reasonable and accepted it readily after he also agreed to her usual payment and termination terms. Finally, they touched on the project-reporting cadence briefly. They agreed to meet again in three months' time, the first review milestone per their just established cadence.

"That's the easy part. Now comes the hard part of delivering the baby," Beth reflected after with a mixture of quiet satisfaction and dreadful anticipation.

Beth also read her publisher's mind: any longer, the subject might not be as hot, despite relationships, sex and secrets being evergreen topics that would attract a ready audience anytime. All the time actually, going by the extensive catalogue of gossip magazines and trashy tabloids available in the market. However, his journalistic publication targeted the intellectual and societal elites, so proper positioning and timing mattered a lot. In addition, fresh quality content of course, this would be indispensable.

As a personal practice, Beth would normally publish exclusively with the first publication that accepted her concept and terms. She had a prioritised list of publications among her retainers, and she had kept this, among other things, in the innermost sanctum of her heart. No one else had the key to this sanctuary, not even Ming. *Surprising?*

YJ Chin

Another Closet of Secrets

"I said before I don't want to talk about my past. Which part of what I said don't you understand?" Beth was acerbic in her retort and intimidating in her countenance.

Instinctively, she looked away from Ming and far into the distant, focusing on nothing and feeling sorry for him at the same time. Beth was trying very hard to be insouciant actually. It was impossible! She was obviously testy and she could not help herself. She avoided looking at him, as she knew it would weaken her to see the hurt she had just inflicted on him.

Beth was strong and determined mostly. However, we all have our weak spots. She knew that one look into his doleful eyes, ideas so clear to her a moment before would become vague, firmed decisions would become uncertain, and whatever resolve she had would melt away at once.

"I'm sorry. Forget that I asked," Ming grimaced regretfully. The sharpness of Beth's tongue pierced deep inside him. Crestfallen, it showed in his downcast eyes. Nevertheless, he decided to try again at some other time.

Beth could be insensitive and extremely curt when she felt pressured. At such times, her mercurial nature would drown out her empathy completely. Foremost, she had always insisted that all her relationships be on her terms. If things were not going her way, especially when her security was threatened, she could become highly volatile. She would react like a cornered animal and bite back defensively with hurtful words. There would be no lack of these given her mastery of the language. Ironically, the people she hurt most were those who loved her and meant everything to her.

"If they really love me enough, they will accept me for who I am and learn to live with my foibles," she would say in hopeful self-consolation after each outburst.

In the beginning, Beth was reticent about her past. She would not talk about her marriage and her husband at all. They all originated in the past, she had rationalised to Ming. Despite the apparent sophistry, Ming got her intention clearly and tried to flow with her mostly. However, their relationship had progressed beyond the tentative stage. He had separated with his wife and was living on his own now.

"Surely, it's time for more transparency."

"There should be no secrets between us."

"Did we not profess mutual honesty some while back?"

The voices would drone in Ming's mind every now and then.

After Beth's own unravelling, Ming had a superficial understanding of what occurred between her and her husband. Beth had volunteered very little information. For sure, they were still married under the common law. Anything further, Ming could only surmise from her moods and behaviour. These ranged widely, unpredictable altogether. Ming's overall impression: they were living separate lives under the same roof.

All the same, the duplicity was unnatural and wearisome for Beth, causing her to become irascible and supplanting their happiness little by little.

"Ming must make his own decision regarding our future, my situation notwithstanding." Someone heard Beth said as she was going about her humdrum the other day.

"It's not clear which path he plans to take." Someone-Else also paid attention now, and wondered if Beth would break out of her circular thinking this time.

"If he decides to divorce his wife, our future together will be on firmer ground. Make sense?" Someone was not sure if a reply was expected but considered this to be the same sophistry nonetheless.

"Well, going by Beth's decisions, she certainly considers her arguments most sound." Someone-Else shared this sentiment.

"But Ming's marriage has already unravelled when you shifted here—a result of his independent decision, using your frame." Someone could not take it any longer and interrupted Beth's train of thought finally.

"And Ming shifted to his studio before you moved out even," Someone-Else reminded plainly.

"Why are you still withholding information from Ming?" Both asked in unison.

"He's only separated from his wife. It's *still* not clear which path he will take!" Beth repeated her defence, becoming irritable at the same time.

"*Aren't you the same?*" The voices accused her categorically, refusing to let the matter rest this time. Beth was quite clear where she was headed but no longer as certain of her so-called sound arguments at this point. At last, stumped and unable to deflect the difficult issues (there were no easier ones to substitute this time), Beth dismissed all her voices summarily. She felt very tired just then.

With their secret now exposed to their spouses, was Beth keeping another closet of secrets in a sanctuary accessible by a secret society with one member only? Like air rushing to fill an empty space, was another duplicity filling up her innermost sanctum, replacing the one that had just cleared out?

"So what's the future for Ming and yourself given the current development?" Someone knocked Beth out of her reverie. Concurrently, she heard a *thug* sound: the magazine with the article, which might contain fodder for her project, had fallen from her lap.

Truthfully, Beth had not thought very much about their future lately. They had been evading the subject also, more for her than for Ming. Nothing came about when they tried to engage each other on the subject a couple of times before. Beth knew very well that total transparency, the elephant in the room, must underpin any meaningful dialogue. It would be pointless unless she was ready to take this head-on.

Beth was a worrier. She liked to be in control of herself especially, though not always successful given her whimsical impulses. Still, she would try very hard, and this had gotten better with age. For her, control included knowing everything (overthinking things?) before she could decide on anything.

"Can she get out of her circular quandary ever?" Someone threw its hands up in desperation. Someone-Else kept quiet now. It knew—kind of, but not exactly—that nothing would come out of their inquisition. Definitely not before Beth found her way out of her own perplexity which only she could, unfortunately.

"What is it that makes one leave the familiar to experiment with the unknown?" "Enough of predictable tedium?" "An escape from a dull existence?" "To feel alive again?"

"Is our need for safety also the impetus for risk-taking, like action and its equal and opposite reaction in physics?"

"The chemistry in our brains maybe, which reactions we have little control over?"

"Perhaps it is our psychology, hemmed in by our biology—we do what we do because of who we are, and that is all there is to it."

"The questions arise because our intelligence needs reasons and causes to rationalise, even justify, our natural proclivities and wants."

Failing to extract any answer from Beth, her shadows speculated among themselves. However, were they asking the *right* questions?

Discreetly, the slightly-husky-yet-feminine voice of Hillary Scott nudged at Beth. She felt suspended between the present with an unsettled future and her earlier reverie. It was a quarter to midnight, and the night was cool and still. Ghosts seemed to haunt the place as the song 'Need You Now' drifted from her audio system. Her aloneness accentuated her loneliness. Suddenly, she was missing Ming intensely. Was it the circular reminiscence, or the harmonious sounds of the Lady A trio, or the heart-tugging lyrics of the song? Not thinking any of these, she simply felt what she felt.

"Maybe I can drive over right now. It's only ten minutes max at this time of the night," her loneliness suggested. Beth perked up instantly on the idea.

"Are you crazy? He'll be wondering what's happening and start asking questions. Are you *really* up for this—truth or lie?" Someone became alert again, clearly on Beth's side this time.

We prefer lies, sometimes we do, *really!* Better still if we cannot tell a lie from the truth—a lie we want to believe in, a truth we are not ready to accept. Beth thought she had a fabricated lie, or more like a truth-lie combo. Maybe she had become obfuscated or worst, delusional. Maybe the lie had become so familiar in her mind that it had become indiscernible from the truth.

"The liar totally bought-in by her own lie now—this would be the ultimate, eh…any different from post-truth or fake news? Similar to the biases that fills our brain, accepting only information that conforms with or confirms those biases?" Someone-New interpolated.

"You are right! Better not. Forget it then," Beth admitted she was not ready for the drama *yet* and slumped back into the sofa, dejected. Her truth-lie combo was skimpy at best, she had not thought through the details yet—that much she was self-aware.

"Now that I'm on my own, there's no reason why I can't see Ming on weekends. Think I will go over next weekend; I can always bring my work along. His studio feels nicer actually. Just ease in and start a new routine without inviting awkward questions from Ming. Once habitual familiarity sets in, voila! A new normal." Clearly, Beth's brain chemicals were active now: her emotions lighting up her prefrontal cortex. Regardless, she perked up again, and she missed Ming even more.

Exhausted from her brain-trip to nowhere, Beth got up and ambled lethargically to her bedroom. She did not bother to clean up the kitchen anymore. The whole of Sunday would be available to do that.

Beth was so tired that she forgot to turn off the radio. Ryan Tedder, the lead vocal of OneRepublic was now belting out *'Secrets'* from the station. Coincidence? At midnight, it sounded louder than it did earlier despite the volume standing still. Even then, Ryan's words were lost on her. Everything was becoming one massive blur again; or messy; or both.

An Atomic Bomb Was Detonated

Mei woke up with a start and a déjà vu of her sitting on the sofa reading. How did she end up in her bed? It was late morning but the standing lamp was still on though perceptibly dimmer in the light of day. So too the indistinct sound of the radio now drown out by the birds outside, which were having a riotous time in the small public gardens opposite her house. Her dream-filled sleep had robbed her of needful rest. Diffused pictures preoccupied her mind as she tried to recall her dreams—Keat in a mushroom stalk, and herself in some extreme pain, otherwise no other details. She forced the memories to form and associate in her brain but gave up after a while when nothing cohered.

"What the hell! Forget it…everything has changed now," she swore aloud but there was no one else in the room to take the hit. Sitting up on her side of the bed, she picked up her phone habitually to check for anything that might have come in while she was asleep.

"Hey, I'm at the gym" Keat had texted earlier in the morning, as he got ready to start his regular gym sessions on Saturday mornings.

"I'll text again when I'm near done"

"We can grab lunch together if u want"

"We shud"…"U need 2 eat anyway"

These were the initial flurry of messages from Keat. Then two hours later, which was a couple of minutes ago, another bunch of texts from him.

"Hey, u up? Lunch?"

"Juz done, gonna shower now"

"Pls let me know. Either way"

"TQ"

Mei considered for a while, she was flustered still though the anger from last night had subsided almost completely. A low intensity throbbing headache had now taken over instead.

"Meet u at the usual"

"B there in 30 mins"

Mei texted back after some hesitance, and then got up and headed towards the bathroom to wash up. She switched off the now smaller standing lamp as she passed it. *The Handmaid's Tale* was still on the sofa. However, the paperback now looked like an unread book with its back cover facing the ceiling. Margaret Atwood was smiling at her.

Mei decided to go with what her intuition suggested, preferred even—it would be effortless, just flow with the established rhythm for now. Domesticity can be a powerful set of familiar routines that orders our days and gives structure to our lives. It is cognitively easy on our brains, and automatic for our bodies. Circuitous moping can be enervating. She decided to leave that behind for the time being, in return for some serendipitous lightness.

Lunch was at a familiar place: not too long a drive from home, and far enough to give them a feel of the countryside. One of their favourite haunts on weekends actually. However, the mood was anything but familiar, tainted by their brief and sharp altercation the night before, each other's icy cold stares etched in their minds.

Mei ambled towards a table at the alfresco part of the café, flanked by a low hedge of fuschia and white bougainvillea punctuated by frangipani trees full of pink and yellow flowers at the left end of the hedge. Flitting butterflies and buzzing bees were fussing over the colourful flowers. Beyond the hedge, a large field in front and a children's playground on the right side. Keat tagged behind her like a tamed dog.

On any sunny Saturday, some boisterous children would be chasing each other around the entire field; other restless ones would be milling at the playground under the watchful eyes of their gregarious parents, mothers mostly. Not today. The field and playground were utterly devoid of life.

The ambiance was a little foggy despite it being mid-day, a carry-over from the heavy downpour just a while ago. The whole field shimmered unevenly from the multitude of invisible rain beads carpeting the countless blades of manicured grass. The blended aura of cool after-rain air and warm fuzzy sunlight was a welcomed respite. Taking in the smell of the fresh flowers, and green grass as if newly cut by streaks of sunrays piercing through the misty atmosphere, Mei felt her shoulders loosened up instantly. A symphony of bird songs was audible only because all the children were indoors. What a beautiful serenity to diffuse the tension. Quietly, time suspended instantaneously as it collapsed around the moment.

As Mei and Keat sat down opposite each other, Mei caught sight of two squirrels frozen in their tracks by the hedge, eyeing them cautiously. The little fur balls scooted off hurriedly in the direction of the frangipani trees after Mei smiled gently at them, which they seemed to have mistaken as a threatening gesture. Better to be safe, one squirrel likely whispered to the other just before they scrambled away.

Meanwhile, Ms Edgy and Mr Tetchy also took up their seats beside Mei and Keat respectively. So quickly, the mood changed. An imminent replay of last night? At once, Mei felt a sudden odium for Keat and wondered if she would have been happier lunching alone.

He seems so fresh and light, Mei thought, clearly disgusted. The bliss had flitted away.

"Quickly, please order something, I'm starving," Mei instructed Keat in a bid to dispel her sulky mood.

Usually she would be the one ordering but nothing had been usual lately. Just as well, Mei was finding it easier to respond to her stomach than her heart right now, substituting the unhappy thoughts with questions, which answers were readily available on the menu in front of her.

Spontaneously, Mei and Keat retreated to the familiarity and safety of their mobile phones while waiting for their food to serve. They avoided conversation mostly, merely making some inconsequential and safe commentary on the surroundings and the weather otherwise. Despite the gloomy overhang, Ms Edgy and Mr Tetchy maintained their decorum and self-control.

Mei realised that her starting volume last night was not in keeping with her personality, and neither helpful to her dignity (first) nor their predicament at all. After all, she was a proud woman, and she was deliberate in her actions, mostly. She resolved to be more in control the next time. She also determined to deploy her now-loosened liberal language sparingly for more effect. She recalled approvingly her final rejoinder to her initial outburst.

"Is this it? Why bother? Eating alone would have been more relaxing and free," Ms Edgy complained while Mei heaved a gentle sigh. Mr Tetchy was too engrossed in Keat's newsfeed to notice anything.

Was Mei hoping for something more than just a routine lunch? She was not sure. For sure, she felt extremely tormented and burdened since the secret of Keat's affair was exposed and acknowledged. Impulsively, she stole a glance at Keat through her bug eye sunglasses. At once, a tender love for him welled up within her, as if none of what happened had transpired at all. She felt the urge to reach out and stroke his face but managed to prevent its realisation at the crucial moment. An irritation ensued instead. She still loved him; however, her liking for him had dissipated for the time being.

Mei was unsure of her path forward. Questions had been swirling in her head since the unravelling but no answers were forthcoming, at least no straightforward ones. What she had suggested to Keat last evening might seem like a path she had decided on. Probably. However, she had been vacillating forever since the wheels fell off. It might change yet again later on.

Mei stared at her phone with distant eyes. She saw nothing of her Instagram feed on the screen, only images of Keat playing back in her mind—their first few meets, him playing with Kim and how he looked over the years. Not much had changed actually, at the edges mostly, except his hair of course. More and more of ourselves come to the fore as we age, do we not? There is less to hide, even lesser to prove.

Mei imagined him ten years, twenty years from now. Having peaked in our lifecycle, are we not all our ages at the same time by now—will he be any different then? "Would she still have him around to validate this truth?" Everyone wondered aloud.

For couples who have been together long enough, we do not really think about the other very much after some time. There is always time for this later, we tell ourselves—lulled into familiarity, consumed by exigencies—we believe time is on our side, and we count on what was would still be around when we have the time. However, this change dramatically, when one is leaving the other— in some cases, after one has left the other—and we wonder about the other more. Now, Mei's recollection flooded her brain, jolted out of familiarity by an exigency. Time is by your side only for that infinitesimal moment that you have it—coming at you and leaving you all at once. Neither a friend nor a foe, it is on nobody's side actually. Presently, her every thought was rushing in, as if trying to slow, if not stop altogether, the grains of fine sand in the conjured hourglass from running out.

Meanwhile, Keat was down his own rabbit hole also despite the façade. Like Mei, he had a rough night too. Unlike Mei, he was feeling light and relaxed. The gym had helped; his brain was flushed with happy hormones for the time being. Our inclination towards familiarity and safety comes naturally. Lunch with Mei was familiar territory, and relatively safe despite his experience last night. Ironically, he felt settled in her company.

Keeping separate lives and secrets was harder and more tiresome than Ming had imagined. Despite the upheavals that followed, the relief Ming experienced was monumental the moment his secret unravelled. Then, someone had lifted an unfathomable weight off his chest. Beth had experienced similarly six months before.

"Unfortunately, that someone is their spouses who bore the terrible brunt of their unburdening; their secret fell like a tonne of bricks on them." Someone sympathised. (Unintended consequence; sadly, it happens all the time.) Their spouses became unwitting participants in this game of chance and love, and made to suffer at the hands of Beth and Ming's impulses and choices.

"Where is the fairness in this recently created universe of four?" Someone then shouted angrily.

Someone-Else trying to restore some calm, asked, "Is there a mathematical formulation to describe this experience: burden shared divides, into halves, or various proportions that add up to the original whole? The after equals the before?" It did not seem so to Beth and Ming although they each felt much lighter after.

"Definitely not for their spouses: the combined weight of the burden feels immensely heavier to them, the volume of unrests altogether has also expanded many times over like a nuclear explosion, as if an atomic bomb was detonated at the point of revelation." Someone-New posited with empathy.

Now, the present was capriciously fragile like a piece of tempered glass still holding together despite countless visible fissures produced by a devastating force. The splintered pieces of their lives held together precariously by the inexplicable glue of the volatile mind. Everyone felt delicate and vulnerable to the idiomatic straw that broke the camel's back. Everything could be shattered in the blink of an eye.

The Creative Brain

S hortly after Ming relocated his life to his studio, he took to reading the novels written by Beth, which was a different fiction genre from his usual staple of spy stories, psychological thrillers and science fiction mostly, but also included literary novels occasionally.

At graduate school, Beth's research thesis centred on the psychological make-up of the young adult segment. A part of her thesis considered the idea of stories that would provide an escape for their teenage-going-to-adulthood kind of raw dreaminess juxtaposed with the coming-of-age kind of angsty adventurism juxtaposed with a what-is-the-world-coming-to kind of rude reality.

At the start of her writing career after graduation, Beth decided to develop this idea further. Hence, her experiment with stories that combined fantasy, science fiction and realism—an emerging space that appeared to be on the verge of explosion among junior college-graduating teens, undergraduate youths and young adults starting out in the workforce. She thought a ready and available audience from each of the discrete genres could be potential readers for her novels.

As luck would have it, Beth's hard work paid off after her pseudo-realistic fantastic world of *Therasudorsa* took off with the release of her third novel—*The Deadly Mace of Barabudur*—that exploited this direction of story development and an almost-new genre that apparently was gaining definition and traction in the creative writing space. To her pleasant surprise, this also reinvigorated interest in her first two novels. This led to reprints of her earlier books, which kept pace with the sale of *The Deadly Mace of Barabudur* as readers clamoured for the back-stories of the characters in and the beginnings of the *Therasudorsa* universe. Consequently, she acquired a cult status of sorts among her small but growing base of loyal readers.

"You are too old for the stuff I wrote," Beth commented a couple of weeks later.

"It's a window to you and your soul, don't you think?" Ming disagreed that the generation gap was any barrier at all.

Ming was right. The ideas and characters in her novels would be fodder for scintillating exchanges on their worldviews, preferences and biases, and their relationship would evolve to encompass a different plane. More discoveries on both sides—sufficiently similar to keep them together amidst volatile times, sufficiently different to keep up the mystery and surprises—adding to the attractiveness for each other. However, when the conversation segued towards Beth's past, she would veer away, determined not to go there.

"The past is passed, inconsequential to our future, let sleeping dogs lie," Beth would say and change the subject firmly. Ming would let it slide most of the time, albeit with a hint of disappointment each time. Beth would see this in his despondent eyes and felt her own anguish at the same time.

"I will have to endure this if I want to have it my way." Beth would tell herself regarding her self-inflicted chronic ache of sorts.

Some months later, Beth's eating routine popped up randomly in her mind. More likely not. Perhaps it was lighter to entertain inconsequential thoughts compared to the heavier stuffy gyrations when she contemplated the state of her happiness. The latter complicated by the uncertain fate of their relationship; its fuzziness had been weighing on her with ever-increasing heaviness since her own unravelling.

Regardless, it happened all the time, random thoughts popping up in her mind that is. Unless Beth was attending to something important or urgent that required continual focus and effort, she would entertain these mental interruptions or sensory flirtations. Her mind would wander for a while to see where these might lead. Something interesting can come out of this randomness; such is the process of the universe and evolution, is it not? She induced. Is this a cognitive illusion?

Indeed, Beth had experienced some epiphanies when the randomness seemingly mixed up with stuff already in her brain to spotlight an insight or observation that might have been under her nose all along. At other times, she discovered solutions to unresolved issues in her mind, or trouble that seemed to be brewing beneath the surface. Actually, some ideas for her imaginary *Therasudorsa* universe had arisen after some mental meandering, which of course had found success after a while. Is this how the brain's creative centre works?

"Creativity is mindless meandering and mindful herding of cat-like thoughts of sorts, you think?" Ming pondered aloud to Beth out of the blue one weekend. It was late morning and Beth was sitting on his bed, working on her special project. She was trying to take stock of her notes and research materials strewn on the bed all around her.

"What makes artists like yourself apparently more creative than the rest of us?" By now, Ming had put down the novel he was reading: *The Fiery Sabre of KangoWatu*, the first book in the *Therasudorsa* series. He was staring out of the balcony into nothingness, or perhaps infinity. Beth realised he was in a mood for some serious discourse. She stopped her project work and removed herself from the messy bed to join him at the sofa.

"I think you are creative as well. I thought you wouldn't have counted yourself out," Beth offered inclusively, her voice more womanly than manly. She reached out to cup Ming's cheeks with both hands as she neared the sofa, intending to give him a kiss but changed her mind at the last minute. Instead, she felt his light stubble briefly.

Then Beth settled down to a comfortable position at the opposite end of the sofa after picking up his huge ceramic mug on the table. She took a small sip of water from the mug, her Christmas gift to Ming last year, as she pondered his question.

I've not asked myself that actually. I know I am and I just bloody get on with it. The thought bubbled up from her brain and seemed contented to stay inside there.

Still cupping the mug with both her hands as if conjuring some hocus-pocus from an opaque orb, Beth wondered aloud, "Hmm…what led me to writing?" Unconsciously, she had substituted a difficult and general question on creativity with an easier and more specific question. Intuitively, her familiar and personal experience as a fiction writer would reduce the brain-effort she needed to answer her own question.

"Did I become a writer because it flows easier with my creative nature?"

"Or did I become creative after acquiring and honing my skills as a writer, the creativity is then a learnt and practiced skill?"

"Classic nature versus nurture question, isn't this?"

Beth tossed the questions out of her head. (Did she just mirror the *thinking aloud* habit of some corporate honchos she knew?)

Naturally, her mind started to drift.

…

"What are you doing, Bethie? It's time for afternoon tea," asked Beth's aunt, about two hours after she was back from her pre-school.

"'I'm playing…A new boy joined my class today, I'm adding him to my story and playhouse. He's going to be the doctor to everyone else in the group…" Beth replied cheerfully.

…

"Bethie, come and sit by my side. Let's chat for a while, shall we?" Beth's aunt called out to her softly when she came into her room. Beth was hard at work, trying to finish her homework for the day. By now, she had outgrown her bookshelves. Pyramids of *Encyclopaedia Britannica* were scattered on the floor by the bookshelves. So were her old storybooks and newer novels. Her aunt shepherded her to a couple of large green and blue leathery beanbags by the bookshelves.

"Okay, auntie Lei. What's up?" Beth asked deferentially, looking a little puzzled and searching her aunt's soft gentle eyes for some clues as she settled down on the green bag. Lei took the blue bag beside her.

"Bethie baby, how are you finding school? You're enjoying this one better?" Lei enquired with trusting eyes and an inviting smile while stroking Beth's shoulder length hair lovingly, as a mother would towards her own child.

"Yes, auntie Lei, very much. The teachers are more helpful, they try to answer my questions even though they seem puzzled by them sometimes. Why? Am I in trouble?" Beth rejoined, more curious then before, and clearly in a tone more matured than one would expect of a ten year-old girl. She had been at her new school for half a year now, having transferred here after she qualified for the gifted child education programme.

"Well, I met with your teachers this morning. They know you are a bright girl. Just that they think you daydream a little too often during lessons," Lei disclosed finally, softly cupping Beth's hands in hers in a reassuring way.

"But I kept up with what they were teaching, did I not? …The topics and the discussions aren't always as interesting sometimes," Beth replied defensively, looking for forgiveness from her aunt, or understanding or a mixture of both

"Not if you are asking questions that shows you have not been paying attention…look Bethie, they are happy to answer your questions especially those that are a little beyond what they have covered. They just need to make sure things do not veer too far off and disrupt the learning of everyone else in the class…they are generally happy with you. It's mostly good; you know that, don't you?" Lei concluded on a comforting tone.

…

A wormhole had pulled Beth back to her childhood. Unusually, she was vocalising most parts of the conversations that the reconstructed episodes were playing back in her working memory.

"I was curious and hungry to learn, still am actually…important to keep an open mind to all things, you think? …my goodness, I even entertained random and bizarre thoughts for their own sake," Beth laughed with self-deprecation at what she just said as if someone might consider her nuts. Her gaiety was contagious; Ming mirrored her demeanour as well.

"And I enjoyed imagining possible futures besides the one that everyone seemed to think were inevitable at that moment. Helped me build *Therasudorsa*, which is a wonderful thing, isn't it?" Beth continued to verbalise her introspection unawares.

"Though most things seem obvious from hindsight, nothing is inevitable in life ever, agree? I have chosen a craft that allows me to do what I want with my creativity while earning a living, and a very good one obviously." Beth voiced with animated satisfaction. Ming nodded with exuberance; her vivacity was captivating.

"A rare opportunity to listen to her talk about her past though nothing seems shocking so far," Someone informed Ming. He knew Beth to be intelligent, inquisitive, creative and empathetic. Of course, he had suffered her capricious moodiness at times, but this was completely absent presently. Ming was enjoying every minute of it. Beth felt extremely safe and secure with Ming also.

What do you talk about when you talk about the creative brain? Everything, it seemed. Their dialogue flowed freely and easily, melding their hungry minds ever more tightly. They forgot about lunch altogether, instead choosing naturally to feast on each other's mental ruminations and intellectual curiosities, which appeared most appetising for now.

Hotel California

'*Lost in Your Eyes*' started to play on the Bose sound system and interrupted Faye's train of thought. She had put on the player just before she headed for her shower earlier. The song by Debbie Gibson was from a new collection of 70s/80s pop music that she had purchased and downloaded from Apple Music about a month back. (When did her interest in music from this era ignite? How? Why?) For convenient and easy listening at home, Faye had pressed those songs into a CD that could be loaded into the player's 5-disc CD changer subsequently. Of course, she could stream the songs wirelessly from her iPhone to the Bose system but old-fashioned CD appealed to her still. The sound quality is better with CD, and without the random irritating static, she justified.

"Don't even mention the Luddites now," Someone warned, "she hates them. You'll be asking for trouble if you associate her with them."

The song, aurally perfect despite the relatively low volume, put Faye in a dreamy mood. The music resonated in the spacious living room. It was a cool and quiet night; an echoey surrealism permeated the ambience. Was it the piano preamble? The lyrics? Debbie's sweet and clear vocals? Faye was not thinking any of this. She was still slumped on her plush comfortable sofa bodily, but her mind had left her apartment already.

...

"It was such a tumultuous period, to say the least, after Mei found out," Sean recalled in a soft and restrained voice. His mind was in a time machine, conjured by the marvellous brain, traveling back and forth between the past and the present at unfathomable brain-speed. Involuntarily, his pupils dilated and his muscles tensed. Faye perceived his ache and anguish at the sight of his jawbone tightening, so slight that it would have passed unnoticed if she had not been training her eyes on him, her sensibilities sharpened by her profession notwithstanding.

Sean was calm and in control, he took his time to access his episodic memory, tapping on the associative network in his brain to retrieve the interrelated and cascaded bits and pieces distributed all over his grey matter. His hippocampus was reconstructing the visual setting, adding the script and emotions, rehearsing for rough order and coherency in a cerebral spatial and temporal dimension, all at once. Sean's brain was choreographing on the fly what was playing, how the drama was unfolding at a particular point in his personal history.

"She was terribly hurt...she reacted with such anger...I'd never seen this side of Mei all the time we'd been together...how is it possible to change into a completely different person so suddenly...I'd anticipated that there would be pain...but the depth and breadth of it was beyond my imagination. She tried to put up a brave front...she's a proud woman...but I knew she couldn't stop crying when she was alone, she couldn't hide her eyes forever...it's clear I'd broken her heart...and her spirit...and probably her mental state too...I was quite blind then, realised it only after all the wreck ...so cruel, am I not?" Sean asked repentantly without expecting any answer nor sympathy.

His brain was also working hard to maintain control over his emotions. It would be much easier for Sean, natural even to just let loose and cry. However, people in our society who betray their vulnerability, especially men, typically cause us discomfort. The public display of raw tenderness is a sign of weakness we strive to conceal. We crave acceptance and the approval of others also: losing control is unacceptable and will not win any approval.

"It's ok Sean, take your time. We are safe here," Faye commiserated and watched him with forgiving eyes. There was no need to parrot what she had heard (a technique she would use when necessary to help her clients and patients clarify their thoughts or develop a more complete view of an issue or just to move their train of thought along). Obviously, Sean was mirroring Mei's pain, ebbing and flowing in tandem with his disjointed sentences, modulated by the specific words his semantic memory was throwing out. Faye saw this in his bottomless eyes and the twitch of the muscles flanking them. She could also hear this in his asphyxiated breathing—sometimes shallow and grasping, other times thrusting yet frail, almost hollow—as if his lungs were at the brink of collapse.

At the spur of the moment, Faye got up from the armchair where she usually sat during their sessions, and settled down beside Sean at the two-seater sofa. She kept a slight distance from him as if the partition of an invisible confessional separated them. There she waited patiently for Sean to unburden his congested heart further.

"Mei was clearly vacillating…wildly," Sean continued, raising his voice a bit. Did someone said his voice was tailing off? Certainly not Faye, she was quiet as a country mouse, all her senses entirely focused on Sean.

"I was torn too…between…innocent words…became… double-edged swords…worlds just collided …spun out…of control …Mei accused me…said I had a forked tongue…misinterpreted… everything…became…a suspect …accusations …the past oddly… put together…totally…out…of…context… revisionist…ridiculous …I became angry too…naturally…just spiral…everything… downwards…imploded exploded…hurling splinters…everywhere …pain…just hurt…more pain".

Sean was babbling, choking on his words every now and then. His speech was in bursts of mere words or monotone phrases. He was trying very hard to stay coherent but clearly obfuscated. Was his pain interfering with his semantic memory? Was his episodic memory trying to match the emotions with appropriate words, sometimes finding no word at all? Is this what 'ineffable' looks like?

Then Sean quietened down. Everything seemed to have bled out of him for the time being. Faye could sense his deep pain and a seemingly abysmal void. Despite the disjointed sentences with multiple pauses and near gibberish words, his expression evoked an uncanny sensation in her as if everything had just happened actually. Strangely, so intimately familiar as well. Did Sean just unearth an unconscious unresolved neurotic conflict in Faye? She was not thinking this. Nevertheless, a sense of déjà vu seized her.

What was Faye thinking? The innocuous, perhaps professional notion that she could help to comfort Sean and alleviate his indescribable pain there and then. She knew the needful role sensory stimuli and physical sensations played in a person's well-being—insights from *Touch: the Science of Hand, Heart and Mind* (so long ago now since she read this book by David Linden) had been assimilated into her belief system. Faye believed in the magic of touch: it could heal a broken person, or at least help with pain relief for a while.

"Sean was not physically or sexually abused in any way before to the best of my knowledge, so touch should not traumatise him," Faye extrapolated further in her mind.

As the conscious mind was preoccupied with justification, Faye's hand spontaneously reached out to find Sean's concurrently. Almost immediately after, she extended her other hand to cup his cheek on the far side, then gently stroked his face from ear to chin, feeling his stubble lightly. Impulsively, Faye leant in towards Sean.

The reassuring feel of warm and tender flesh on his skin, an abrupt release of chemicals and electricity in his brain: Sean was overwhelmed instantly. With primal instincts, Sean reached out and gently held Faye's pink-blushed face with both hands and proceeded to kiss her on her glossy and full but closed lips. He tasted mint on her supple lips (real? imagined? where was he now actually?) and imagined they would have been poutier and fuller when she was younger. Faye was attractive even at her age. Did Sean think this?

"The line has been crossed, you are clearly in the inappropriate behaviour territory now," the voice yelled at Faye, half accusing and half admonishing her.

Faye just dismissed it utterly. With a noticeable intake of his scent, she kissed Sean back, now with parted lips, tasting and drawing him in all at once. Faye experienced a surreal transfusion of life as she breathed Sean in.

What was Faye thinking now? Nothing really, at least not consciously. However, she felt ecstatic—her heart was wispy and airy as a cloud, her lips bathed in a soft and warm moisture, her pale pink cheeks safe in his strong steady hands. A feeling she definitely had not experienced for a long time. A feeling she was most glad to melt into, forever if she could help it.

What was going through Sean's brain? Mentally exhausted and emotionally empty at this point, his mind had relinquished all self-control. His brain was in autopilot mode with its guard down: no longer evaluating options, or considering the consequences of his actions, or anything of this sort. Sean was just reacting to his need for emotional security, like a little child who was deeply hurt, feeling an unstoppable torrent of pain at the same time.

Unconsciously, Sean still needed to be sure that the coast was clear. This basic human need underlined his instinctual search for signs to inform him: her approving eyes, quiet inviting posture, and tender touch. He sensed safety: he had her permission, and assurance of protection from consequences and reprisals, if any. By Faye's response, his instincts were probably right on the mark.

Had it been seconds only? Minutes more likely. It felt timeless nonetheless. Funny how a minute can vary so wildly between wake-state and dream-state, between daydreaming and night dreaming. The mind knows no absolutes at all, not even time. Yet, we have such absolute confidence in the immutability of time that it has come to dictate and structure every part of our wakeful existence.

The Bose system was effusing *'Hallelujah'* now. At its chorus, a band of backup singers fused with Leonard Cohen's deep, low, gravelly whispering-talking-voice to hit a crescendo of sorts, which woke Faye up instantly.

Faye felt a chill down her spine and goose pimples all over her arms and shoulders. She realised she had fallen asleep on the sofa. Incidentally, Sean had mentioned at Session No.5 today that *'Hallelujah'* was one of the soundtracks in the *'Watchmen'* movie released in 2009. When and how did this come up? She could not quite remember. *Yes!* Faye remembered the movie definitely, and the song vaguely. She had enjoyed the cult movie very much (being somewhat carefree at medical school then) but she was unaware of the singer/songwriter at all.

As wakefulness seeped back in, Faye recalled her intention to review Sean's session for the day. "I have brought back his dossier for this purpose, didn't I?" She bellowed as if to nudge herself out of her grogginess. Almost simultaneously, snippets of her night-daydream a moment earlier flitted across her mind. Her torpor played havoc with her fuzzy memory somewhat. The part with Sean and her kissing was completely absent from her recollection.

"Did it not happen just an infinitesimal moment ago?"

"Can her brain not rewind just a bit?"

"Has it blotted this scene out altogether?"

As the frantic voices in her head fussed over what just happened, Faye became self-conscious: she felt wet!

Without a second thought, Faye got up from the sofa and decamped to her bedroom. She sprawled herself on the bed, as if trying to occupy everywhere all at once. (Suppose that was how she slept alone in a king-sized bed.) Then, she self-helped.

Shortly after, Faye came, in exuberant waves of vibrant fireworks, and fell asleep soon after all the euphoria had vanished from her brain. By then, a narrow vertical beam of moonlight had streaked into her bedroom through a crack in the curtains, softly illuminating her naked chest, accentuating her sensuality even more. What a sharp composition of nude photography! Just then, the seductive guitar prelude of *'Hotel California'* (by the Eagles) echoed faintly in the air, immersing everywhere in a complementary Sen-surround.

Meanwhile, Sean's dossier was still in Faye's busy briefcase while the kiss she had fantasised with him was still encoded somewhere in her now blissful brain. The dossier filled with precise and reliable recordings that could stand the test of time. Her brain filled with contextually subjective memories that could lose its reliability with age and the passage of time. For now, nothing mattered, Faye had already checked into the ethereal hotel. She would battle her demons deep inside there, which coincidentally seemed to resemble the dark and dreadful dungeons of *Barabudur*.

YJ Chin

Urgent Leave

"My goodness! I look terrible. How to go back to office like this?" Mei concluded as she looked at her pathetic self in the mirror while washing up. Two days had passed since Keat's secret unravelled—his two-year old affair with another married woman. Though Mei had a nagging feeling that something might be happening as far back as a year ago, she was not able to put her finger on what exactly her hunch was telling her all the while.

"Better apply leave…good thing there's nothing heavy this coming week…my guys should be able to cover me for a while," Mei determined quite immediately. As her body was going about her washing-up routine habitually, her mind was wholly preoccupied with what to tell her boss and her people later. All her colleagues might ask too, feigning care and concern to cover for their nosiness. Actually, they would likely be looking for fodder to feed the office grapevine, which had been somewhat dry and dull lately.

"They are inconsequential. I'll bother with them if I have to," Mei winced in disgust, which caused her to swallow her toothpaste at the same time. Well almost! Her reflexive system managed to cough out the foamy residue in time.

Need to think a bit. How to explain one week of urgent leave all of a sudden? Cannot let this cat out yet. Anyway, we agreed to keep this to ourselves until *such time*. And Kim must be the first to know amongst everybody else beyond the two of us. Mei frowned slightly as she thought, her body still going through the motion of the longer-than-usual washing up routine.

Mei and Keat did not actually ascertain what *such time* meant. They did not discuss who would have the final call to determine *such time* when it finally came either. This assumed that there was a way of telling definitively that *such* was indeed the *time*. Kind of chasing your own tail, was this not? No one was thinking any of this at all. There were more pressing issues to deal with for the time being. Maybe everyone was just avoiding the difficult questions. Moreover, every question appeared difficult now. Nevertheless, should this not be priority? It would certainly complicate their situation further if more people became aware of the secret—first Keat's burden only, now a shared one between them.

"I won't have much need for my leave days any more anyway, might as well clear some," Mei justified aloud. Their usual year-end family vacation would not be happening this year. Kim would be flying off to Zurich for her exchange programme in about two weeks' time. She would be there until the end of the year. All the same, Mei could not imagine Keat and herself going anywhere together given the recent domestic explosion of sorts.

Nonetheless, after two days of involuntary bodily reaction to the unravelling, Mei was very lucid now and appeared to have reclaimed some self-control. Perhaps she had exhausted herself of the matter for now. Around mid-day, Mei texted her boss to apply for leave for the whole of the upcoming week. She stayed sketchy in her texts deliberately, and kept her language formal.

"Good day Boss. Hope you are fine"…

"Need to apply urgent leave this coming week"…

"Something urgent came up at the home front. Can't wait"

Then Mei left it at that.

…"Appreciate your understanding." Mei added a while later to tug at his compassion. Just as well, to telepath her boss that he was expected to simply approve her leave application as a formality.

After some toing and froing clarifying some outstanding work matters, her boss yielded and gave his approval.

Subsequently, Mei spent the better part of the remaining day texting with her staff and talking with a few of them on the phone to frame everyone's priorities for the week ahead. They would need to collaborate on some pieces of work and submit the output to her boss by the end of the week.

"Great. They are adequate. The output will be up to standard," Mei whispered confidently when she was finally done. She was glad that her work had taken her mind off her marital woes for the time being. She felt light and somewhat centred as if the work had anchored her to some purpose and provided a way forward to pin her hope on.

However, this did not last long; a maelstrom of churning emotions revisited Mei during the week while she was on leave. Her demons were especially present when she was alone in the house. Mei was not one to give in to depression but she could not help herself, she was never as traumatised as now. She would experience many firsts, not the kind anyone would wish upon himself or herself, or anyone else. It can be hellish when we are in it. Most of us come out of it after a time; some just take longer than others do. Tragically, some never do.

"This cannot be…it cannot be real"

"I can't believe this is happening to me"

"Why me?"

Mei was in denial initially. About forty percent of men would have at least one extra-marital affair at some stage of their lives— this statistic flashed in her mind out of nowhere. She had no idea it was even there or who had dredged it up.

"Which country was this?" Mei asked woefully to anyone who was listening. Never in her life did she imagine that Keat would be lumped with this statistic, this group of unfaithful men.

"Does it matter now that it has happened to your husband?" Someone asked rhetorically.

"Where you are concerned, it's a hundred percent, isn't it?" Someone-Else added matter-of-factly but the tone sounded sarcastic.

"Damn you, Arsehole! That cuts really deep, thank you for being so bloody blunt." Mei felt a stab in her chest. She was also becoming quite uninhibited in her language.

"There is a hint of truth to what Arsehole just said, is it not?" Someone-New suggested, trying to be objective. "We have a tendency not to deduce a particular situation, especially ourselves or someone we know even remotely, from a general statistical fact though that fact covers us generally."

"However, we think otherwise after that fact happened to people we know or us particularly; we suddenly become alert to the statistic and infer the fact to be generally applicable now." Someone-New added.

"It seems facts can sway us easily and readily when we can associate causal stories with them. Mere statistics alone, however relevant, hold little significance for us." Someone concluded also.

However, Mei was not paying any attention to whoever was sharing that insight right now. Her heavy heart had occupied her brain fully already, there was no room left for anything else.

"Did you have any idea you were on the way to losing your husband?" Someone interrupted in a genuinely puzzled tone. At once, Mei imagined herself being a cuckquean but she just could not wrap her head around this possibility, self-denial aside. She definitely had no inclination of any sort. Nonetheless, she felt another strike to her heart. How she hated that word! She cursed the idiot that invented or added it to the English language.

"You should have taken my nudge seriously when I alerted you to the bit-by-bit changes in Keat's mannerism over last year," Someone-Else tried to answer the question but this was not helping Mei at all.

"How can I be so daft and so blind?" Mei acknowledged in the end with shame burning through her. Her brain had darted haphazardly from one episodic memory to another in her attempt to pinpoint what those bit-size changes could have been. Some of her recollection process became circuitous and others became entangled, all led to nothing tangible in her mind. Mei could not construct anything even remotely plausible. Her mind became so wound up and tight that she acquired a headache in the process. At the same time, her emotional strings were in complete disarray, agonising her tortured heart all the way. Finally, her disjointed mind map and heavy heart just fell on its own weight and collapsed on her altogether. At that point, she felt confused, defeated and spent. It would have been easier simply to admit she had been blindsided right from the start.

"What's wrong with me...am I not good enough for him?" Self-doubt overtook Mei when she realised no amount of self-denial could undo the past. There was just no turning back time. They were not in a simulation. Her self-esteem took a further blow when she recalled Keat's confession that he was still seeing the other woman despite his conflicted desire to stay in their marriage. At once, the thought of the other woman filled her with a searing rage, displacing her numbing pain for a while.

"What is so special about her...what does she have that I don't?" All of a sudden, an enemy formed in Mei's mind vividly—faceless and nameless though—with a sucking sound audible in her mind only. The enemy was now an imaginary black hole, stripping everything away from her: her husband, her life, her identity, her hope. A dry bitterness filled her mouth as an angry resentment for the other woman took hold of her. Unawares, it started consuming Mei bit by bit.

"I've been such a supportive wife...I've kept the home in order while holding down a full-time job, so that you can focus on building your career. Look at how successful you've become, didn't I play a big part in this?" Surreally, Mei seemed to be pleading her case aloud in front of an invisible Keat. She was part crying (again) and part gasping for air, feeling terribly disgusted with her own weakness at the same time. Her thoughts caught in her throat rendering her vocalisation somewhat unintelligible. This did not matter; she was alone anyway.

Who are you? Some of her own ugly behaviour shocked Mei, and she detested herself for that. Mei was an intelligent and confident woman, she had done well by herself professionally, and could have achieved more if not for the conscious trade-offs she made for Keat and Kim. However, she was not relishing in any of her own triumphs, not in the least bit right now. It was so unlike her to feel so defeated.

Watching her pitiful self-exoneration is so heart wrenching and stomach churning. Someone empathised with a heavy sigh.

More so, when you consider how much Mei has invested in her marriage with Keat, Someone commiserated further.

"Why are you taking all this upon yourself? Are you thinking it properly? Keat is clearly in the wrong. Why are you not holding him to account? What a shitty man to leave a child that he dotes on endlessly," Arsehole interjected again, trying not to be an arsehole this time, trying to pull Mei out of her emotional rut, and break the spiral of negative self-condemnation that was drowning her in a mental quicksand of sorts.

"Not to give anybody a free pass at personal responsibility or accountability, but does luck and chance have anything to do with this whole saga at all?" Someone-New conjectured aloud to everyone else, as if the problem was not already complicated enough than to add another dimension or variable to the mix—a fuzzy one to grapple with, if not an impossible one to determine altogether.

"*Who knows?* Great! Now I am talking to voices in my head, have I gone mad or what? Why is everyone asking questions and no one providing any answers?" Mei's encircling self-trapping introspection was hemming her in. On some days, it would disorient and incapacitate her for hours on end. At other times, she would meltdown uncontrollably when more voices than she could deal with rioted within her. Someone would be blaming one another for this or that. Every now and then, somebody would be arousing pity for someone or anger in someone else. They would drone on endlessly in her mind like a vinyl on a turntable that could not stop. That would not stop even if it could. Would it have been better for Mei not to take leave at all? Any distraction would be helpful right now. Work would be an excellent distraction actually.

Since the unravelling, Mei had been crying almost non-stop; she could not help herself. Her sleep was fitful on some nights and restless on others as intermittent insomnia gripped her. It was a wonder if she managed to sleep at all. Her eyes became all puffy and blood shot as a result. Dark rings appeared under her eyes as well, as if she needed a complete set of evidence to show her boss that her urgent leave had been a legitimate request.

"No amount of make-up could conceal this ugliness," Mei examined herself sullenly. To begin with, she normally used make-up very sparingly; she had a natural beauty that did not require a lot of embellishment or artificial augmentation, even at this age. Any make-up heavier than usual would surely attract nosy eyes, gossipy mouths and itchy ears in her workplace. Unlike a swarm of restless bees buzzing non-stop around the hive producing honey, her colleagues would be lingering by the water cooler, busy whispering tales.

"How to go back to work in this awful state next week?"

YJ Chin

Shall We Prepare Dinner?

When Ming stepped into the studio, Beth was sitting on the sofa by the balcony with her legs pulled up towards herself; her arms wrapped around her legs. A half glass of red was resting on the coffee table. She looked forlorn, her eyes softly focusing on the darkening sky outside.

Beth was still hungover from celebrating the awesome sunset: the fiery crimson turning to reddish orange and then a cascading mixture of red, orange, chocolatey brown in its myriad shades from milk to dark, and then graphite grey. The rolling colours were slow dancing to a sublime symphony, perceptible only to one attuned with the moment. The air cooled as the powerless grey dusk yielded the expansive skies to the invading black night reluctantly. The ambiance became cooler as the year approached October. Its smell and its gentle caress on her skin: always a delightful sensation.

Some nights, the stealth darkness would overwhelm except for the iridescence of faraway stars that insisted on holding court in cloudless skies when the moon had agreed to stay away for a time: always an awesome sight.

Dinner was a fluid concept for them where real atomic time was concerned; it also depended on whether they were eating together or separately. However, it tended to be late if they were eating together, as in after 8pm most of the time due to Ming's perennial hectic schedule. Beth did not mind the lateness though she had grown up with dinners around 7pm, sometimes earlier at six, which she had carried over habitually to her adult and married life mostly.

Incidentally, Beth had adopted a pattern of small and more frequent meals about the same time when she started taking on assignments from media publications. This would normally include a light snack around late afternoon, usually mangoes or bananas and assorted nuts with tea, sometimes coffee. She tried hard to avoid cheese and wine at such times but she could not help it sometimes. When she was hard at her writing, her brain would need her sugar replenished by then if she was to persevere and progress further.

Consequently, late dinners were no trouble for Beth at all. Generally, people are eating later anyway. Her anecdotal observations informed her.

Today was an exception. Ming was back earlier than usual. However, it was not nearly enough to catch sight of the exceptionally colourful sunset in person, which was in its final moments when Beth heard the turning of his key unlocking the door.

"What a waste!" Beth let out softly.

Unawares to Beth, Ming did catch a bit of the awesome sunset while driving home. He loved beautiful sunsets too. Luckily, he was attentive enough this time. (Most times, his brain would be preoccupied with work even while driving back.) This took away the worries of his workday just and refreshed his mind quite a bit.

So looking forward to dinner with Beth, Ming thought excitedly, as he parked his car.

"You started on the wine already? Did you eat something to line your stomach before that? You must be careful, you know. You don't want another nasty gastric attack, do you?" Ming blurted out impulsively after spotting the glass of red on the coffee table while walking towards Beth.

Beth was in his comfy cerulean-white checkered flannel shirt, sleeves rolled-up—slightly baggy and oversized for her as the top of her head touched Ming's chin only when they stand face-to-face—

and her nude coloured knickers only, clearly exposed from the way she was sitting. She had woken up just before the start of the leisurely-transforming fireworks display put up by the heavens, and had intended to change out before preparing for dinner.

"Just back and he is fussing already," Beth huffed under her breath, feeling petulant at the same time. She recognised Ming's concern for her and appreciated his thoughtfulness. *Really!*

I am old enough to take care of myself; of course, I don't want another bloody gastric pang, I'm not nutty nor masochistic; why don't you ask and check instead of assuming and before jumping to conclusion; the wine is untouched, you idiot! Beth reacted spontaneously. She could not control what her irked mind was throwing out impetuously.

Was it the anti-climax to the wonderful sunset experience Beth just had or the disruption of her peaceful disposition, both the result of Ming's inconsiderate questions? Maybe her lousy day had seethed her volatility, except for the sunset episode of course. She surely was not thinking any of this. However, unlike him, she was able to keep her mouth from shooting off uncontrollably. This, she did exactly despite her mercurial nature.

"What is troubling her then?" Someone-Else asked.

"Must be her writing block and the looming deadline for her special project," Someone proffered willingly.

"Shall we prepare dinner?" Beth suggested, doing her utmost to sound convivial and dismissing the annoying questions altogether. She was quite prepared to do this all by herself despite her entreaty. It did not matter actually; she knew Ming did not like to cook anyway.

All of a sudden, Beth was unsure if she would enjoy her dinner with Ming now.

"Sure," Ming tasted no wine as he bent down to give Beth a longing kiss on her quiet pursed lips. At the same time, he squeezed her upper arm gently to feel her temperature, and hoped to transmit some of his light-heartedness to her also.

"Let me grab a shower first." Ming whispered into her ears. Then he quickly disappeared, after apologising with his penitent eyes while surreptitiously picking up her irritation also, to wash it off when he showered later.

Beth warmed up to the affection. Ming's pheromones and touch worked magically on her. Heartfelt kisses, even chaste ones, rhymed with her too. Intuitive and intriguing, the magnetism of entwined hearts. Wonderful to feel so loved. Just as well, she was exceedingly pleased with her own self-control.

It's going to be a lovely dinner after all, Beth sensed now.

Beth got up and strolled to the kitchen, took her own sweet time and not bothered to change anymore. She felt utterly comfortable in his flannel shirt: its contours reshaped by her full naked breasts underneath, and its over-washed cotton fabric, soft to the touch, adequately concealing her taut body.

An amazing body, thanks to good genes; nonetheless, one most women at forty-three would die to have.

It Can Happen to You Too

Following the exposé, it became no-holds barred on the domestic front. Invariably, the quarrels between Keat and Mei escalated as time progressed with weeks of unrests. Seemingly, innocuous worms crept out of the woodwork and instantly transformed into venomous cobras. Each trying to intimidate the other with its blood-sucking fangs. Into submission? Into repentance? No one knew (consciously) the reaction each was trying to incite in the other. *Really!* Nonetheless, the vocabulary deployed in their verbal assaults continued to expand with accusatory, shaming and all kinds of hurtful words they had known most definitely and used somewhat sparingly until then, but never directly at each other before.

Unimaginable, the scornful fury unleashed. The speed at which a marriage could disintegrate into such vengeful spite was equally shocking. In the heat of the moment, they forgot they could never take back spoken words ever. Like a double-edged sword, inflicting excruciating pain when pierced deep into the human flesh and leaving ugly wounds after withdrawn. The subsequent scarring, which the body intended as a recovery for the injury, nonetheless left an indelible tattoo as a testament of the pain suffered.

We may forgive but we will never forget—a cliché that is both accurate and worth a reminder.

One time, as if to add cosmic incredulity to their awful state, Eminem started to rap *'Love the Way You Lie'* as Keat and Mei were in the midst of an intensely aggressive brawl. The universe was ludicrously vocalising their thoughts on their behalf, adding a rhythmic beat to their argument as if trying to lighten up the gravity of their situation. Were they part of a Broadway musical act then? They were not even aware that the radio was playing in the background. If they were, would Mei have loved for the lie to continue as what Rihanna had just sung? They were not fans of rap music but they could not control what the DJ was spinning in his studio. Moreover, no one was thinking of calling into the radio station to make a request then. They could turn off the radio but they were too embroiled in their physically unarmed but psychologically destructive fight. The focus was on slitting the other's throat though each was mindful enough to contain that impulse in their imagination. Still, the altercations continued and became more often and intense after Kim left for Zurich. Thereafter, the words grew more vicious and unrestrained; each helped by their own demons.

Expectedly, the devils were out in full force. However, whose side were they on? Nobody's, clearly. They were their own side, simply out to create hell on earth for everyone else. Then watched with heinous glee, the verbal blitzes and unfolding madness all at once. They then cheered the resultant mayhem, claiming the life-shattering destruction as their prize.

At other times, they displayed cold passive-aggressive gestures at each other: seeing or feeling words only, not speaking or hearing them. Like the look as they brushed pass each other in the house, which appeared to have shrunk space wise. (There seemed to be no space where one could take refuge in whenever both of them were at home, where no sense of the other could be.) Like the loss of consideration for each other: packing away some extra food when preparing simple meals for themselves in case the other had not eaten after a long and hard day. Like the neglect in simple shared chores: the slight greasy feeling on washed plates, household or grooming stuff missing from where they were, the misplacing or just the pure disinterest in taking care of each other's snail mail. The house, no longer a home, was becoming unkempt—its dishevelled mess mirroring the state of their union.

After three weeks, Mei and Keat stopped sharing meals entirely. The domestic atmosphere had become too toxic, its ferment an ideal ground for conflict to germinate. They had become mere lodgers in a shared accommodation.

"Even Airbnb lodgers enjoy more courtesy and friendliness amongst themselves." Someone commented quietly, feeling extremely unsettled at the same time. For Keat, the house was now a bed for the night and a quick change of clothes for the day. Moreover, the showers, now quick and completely disagreeable with him, added to his misery.

Mei's internal struggles would start whenever she was alone at home, which emptiness more poignant now with Kim away in Zurich and Keat hardly around. She had stopped crying—the well of tears had run dry, perhaps self-pity had hit rock bottom also— but she had not stopped brooding. Her mind would bring her to the same old places and some new ones each time the excursions started. Psychologically, Mei simply could not extricate herself from the thrall of her marital woes.

"I've allowed him free rein…knowing his free-spirit…is this the problem…should I have been more inquisitive about him…more probing of his activities?" The more Mei considered the way she had conducted her relationship with Keat, the more she became unsure of her ways and herself, hitting her self-confidence bit and bit.

What followed was an endless redrawing of what-if mind maps. First, it was reimagining the past: going back in time and constructing new possibilities or evolutions between Keat and herself—things she might have done, decisions she might have made, paths they might have taken—that might lead to an alternate reality. One where Keat would not have strayed at all. Alas, the past was history now, the chips had fallen, and there could be no undoing any of that.

When Mei recognised that her past had cast in stone, she turned her attention to imagining the future. This may have a chance of happening, or so she hoped. She contemplated the possibility of a physical reality where multiple centres of gravity could coexist together as in Escher's *Relativity*. The lithograph oddly juxtaposes multiple depictions of quotidian life. Each setting appears normal, sensible in itself but seems ridiculous and impossible when viewed altogether.

Is such not the reality now when including the other woman? Each of them a distinct centre of gravity of sorts seemingly coexisting in time, and going about their quotidian activities in mutually exclusive parallel universes. Is this not how humans have lived since like forever: one in Nairobi, another in Liverpool and the third in Singapore, everyone living independently yet sharing the same earth at the same time? However, these parallel settings sometimes intersect by chance and interfere with each other's routine, even more likely nowadays with the world becoming smaller and borderless.

"*Exactly!* Like what is happening to us right now." A slow, low-intensity throbbing headache would build up every time Mei pondered all of these.

"Can I share Keat with the other woman? Can I live with knowing that Keat will be functioning in two spaces—mine and hers—or three: both of us in his though not at the same time?" Mei asked herself earnestly, wondering if there could be a middle ground, a possible scenario for coexistence.

"Don't kid yourself. It will be a worse living hell than the current one. You will be dying to know how his life is like with the other woman. You will not want to lose out naturally." Arsehole jumped in immediately. "The jealousy will grind you down and make you a bitter person most probably. Don't forget to consider: will the other woman accept such an arrangement?" Arsehole was keeping watch silently, diligently parsing every thought bubble inside Mei's brain. Now it was directly in her face: Mei must see everything as clearly and honestly as she possibly could, and whatever was before her must feed into her decisions. Nudges no longer worked for her. Mei jerked suddenly at this as if she just had an epiphany.

"Does she even figure? Do I care?" Mei rebuffed with a head full of hostility. She felt extremely good and superior to have someone to direct her animosity at for the time being. At the same time, she could sense the answer fully—it was either all or none of Keat, there would be no sharing. Shared loyalty would be emotionally impossible, no matter what. This would be an absolute and unwavering certainty, as sure as the sun would rise in the east each morning.

"Does he want to stay in the marriage? If so, should I give him another chance? ...only if he relinquishes all contact with the other woman—completely, immediately and permanently! ...and commit to never repeat again." Mei decided, also with absolute certainty, but sceptical of Keat's readiness to yield at the same time. She sensed his inner conflict between what he wanted morally and what he seemed to tend towards naturally.

"What if he doesn't want to let go of the other woman? ...what do I want? What can I live with? ...what about Kim? How can he bear to leave her? Does our daughter not have a say in such matters as well? ...what will this do to her?" These questions knocked Mei off her steady perch and she started to waver again, her feelings on a roller coaster.

For a moment, Mei flashed back: Kim and she were having dinner. Mother was cuddling her distraught daughter tenderly in her bosom. The younger Kim terribly perturbed by Natalie's parents' divorce and her best friend's inconsolable state. The audio in her mind played back her words as the out-of-sync video rolled in slow motion: do not worry baby, it is not going to happen to you.

Was that a promise? How could she be so certain then?

At this, Mei's eyes puffed up as full tears began to form again. In slow flowing trickles initially. Then in streams running down her cheeks as the ducts let loose when she could no longer control herself. She wailed as never before, and became utterly inconsolable herself. Unawares, the wells of tears had refilled themselves without anyone asking. What was all this turmoil doing to her fragile heart? Helplessly, Mei realised she could no longer protect herself, much less her innocent child.

Young Kim's original thought bubble had now lost its question mark. Mei would need to figure out what to do with herself and her girl. There would be no escape from and no substitute for this onerous question this time.

"Sorry baby, it can happen to you too." Mei found herself whispering, as if she was still holding Kim in her bosom. However, her throat cramped up, and her words became all jumbled up. It did not matter; Kim was somewhere else.

Notwithstanding, Kim would know her parents' secret in time to come. Fortunately, her parents would be the ones to initiate her into their secret society, after which its members tally would increase from four to five.

If It Doesn't fit, it is Not Going to Fit Ever

Today was one of those days. Beth could not seem to organise her thoughts or marshal the appropriate words to print them on her word processor. With glassy eyes, she gawked at her research notes. The words devolved into letters, the letters into a mix of shapes and lines and dots. Not distinct enough for her semantic memory to associate meanings with. Nothing flowed even when she held her pen to paper; this was highly unusual. Her mind completely parched dry. Her fingers completely immobilised as if seized by a painless form of trigger finger. Worryingly, she seemed to be having quite a bit of these dry spells lately. Had the chemical climate in her brain changed? Unawares, until now. Can Beth conclude on her special project, her final one, as her brain seemed to have prognosticated some while back?

Beth should have started on her draft almost a month ago but had taken refuge behind her reading and research. On a few occasions, she had hit a block when she tried, as was the situation right now. However, there was no escaping her current predicament any further. Beth needed to write something quickly. A rough construct of her essay minimally. The date to publish was just two months away. Her publisher would expect to see some kind of a draft, however sketchy it might be, at their review in a week's time. Sufficient time? Everything rested on Beth unleashing the writing centre in her brain while keeping her worry centre under control concurrently. Regardless, that would be the only kind of good news her publisher could appreciate. Moreover, she had promised him that in her most recent text to him.

"Shit! What's happening?" the manly part of her mercurial voice yelled at its womanly counterpart. Beth felt more and more incapacitated as the date of her review loomed nearer and larger. Clearly, her worry centre was having the upper hand.

"Have I lost control of my craft all of a sudden? I used to be able to produce a novel with a hundred thousand words at least. I only have to lift my pen and they would flow like water from a faucet when turned on. Now I can't seem to produce an essay of five to ten thousand words, not even an initial two to three thousand for my draft." The worry centre lamented aloud.

"Have all the editorial work reduced me to just perusing and correcting other people's semantics, syntax and grammar? Structuring their thoughts and organising their ideas? Has the columnist work cut my production capacity down to mere article-length of a thousand words or two? Three thousand max!" The worry centre was rousing regret in Beth's decision to move into media publication work.

"Is she looking for someone to blame?" Someone-Else asked, just as concerned that things were not going according to plan also.

"In this state, don't think I could ever get back to writing novels, not even short stories." A hint of self-doubt impinged on Beth. Her anxiety was coming to a boil.

In desperation, she pushed her worry centre aside. Then, she pulled her writing centre away for a pep talk for the first time since the start of this special project.

"You know that time is running out, don't you?" She needed the centre to appreciate the exigency of the moment.

"I do but I'm really struggling to write something," her centre replied meekly and apologetically, hoping Beth could understand that piling on more pressure now was not going to help anyone.

"Besides, there's nothing substantially new; everything points to same-old, same-old so far." The centre pointed out this fact.

"Yes, you can definitely overcome this. You've done it so many times before," Beth reminded her writing centre adamantly, ignoring the fact completely. She could appreciate its struggle but she was not accepting any of it.

"Why did you even put forward the idea to him in the first place?" The centre was defensive now.

"Why do I have to suffer at the hand of your vanity?" It needed to deflect its responsibility and divert the unwanted attention.

"*Enough!* This is no longer up for discussion. You know this perfectly well. You're not an idiot," Beth cut her writing centre off sternly. She felt slighted nonetheless.

"I really need you to focus on the task at hand. C'mon, you can do it. It's going to be the last time, I promise," Beth pulled back after a pause and switched to a softer tone when the writing centre stayed quiet. She seemed to be pleading with the centre now.

"*Please.* Don't make promises you cannot keep or don't intend to." The centre's words struck Beth again, this time deep into her innermost sanctum. She remained silent for quite some time. The words had unwittingly dredged something out of her sanctum.

"Why don't you go amble in the park and leave me alone to wander for a while, the pressure is just too intense." The writing centre followed up in a reconciliatory tone after what seemed like a lifetime. It felt terrible to have struck Beth with such a painful punch actually.

"But cutting to the core is the only way for her to let go of me for a time. Determination is not *it* now, you agree?" The writing centre was trying to win the sorry department over to its side.

Beth slipped into a meditative state. Perhaps some relaxation and meandering of her thoughts might help. Automatically, she moved from Ming's worktable and sank herself into the sofa. Her research materials strewn all over: the worktable, the sofa, the coffee table and on the floor near the balcony. (It was not a very large space to begin with.) Quite a mini battle zone really: must have been a tragicomic struggle with her writing self.

Then Beth caught sight of *The Deadly Mace of Barabudur* on the coffee table. Her mountain of stuff had buried it partially. Ming was done with it; he had left it there still. Spontaneously, she reached out for the novel, exposing *The Fiery Sabre of KangoWatu* just below the earlier novel she saw. Picking both up, she held them close to her chest.

Silently, the romanticism of her life as a novelist crept into her heart—the flexibility and carefreeness she used to enjoy was now even more appealing. Then she was answerable principally and mostly to herself only. Now she felt an emptiness inside her. Her work was presently more topical and faddish, much less creative and original—she felt as if her creativity had hollowed out. She missed those times; they allowed her to be as close to a free spirit as she would have wanted. The nostalgia weighed heavy on her heart.

When Beth started her writing career, her rich imagination and hard work led to a modest oeuvre based on the *Therasudorsa* series. This had distinguished her and brought her success that might seem inevitable from hindsight (though there were no guarantees at the beginning).

Vision in spotting the psychological needs of the young adult segment—a teenage-going-to-adulthood kind of raw idealism juxtaposed with the coming-of-age kind of angsty adventurism juxtaposed with a WTF-is-the-world-coming-to kind of rude reality—was one thing. Producing fiction that could speak to those needs and the heart of the readers was an entirely different endeavour. Clearly, Lady Luck helped with aligning the stars for success to spark. It also helped that she clicked instantly with the marvellous agent she found who believed in her and was able to sign her up with a prestigious publishing house. Equally, her editor at the publishing house was most effective in guiding her and very relentless with steering her works towards commercial success.

Indeed, she was grateful that the success of *Therasudorsa* had enabled her financial independence, afforded her a comfortable lifestyle and a small accumulation of wealth along the way.

Unlike some artists she knew, who had squandered their earnings on whatever they fancied the moment they achieved fame (only to regret it later), Beth had been prudent with her finances. Sadly, she also knew some whom had wasted away completely after struggling in vain. In this sense, Beth's sensibility to defer or trade short-term gratification for long-term benefits was unusual, even surprising, given her bohemian personality. She even figured that if she stopped writing after her eighth novel, she would have sufficient savings to afford her lifestyle for the rest of her lifetime.

"I'm not high maintenance in the least bit, and there's no one else to support or to leave my stuff to after I die. Materially, no worries at all." Beth would inform herself whenever she thought about her financial security. Of course, this analysis had included future earnings based on the current market momentum of her extant works. She also betted that *Therasudorsa* was not merely a fad in time. That it would continue to appeal to future generations of the same target reader segment—junior college-graduating teens, undergraduate youths and young adults starting out in the workforce.

Beth's audacity and flightiness aside, her financial security might have underwritten her decision to break away from her novel writing and *Therasudorsa*, at least for a time, and explore other options in her writing career. Did she feel she has to get away because she was approaching some kind of a wall?

Rationally, Beth branched into editorial and columnist work for some publications in both traditional and digital media. Beth considered this would provide a steadier stream of income—might not be as rewarding as when she released a bestseller or a novel that sold reasonably well from her experience but good enough to cover her lifestyle.

"Artists do have to feed themselves, you know. Media publication work will be more predictable than the feast and famine cycle of novel writing, my financial prudence aside," Beth figured.

Of course, if she could defer the drawdown of her accumulated wealth to as late a time as possible, even more beneficial—she justified further.

"She is very sensible indeed," Someone-New said.

Beth's agent readily took on the straightforward task of engaging her with potential publishers. When her agent sent word out that Beth was interested in editorial and columnist work, he was not surprised with what came back. For the publications that courted Beth, they clearly saw the benefit of having her on their editorial team or panel of regular contributors: her faithful followers as potential customers. Once the network effect took off, the advertising revenue would torrent in. Just a matter of time—they all seemed to think the same way.

"May be good to use this opportunity to figure out what I want to do next. Whether it's writing or otherwise," Beth had reasoned to herself when she was evaluating the offers then.

"The flip side would be the regular deadlines that are a lot less flexible compared to writing on my own, I'll need to be prepared to subject myself to more structure and demands. They don't pay you to sit around, do they?" The writing centre advised Beth warily. Its concern: could I handle the production pressure if push comes to shove.

"Do we *really* need to do this? The somewhat laissez-faire novel-writing regime suits me perfectly fine. Have you decided already?" The centre had beseeched then.

In life-changing decisions, Beth was always careful to make sure she knew what she was getting herself into, consciously deciding what she could live with and what she could do to mitigate those she might have problems with later on. Intuitively, the decision seemed preordained already. Was this overthinking then since she had apparently decided, unconsciously? Nonetheless, her worry centre needed to cover all angles as usual. At the same time, she was fully conscious that whatever she could see of her situation was all there was to it.

Beth was so full of life when she first started, slightly over a year ago now. For a while, she completely immersed herself in her work as she picked up the ropes of her new industry. She was learning new things and she liked that very much.

However, Beth was a quick learner. The old-fashioned structures and predictable work routine soon became a bore for her not long after. The constant deadlines became bothersome but unavoidable chores to her. Now, she was on a treadmill—constantly on the run but not going anyway—and answerable to whoever was writing her pay cheques. There were two of them for columnist work currently and their demands were not always in harmony, which could be a struggle sometimes. In the mix was also part-time editorial work that she took on with a digital print agency. Consequently, she became edgy most times.

Even Beth's large readership that followed her columns fervently no longer gave her any satisfaction. In fact, her readership was becoming burdensome with the continual need to drum up stuff to keep them happily engaged.

"Keeping them happily engaged is what you have signed up for, isn't it?" The worry centre asked, concerned that Beth might blame it for missing out something. While Beth had anticipated the potential drag of corporate structure and demands, and the mentally predictable and unchallenging work, she thought she could last longer in the industry. Perhaps she was not as self-aware...but this was just a moment of self-doubt when she was feeling depressed or overwhelmed.

"If it doesn't fit, it's not going to fit ever. The industry is not going to change for me, and I am definitely not going to change to fit in. Better to be in control of my own destiny and plot my own transition to something else." What else? Beth did not know yet.

However, she knew she wanted to be good to herself, she was financially secure and she could afford to do that. She was quite content to be serendipitous at this stage of her life also.

Beth's intuition must have impressed upon her that this special project would be her final one. Do we not depend on our gut feel ever so often?

"Her final one?" Someone asked peevishly, feeling a little left out.

"The fast thinking part of her brain has decided to exit the industry already," Someone-New shared knowingly.

"Huh? When was this?" Someone-Else was also curious now about Beth's secret plan.

"Shortly after the project commissioned, most probably. Don't act surprised, she's quintessentially human after all," Someone-New summed up the whole episode before anyone had a chance to react.

Thereafter, Beth's conscious mind would work out the timing and details of everything that followed.

Everything Hangs on Your Work

He called at exactly the wrong time. Beth was in the middle of a destressing activity when her mobile phone went off in the living area. Now, she felt terribly upset. The phone rattled on the coffee table while giving out a near convincing baby cry, a sort of incongruent ring tone when one regarded Beth. One would have mistaken the squall for real if not for the electronic feel to the sound. The phone seemed to have gain agency now, it was crying its eyes out for immediate attention as from a hungry baby in its crib, rising in volume and inundating the whole place with annoying echoes.

Ming had asked her to change to a different tone countless times before. Plainly, it irritated him whenever he heard it. However, voice calls were becoming scarce, and they were not always together when her phone cried, so it was not really that often that Ming would get to hear it, for crying aloud. Beth just ignored him, one of many things she had been doing concerning Ming. It appeared to be a growing list but Ming did not seem to notice it, or if he did, this did not really bother him.

Nevertheless, it bothered Beth that Ming seemed not to be bothered. Did her mercurial nature tame his behaviour?

"Has Ming become fearful of me (somewhat)? This is not helpful in our relationship surely." Beth wondered aloud. Some fear is good but it needs to be of the right kind, she believed. What surprised her was not how much he demanded of her, it was how little he demanded of her actually.

"In relationships, one's demands, interchangeably with expectations, morph into responsibilities on the other, if accepted. Agree?" Someone asked on Beth's behalf.

True to her bohemian personality, Beth wanted as little responsibilities as she could get away with. For Ming, he preferred the relationship to be light on responsibilities too. He had enough of them elsewhere already. Regardless, it was almost impossible to please Beth—she disliked any demand placed on her, equally she disliked insufficient demands placed on her.

"Damned you do, damned you don't really." Someone-Else said with a sigh. For the latter, Beth wondered if Ming was serious about them at all for surely concomitant demands were part of any serious relationship; this could be her *real* bother. The thought that Ming might have given in to her too easily did not please her in the least bit either.

"What the fuck! Who can it be at this time of the night?" Beth shot her mouth off. The phone was way out of sight for her to see the caller-ID—light could not bend, not so near the earth's surface anyhow. She contemplated if it would be worth her while to answer the call—her brain intensely doing the cost-benefit calculations automatically, re-directed from whatever else she was doing just before.

"Fuck it!" Her swearing was her conclusion. Whoever it was could wait. Whatever matter it was could also wait. About then, the baby stopped crying, as if it had cried itself to complete exhaustion. More like mommy would not give a damned shit to anything else right now! Beth recommitted to what she was doing before but gave up after some half-hearted effort.

"Fuck it!" Same swearing but a conclusion of a different kind, and with a voice more manly than womanly this time.

"Was she in a fucking mood or what?" Someone asked, utterly disgusted. The unwelcomed interruption had killed her fucking mood. Now, she was even more frustrated than before.

"Some wine will help," Beth exclaimed as she got up from the king-sized bed and shuffled languidly to the kitchen in her birthday suit. She did not bother to get dressed, there was no one else in the studio—Ming was away on a business trip for a few days and she had decided to stay the night.

Beth would not stay the night when Ming was in town. She would always drive back herself no matter how late the night. Beth would also refuse Ming's offer to fetch her home no matter what. He still did not know she had physically separated from her husband.

All the drawn curtains shielded Beth except for slight cracks between them. However, there was no one beyond the curtains. Intuitively, she was counting on the laws of physics to work as expected—light traveling in straight lines and its reversibility principle. Since she could only see the night sky beyond the curtain cracks, only the stars and maybe the moon could play voyeurs and catch a glimpse of her still winsome body and her full breasts. The stars did swoon, as did the crescent moon. Beth was very body-confident and she enjoyed her own nakedness thoroughly. However, she was no exhibitionist.

Suppose our primal instinctual needs—good food (including wine), sublime music (and light easy conversations), agreeable sex (including self-stimulation) and maybe sleep—are substitutable in some ways, especially when the brain is exhausted and in need of instant gratification. Without self-control, it will plot its way along the path of least resistance towards self-fulfilment. Beth seemed to be doing precisely that right now.

Beth made her way to the coffee table with a glass of wine in hand. It was her second glass already, and she was at ease now, just a tiny bit.

"Who's the idiot?" Her tone a little cantankerous. She was on the verge of seeing the lively colours dancing in her brain when the baby squall crashed her party of one.

To Beth's surprise, it was her publisher. She half expected it to be Ming; he would usually call on one of the nights while he was away, at the least.

"The first time he has called so late in the night," Beth could not recall any other time. Though she would not be surprised if her publisher was calling from his office as he kept ridiculous hours at work. However, it was not him, it was the media, advertising and publishing industry—a crazy place. Maybe she should really get out while she could, on a high of course—this thought had been gathering momentum in her conscious mind of late. However, her unconscious mind had decided already.

Beth played back her publisher's message from her telco's voicemail. So ancient, she thought dismissively, people hardly leave voicemail nowadays. "What can be so urgent as to warrant a call at such a time?" Testy indeed!

"Beth, remember what you promised to write for me, we are supposed to talk about it next week? Please return my call. To confirm. Thanks." Her publisher stiltedly informed the voicemail system of his demand earlier after his call to the intended recipient was unsuccessful. Then, her telco had diverted him to its backup assistant with an unfriendly pre-recorded female voice.

That was it. Why was her publisher so jittery about their next review meeting, their second one? There must be something more, Beth suspected. His voicemail felt weird to her.

"It's about two months away. Is he having cold feet now?" Beth asked everyone intuitively. No one replied initially, everyone was tensed and cagey of her foul mood.

"You didn't have much to show for during your first checkpoint, remember?" Someone took a risk to remind Beth after a while so that everyone could get on with whatever.

...

"It's only three months and I'm only half-way, more like one-third way into my research—you want substantial and impactful content, don't you?" Beth had said then at the first checkpoint meeting, at one of his usual Japanese restaurants. (The same restaurant again! He thought they had met at a different one where they first agreed on Beth's project. *Whatever!*)

He was an impatient man. Old-fashioned too, he had expected something physical, a page or two of the draft perhaps.

To assuage his concern, Beth showed him a list of the research items she had collated for the project on her iPad, and where she was with her research. She also produced a list of local eminent scientists, medical practitioners and psychologists that she had identified to shortlist for interviews, though she had not arranged for any interview yet. Lastly, she sketched for him her own timeline for the project.

"You are across the fact that your essay is going to be the main beef in our annual special edition to be published in time for Christmas, are you not?" He impressed upon Beth after he had heard her out, as patiently as he could under the circumstance. He expected her to appreciate the significance of what he had just said.

"Everything hangs on your work, you know," he added just to be doubly sure.

"Yes, I am fully aware. Don't worry, I won't let you down," Beth gave the best assurance she could possibly muster at that point. Truthfully, she felt stressed herself; she seemed to have suffered a bit of a writer's block of late. She was doing her best to hide her struggle from him also.

"Let's hope so," He rejoined without much conviction. He was shrewd and sharp enough to see through Beth's half-baked assurance but he left it be. They tried to keep it light for the rest of the lunch with some small talk. What could be lighter and more topical than the royal wedding of Prince William and Kate Middleton right now? As usual, there was nothing interesting on the local scene. Nearing the end, Beth wondered if Prince Naruhito and

Masako might have interested him more. Nevertheless, she let the thought slide as his company was becoming a bit of a bore by then. When they finally parted after lunch, her publisher remained harried still and uncertain of Beth's wholehearted commitment to the project.

Unbeknownst to Beth, his most recent prior quarter sales for his journalistic publication were terrible. The trend for the current quarter had been disappointing so far. Her publisher really needed the year-end special edition to be more than just successful—he needed it to make up for two quarters of deficit in order for him to hit his full year sales target. Ironically, time seems to speed up at those times when you need it to slow down.

"It may be too late to do anything now, I'll just have to trust my instinct that Beth will come through for me in the end," he whispered half-hopefully while alone in the elevator.

Lucky for him, he would be right though he would waver a bit before that. Regardless, he would need to endure a couple more months of tumultuous anxiety while keeping his worry centre under control.

...

"Well, you knew what you were getting yourself into when you started, don't you?" The voice of *slow* reason quickly reminded Beth before her *fast* intuition could have a chance to act up. It was almost midnight now; she was in no bloody mood to pick a fight with anyone, much less with herself.

"If no one has any better idea, I'm just going to WhatsApp him back. I'm in no fucking mood to talk with anyone, publisher or lover!" Beth, visibly annoyed, informed everyone. She was not asking anyone actually. Everybody knew and just shut up, now was not the time to be the wise guy in the room.

"A return call will be superfluous, it's just a confirmation of our meeting next week; it will be too inconsiderate to call at such a time anyway," Beth softened as if her action needed justification. She kept her texts short and sharp, and somewhat formal.

"Got your voicemail. Yes. I remember our meet"...

"Don't worry"...

"I'll have good news for you when we meet next week"...

Beth ended her texts with a smiley emoticon to lighten up the atmosphere between them. She hoped to put her publisher at ease. After ensuring that the message was marked delivered, Beth switched off her phone immediately. She did not wait for any response; she was not even interested to know if he had read it.

Ming would have to wait for another time to talk to her if he wanted to. Beth had made herself uncontactable; she was done with enervating humans for now, even if the connection was only remote and virtual.

At this point, Beth felt an odd mix of relaxed numbness and pent-up frustration. She felt a little moist also.

"Tension-fuelled hormones can get us excited, you think?" Someone teased, hoping to ease everybody with the cheeky remark.

Instinctively, Beth got up from the sofa and strolled to the bedroom. The mellifluous voice of John Lennon with his dedication of 'Woman' to Yoko Ono and Beth, and every other women in the world, transfused the atmosphere all over the studio.

"What a lovely song. How appropriate." Beth smiled as she approached the bed.

"Time to fuck my brain out," Beth visualised as she spread herself on the bed. There was nothing to undress this time. Sometimes, she liked being alone on the king-sized bed. After a while, she lost herself in her world of fantasies. For a writer with a rich imagination, one could easily expect that world to be exuberant and fun.

After yet some while, with no squalling baby to break her momentum, Beth came finally. In a violent wave initially, then followed by some aftershocks. Her body consumed her spinning brain, and bathed her in a fine film of warm moisture with the smell of saline sweat all over her sated body. She shivered slightly as a tingling sensation traversed her naked skin from head to toe, leaving her with goose bumps all over. One could only imagine the conversation her mind was having with her body. No extensive fireworks this time, just flashes of cool blues and soothing greens as Beth collapsed into deep sleep. Her ravished body now exhausted on the expansive bed; her still perky tits softly illuminated by a narrow vertical stream of moonlight breaking in through the crack in the curtains. The crescent moon peeked inside and then hailed— a perfect reclining pose for painters of all stripes!

A smile formed on her wan face. Beth was in a realm of magical impossibilities now. Unlikely to be any in her *Therasudorsa* universe. More likely: a promiscuous world conjured up by all her research materials like jigsaw puzzle pieces fitting into place and telling a fantastical story that could only make sense in her liberated dreamscape. An unconventional world that would only feel safe to betray itself in her brain—safe from human judgement and bias, completely unshackled from societal norms and by-laws.

Lucky Beth, she would go on to write the essay of her life—one that would allow her to go off with a bang, on a mountaintop high as she would have wanted it. Another triumphant experience! However, Beth did not know that yet, she was struggling with her writing centre still. Meanwhile, she had taken refuge in her fantasies; her brain desperately needed an escape for the time being.

Is our intuitive mind capable of prognostication—fuzzily conceived as the sixth sense? It appeared to be a possibility for Beth. Maybe this was another case of déjà vu. Anyways, she would be familiar with this most definitely: 'success begetting success'.

Separate Lives

Finally, Mei and Keat reached a settlement of sorts, exhausted by the unrest, or perhaps in a mutual bid to regain sanity and balance in their individual lives. Most likely, a deadline of sorts imposed by the return of their only child.

"Enough of kicking the can down the road"...

"Kim coming back" Mei texted Keat, a week before Christmas, issuing him an ultimatum of sorts.

"Ok let's find some time 2 chat" Keat conceded gladly. He had thought of this for a while but lacked the courage to initiate it. It was time to man-up to the situation and take some responsibility. After all, he wanted to be good to Kim also, a weak spot for him definitely.

Mei knew this too. Sometimes, she would wish for the same level of attention and affection from Keat. Was she envious? Definitely not in a competition-with-her-daughter sort of way, perhaps more like in a mature I-was-your-first-love kind of way.

...

"Hi, I'm Sean Tang Ming Keat, nice to meet you," Keat extended his hand as a friendly gesture towards Mei, taking in the delicate face framing those upturned almond-shaped eyes looking back at him. They were attending some kind of small group workshop on management and leadership styles that their companies had sent each of them to for their career development. The trainer had started with an icebreaker game and he had randomly coupled them as a team for the game.

He is funny. First person I come across who introduces himself with his full name. Mei thought curiously while straightening her shoulder-length hair a bit self-consciously.

Automatically, she took his hand and gave it an assertive shake. His strong and protective yet comfortable grip gave her a sensual tingle on her nape and shoulders. She felt the edges of her ears burning a little.

"Hmm, you can call me Mei…is that how you introduce yourself normally?" She gave voice to her earlier thought; she could not control it.

"I mean with your full name like that," Mei added when she noticed his puzzled look. Luckily, her hair concealed her now pinkish ears. She touched her hair again to ensure this, unconsciously as well.

Think she is about to lose it, Someone speculated.

"Oh yea. It's a habit. Most people call me Sean. My mother calls me Ming." His ears started to redden too and Mei noticed it immediately. He kept his hair short and stylishly cropped, rendering the slow colour transformation of his ears utterly conspicuous.

"Then I'll call you Keat if it's alright with you," Mei quipped enthusiastically, as though there was a land-grab for his name.

A little presumptuous and premature, you think? Someone-Else commented. Just as well, Mei found it odd that he should mention his mother in such a setting.

Such a mother's boy! Mei teased, in her mind of course.

"No problem at all. This is interesting. You'll be the first to do that." Keat replied with a cute awkwardness.

"What is it we're supposed to do again after the introduction?" Keat quickly circled back to the workshop activity to draw her attention away from his unease.

…

Mei felt nostalgic in her reverie. That was the start of what would become a good thing for her, probably the best thing to happen to her—she had imagined then at the beginning of their relationship.

Now, the unimaginable had happened also! Perhaps Keat's affection had morphed over time; perhaps it was dead now. Suppose he only had a constant capacity to love—in all its forms and manifestations—and Kim had acquired some parts of that over time. Of course, the other woman lately, Mei burnt with jealous anger at this thought.

Maybe the affair had brought to the fore what was latent for quite some time—there were fissures in their relationship unawares, and they had papered over them naturally. When? Could Mei pinpoint the time or times? Maybe that was how she had lost her husband. First, gradually, and then suddenly. Like falling off a cliff unexpectedly after traversing some distance, undulating or otherwise. If we are not watchful of where we are going in the dark, we may just crash accidentally.

If Keat could not relinquish his contact with the other woman completely, the only option left was to divorce. These were the only options available to him. However, he felt torn between wanting to stay in the marriage for Kim's sake and his love for Beth. He felt conflicted when he thought of Mei also.

"Love? *Really?* This would require more scrutiny. Surely, you're not self-critical enough to do this on your own." Someone mocked at Keat.

Could they not approach this like the Japanese? Keat thought in despair.

"What is the weight of twenty years of marriage? What about two years with Beth? Is there a way to compare the two, a scale that can accurately weigh out the difference and throw up the correct choice?" Keat had struggled with these heart-wrenching questions countless times.

Essentially, Keat needed to know with clarity and certainty what he really wanted, what he could live with, and what he was prepared to give up in exchange. Mei had made it very clear in terms of her position and demand—he had to choose between staying in the marriage and giving it up completely if he chose the other woman. There would be no in-between—Mei would not share him with the other woman, *period!*

Is that how you repay someone who has been only good to you and for you? Surely, Mei counted a lot towards my success, doesn't she? Keat felt a shade of self-loathing at the thought of his own ingratitude.

"But marriage is not a life sentence, is it? …and this no longer holds if one or the other decides otherwise? There can be no unilateralism in marriage, or any relationship for that matter. Make sense?" Keat thought aloud, hoping for an epiphany that would suddenly provide a magical solution to all his woes.

Then, there was the inevitable question everyone in modern progressive society seemed obsessed with: "What will make me happier? I deserve to be happy, don't I?" Keat asked unashamedly. Such selfishness!

"If I am not happy, how can I make those around me happy?" …"Don't they always tell you to take care of yourself first before you attend to another in an air flight emergency situation, even if another is your child?" Keat continued rationalising aloud, seemingly without any guilt now.

"Such sophistry, the validity of the question on happiness notwithstanding. Moreover, what a lame analogy, is this an emergency? You must have been flying too much!" Someone-Else joined in also.

"I don't like what you just said." Did Keat just talk back?

"Suck it up, you piece of shit! Truth is hard to like sometimes!" Someone-Else bit back brutishly, clearly angered by Keat's solipsistic concerns.

Back to their compromise, Mei and Keat agreed with amicable maturity that a period of separation would be helpful for everyone. Clear headedness would prevail during this period hopefully and they could keep their individual harrowed state from affecting the other.

Mei was relieved too. Deep inside, she was not sure about divorce—it had a sense of finality and the scent of death, the end of hope. She was not ready for this if she was truly honest with herself.

What is the price of honesty? The dissolution of hope—the hope of a future akin to what was in the past or close to it, the hope that tomorrow would be better than today and a little closer to where we want it to be. If such is the price, I will not pay it. I will lie, even to myself, just to keep my hope alive.

"Is this what you are thinking?" Someone-Else had reappeared to ask Mei.

More chats followed on the mechanics of their separation—more civil this time, and some convivial even. Some light-heartedness had crept back in and they had begun to laugh at some of their childish antics in their past squabbles. On the period of separation, they hesitated from one year to two, maybe three. Why three? Then they could proceed to divorce straight away without any hassle by applying the law of the land, if it came down to that finally.

"I thought you wanted me out of the house," Keat fessed up while they were talking over coffee at home one weekend afternoon. He was genuinely puzzled now; he had assumed this would not be up for discussion. At this stage, he was prepared to accept all of Mei's terms.

"I'm not sure if I can bear staying here. There will be too many painful memories," Mei confessed truthfully while trying to be stoic. She stole a glance at Keat and her heart missed a beat.

"She still loved him. It's crystal clear." Someone concluded, feeling her heart ached at the same time.

"Granted the last few weeks have been harrowing for both of us. However, it has been good on balance, considering what we went through together for twenty years. Isn't this more important? Surely, the twenty years must count for something, much more than the last seven or eight weeks," Keat said gently, trying to soothe Mei's pain and refresh her frame of mind at the same time.

Nevertheless, it is true: we remember the end of an experience more than the actual experience across its entirety. In fact, the duration of the experience do not even figure in the overall memory most times, over time.

Sadly, the end of their experience at this point was painful for them mostly. The last few weeks had completely eclipsed the twenty years before unfortunately, especially for Mei.

For a while, they went back and forth: you-stay-I-rent or you-rent-I-stay. Did they forget Kim? Did they not profess to have Kim's well-being in mind? Maybe we really have to take care of ourselves first before we can consider others adequately. Our needs have a way of sharpening our focus on matters, and calibrating their gravity and priority.

Finally, they agreed on how to execute on their intentions: Keat would seek out a rental apartment as soon as possible for a period of two years, with the option to extend another year. They would talk with Kim together when the father was ready to move out, or earlier if the opportunity presented itself. (Again, no clarity nor any discussion on what the latter meant, and who to make the call.)

Keeping separate lives and secrets can be exacting on the brain and the body. With the cat out of the bag, would it be any easier for Keat? Even less burdensome now with their agreement to separate for a while?

Of course, the secret was also out with the other woman and her husband by now. However, Mei knew none of this. Keat avoided discussing the other woman at all cost. Similarly, Beth had kept from Ming her own separation from her husband all this time.

So how do separate lives happen actually? Does it start in the mind and then transition to the physical? Does it begin with one living two lives, then bifurcate and recombine with two living one life?

How do the equations of separate lives pan out with time?

In the beginning:	$2 \Leftrightarrow$ [chance] $\Leftrightarrow 2$
Commonly with time:	$(1+1) \Leftrightarrow$ [chance] $\Leftrightarrow (1+1)$
Gradually, with more time:	$1 + 1 \Leftrightarrow$ [chance] $\Leftrightarrow 1 + 1$
Suddenly, randomly by chance:	$1 + 1 \Leftrightarrow 1 + 1$
Separate lives, with secret affair:	$1 \Leftrightarrow (1 \Leftrightarrow 1) \Leftrightarrow 1$
Separate lives, with open secret:	$1 \Leftrightarrow (1+1) \Leftrightarrow 1$

Is this the way to think about it? How would the last equation evolve from here? How does the network bifurcate further with time? *Who knows?*

"Nothing is ever inevitable in life, except perhaps time and chance (or luck) which happen to us all. Certainly, death as well, which is when uncertain chance runs out at the end of time." Someone-New was at it again with its string of so-called truisms, or so it thought.

"We ought to recognise the significant roles that random impulses and chance interactions play in our quotidian existence. They can rearrange or introduce new associations in our brains before we even become conscious of them." Someone-New added, hoping to convince everyone.

"However, from experience, we do not." Someone retorted.

"Randomness and chance do not play well to our intuitive tendency to associate things and link memories together."

"We need aetiology—reasons and causes that coherently explain our life events or chance occurrences even where there is none."

"Chance digresses us from our need for accountability over the conscious decisions we make."

"However, we ought to be more mindful with how our brain judges and decides, ought we not?"

A boisterous exchange had erupted among the multiplicity of voices.

Was Mei and Keat's thinking converging on anything? Were the ideas from their inner voices lost on either or both of them?

Regardless, Mei and Keat would enter a period of détente between themselves following this settlement. Both seemed to have hit a bottom of sorts for now. Whither their relationship? Only time will tell, with chance as its faithful companion. Unlike love, chance is not possessive of time.

A Free Pass at Infidelity?

"Actually, you have all you need to get started, don't you?" Beth tried again with her writing centre. Concurrently, she was hoping some cheese and wine might suffice as a bribe for the centre. It had worked before.

Already, Beth had bedded and corroborated most of the facts and evidence, including essential interviews with domain experts and practitioners. She was particularly proud and happy to have access to the top few on her shortlist upon her request. They were all local paragons in their respective specialty areas; they seemed intrigued with her subject matter as well. Now she needed a storyline to tie everything together.

"It's easier for people to wrap their heads around facts and scientific truths when they can see causal links and associate familiar events with characters who resemble bits of themselves or people they know. In other words, tell them a good story that appears relatable...better still, a story they want to believe in...best of all, reflect their stories—speak to their own biases and beliefs. Storytelling, including gossips, is one of the oldest form of education and information sharing technique, isn't it?" Beth's thoughts cohered effortlessly now.

To her pleasant surprise, the writing centre seemed to be playing ball all of a sudden. Storytelling was the centre's forte after all. As well, her adrenalin started to flow as the familiarity of a former life excited her. Beth was getting her moxie back.

"Let's lay out and distil the facts I want to present first, then it's easier to have a big picture of sorts to work out the storyline after that," the centre instructed automatically. Beth gathered the notes and facts that might form part of the opening paragraph for her essay. As in her novel, the opening needed to be powerful to capture the reader's interest. In this case, it needed to go one up and motivate them to pay for the publication or online subscription that contained her essay.

...

"People who are unfaithful to their partner may be genetically predisposed that way."

"Apparently, there is a certain type of dopamine receptor gene—DRD4— which is associated with infidelity and one-night stands."

"Is science telling us that those predisposed have a free pass at infidelity— it's their genes and they can't help it?"

"Need to consolidate the technical terms and de-jargonise the language—will make the essay more accessible and relatable," Beth reminded. "Let's move to the interviews."

"Here, the notes with Dr Kwee (the geneticist) and Dr Nathan (the neuroscientist) regarding our genes and dopamine, the hormone that may have triggered one's promiscuous proclivity."

I will need to include their credentials very succinctly—Beth registered with her writing centre.

...

"Genes: what are passed down from parent to child which determines the child's characteristic. There are variations of these which accounts for the differences among individuals."

"Dopamine: main hormone of pleasure in popular science. More accurately, it plays an important role to control the reward and pleasure centres in the brain. Simply, it starts with an assessment of a reward, like the level of

pleasure that the reward can impart. Then it motivates the actions to realise the reward, and the resultant experience of pleasure."

"Another way of understanding Dopamine: first, it confers a 'desire' or 'want' attribute to a particular 'reward' stimulus. The 'desire' or 'want' becomes the motivational magnet. 'Reward' is the attractive and motivational property of a stimulus. Then, behaviours are induced to motivate the 'desire' or 'want' towards the 'reward'. Pleasure, or the level of pleasure, is the experience of the 'reward', and the fulfilment of the 'desire' or 'want'."

"Dopamine (receptors are) implicated in many brain processes—motivation, pleasure, cognition, memory, learning and fine motor control."

"The anticipation of most types of rewards increases the level of dopamine in the brain."

"Think the second definition for dopamine may be easier for people to understand," the centre suggested as Beth evaluated her scribbles.

"Now, let's get to the causal links or what science has to say regarding the genetic basis for infidelity. This is supposed to be the most interesting and punchy part. There, more stuff, including the interviews with Dr Yeo (the psychiatrist) and Dr Theseira (the psychologist)."

...

"Individuals with a certain variant of the DRD4 gene were more likely to have a history of uncommitted sex, including one-night stands and acts of infidelity."

"The motivation seems to stem from a system of pleasure and reward, which is where the release of dopamine comes in."

"In cases of uncommitted sex, the risks are high, the rewards substantial, and the motivation variable—all elements that ensure a dopamine rush."

"An individual with this gene variant experiences rushes of dopamine. At such times, his assessment of the reward associated with a stimulus tends to

be substantially higher than normal; this effectively triggers his desires for the stimulus. There is also a propensity towards taking more and higher risks."

"In the case of infidelity and promiscuity, the stimulus can be someone sitting across the counter at the bar that one becomes attracted to instinctively, and the motivation then moves the individual towards hooking up for a one-night stand after some seemingly innocuous drinks. The one-night stand being the reward as they decamp to her apartment. Surprisingly, sex is not the ultimate reward when one strays or is being promiscuous, not all the time. Suppose the concomitant sex leads to this intuitive association. But in this case, the reward can be the thrill of the chase, and the satisfaction of a catch, not so much that they get laid in the end."

"The stimulus can also be an attractive female colleague whom a married man is having a late-night meeting with at the office. This can be the start of an illicit affair, which logically can be the fulfilment of the desire or want and the experience of the reward. While affairs generally involve sex, this need not be the stimulus or reward. What keeps the pleasure cycle going may not necessarily be sexual in nature, or not entirely, and certainly not all the time."

"The stimulus can even be just a familiar sight or scent that triggers a want that motivates the engagement of paid sexual services. The pleasure of sex being the reward in this case, as expected."

…

Genetics do appear to play a role in how we behave and the decisions we make in life."

"The studies so far showed that the relationship between the gene—DRD4, or more specifically a variant of this gene—and infidelity is associative. Correlation does not necessary equate with causation. Hence, it means that transgressors are not off the hook. More studies are required."

…

"Huh, is this all? What an anti-climax, you think?" The voice asked Beth, clearly not expecting this at all.

"Science is inconclusive on this subject after all the stress and hard work—no free passes after all!" …"Bloody hell! Where's the reward then?" Someone asked, clearly not interested in the monetary aspects of the project in the least bit.

"That's pretty much the gist of it, I'm afraid," Beth answered her shadows. "The rest of the notes just more elaborations and examples of the same."

Actually, Beth's hope of finding a genetic link to human infidelity and promiscuity had crushed. This was the conclusion at the time when she sighted the article but she was hoping that more stuff would be forthcoming from the scientific community. She had expected that more researchers might be intrigued, or those that were already doing related studies might be motivated to publish their findings.

"Surprisingly, it didn't seem like a popular area of research after all." The writing centre whispered smugly as if to vindicate itself, short of telling Beth straight—I told you so.

Nonetheless, her essay would still be more substantial than the initial published paper—from her interviews with the eminent doctors and scientists, from her layman and more relatable explanation of genetics and the workings of hormones in the human brain. The reach of her essay would also be different. Very different in fact. Of course, her sublime storytelling style would make the subject most interesting and engaging.

Back to the subtext of the essay, it would be nice to have something or someone to blame for our extra-marital pursuits or promiscuous proclivities instead of ourselves for sure! Better still if it was something that one had absolutely no control over. Was Beth unconsciously looking to find an excuse for herself—her extra-marital affair with Ming that had resulted in their current quagmire? What about her unspoken past?

However, Beth could not wait any longer for more research to materialise in the public sphere or otherwise. The deadline to deliver her essay was immoveable. This was one occasion where the future would definitely stay where it was supposed to be.

"Looks like the concluding paragraph is more or less done. The conclusion was such a let-down! I'll have to devise a proper ending; need to think what kind of atmosphere I want to leave the readers with." Beth whispered as she perused the curated material before her and considered the proposed structure of her essay so far. Her writing centre got her drift.

"The story should end without a closure—maybe a cliff-hanger of sorts—since the findings was inconclusive. Yes, that's it: an inconclusive conclusion." She was pleased with the writing centre after it settled on the manner and tone of the closure for her essay, smiling smugly at the play of words too.

"Now to the storyline"…"Well, the distinguished doctors have sketched out some good examples to explain their understanding; I could just develop from these." Beth became pensive as she imagined one possible narrative, from the first example cited by Dr Nathan:

"He starts to kiss her as he fumbles to open the door. His clueless fingers are blindly feeling for the right one among a novel set of (her) keys thrusted into his hand. Why did she pass them to him in the first place? However, he is too tongue-tied to ask any question now. Meanwhile, she openly kisses him back spontaneously and boldly.

Once inside her apartment with the door slammed shut behind them, he turns urgent and animalistic. Like a hungry lion, he is hunting—not for food but for something to feed another primal need his hormones have unleashed. Their adrenalin is hyper-supplied now.

He then rips her silk blouse apart naturally, causing a couple of silver-plated buttons to flip like nickel coins through the air. Her blouse tears at the seams too. It is the most expeditious way to remove the impediment. She did not envisage that giving in to her dopamine rush would be such an expensive affair. In fact, she is not anticipating anything at all. The planning centre in her prefrontal cortex has shut down for the time being. Next, he pulls her nude-coloured brassiere over her head as if he is pulling a t-shirt off her body, exposing her full and firm breasts, and tight nipples. It is perfectly clear to him that she also wants what he wants, no need for verbal consent to transpire between them.

In today's #MeToo era, should one even take such risks? Alas, such is the lay of nature, the propensity towards taking more and higher risks increases with the rush of dopamine and the concomitant loss of self-control.

In no time, he is all over her with..."

"With what? C'mon, the fun is just starting, go on..." The voice prodded with excitement as if it was witnessing the writing-in-progress of a screenplay of sorts.

"Isn't the style a bit too risqué and lurid? Somewhat inappropriate for the publication, you think?" Someone-New asked disapprovingly.

"Why? You have a problem with raw passion and unbridled display of primal wants. *Wake up!* It's the new millennium already!" The voice pushed back hard, coming to Beth's defence like a bouncer.

"Alright, calm down everyone. I'm good for now...just want to get an idea of the story's narrative around the facts," Beth reclaimed control of her runaway thoughts.

"Think I may give literary novels a shot," she digressed and beamed with satisfaction.

"Now, where did that come from?" The writing centre shed its passivity at once, worried that she might be jumping out of the pan and into the fire. Everyone resonated with the sentiment too.

Beth's face shined even brighter with the afternoon sun now casting a pall over the living area and on her. Surprisingly, the heat did not disturb her at all, the air likely cooled by a passing shower just. Beth was utterly engrossed in her work. The slight warmth she felt on her pale skin could even have emanated from her own thoughts of passionate sex, drummed up by her hardworking brain.

"Such audacity to think you can simply switch to another genre after just a couple of paragraphs, all agree?" Someone-New flowed with the writing centre and played the devil's advocate now. "More like erotica than literary if you ask me." Someone-New continued dismissively, trying to provoke a reaction amidst the silence.

"Part of her nature—audacious, flighty and experimental. Isn't she?" Someone replied finally to the first remark to distract everyone else from the second, seemingly protective of Beth.

Beth just ignored everything that was going on between her ears. She continued with her imagination of the narratives, determined to ride her flow to the fullest. Her quick wins throughout the day definitely propped up her spirit, putting her in a very good place.

"Perhaps I'll drop the one with the prostitute, too crass for the targeted readership"…

"Think it'll be interesting to add a rich married woman with a toy-boy relationship—it's real-life though uncommon, can add a bit of high society panache." …" Yes, let's do that"…

"Remember to inject an aura of gossipy secrecy into the relationships, in a voyeuristic sort of way—tabloid-like to tug at our basal instincts but much more sophisticated and intelligent"…

"Oh, I almost forget, need to be inclusive, perhaps a married bi woman who has a dangerous office liaison with a lesbian subordinate"…"or a closeted gay conventionally married but maintains a secret relationship in another city"…

"Now, which is better?" …

"You have a bi-lesbian anecdote, do you not? Art mimicking life, think this will work better!" The writing centre primed.

Coincidentally, Beth did have a real life narrative to go along. "Indeed I do…just anonymise the characters appropriately yea," she reminded, "oh, don't forget the usual disclaimers also"…

"This should really get at people's curiosity"…

"Should be adequate for now…Let's see, what else is left?" Beth seemed ecstatic now; she was extremely happy with what she had achieved so far. Amazing—so much accomplished so quickly when her writing centre was fully on the assignment. After the brief early morning inertia, she got into her flow for the rest of the day, only taking short breaks for fruits and nuts, and more cheese and wine— enough to keep her mind sufficiently productive and her spirit sufficiently high.

"Finally, I need an attention grabbing title that can also be shortened into a catchy tagline for billboards of all sizes and online banners if required. It needs to jump out at one's mind, instantly stop what the person is doing and motivate him to pick up the pub there and then."

"What else? Trigger a dopamine rush!" The writing centre cried with excitement. Beth looked out of the balcony, with darting eyes as if trying to pin down all the ideas criss-crossing her mind.

It was late afternoon and the sky looked like it was setting itself up for a marvellous sunset soon. Sunsets were mostly beautiful during this time of the year. The air was cooler at end-October as well, and made more so by the passing shower a while ago.

Just then, a gentle breeze skimmed her pale skin—a whiter shade of pale under the afternoon light. And *voila!*

"*A Free Pass at Infidelity? What Science Tells Us about Human Promiscuity*"…that is it, that would be *the* title of her essay. Beth had never been this sure of herself. At that very moment, extreme relief overwhelmed her all of a sudden as if an unfathomable weight had lifted from her shoulders instantly. Though not completely done yet, the heavy lifting was over for now. She had about three to four weeks still to write up the whole essay, after she had run through everything with her publisher next week. Just as suddenly, she felt completely exhausted.

Unbeknownst to Beth, Ming had stepped into the studio with his grey cabin luggage, his usual for the short business trips. Beth was sitting on the floor, still looking out of the balcony with her back to the door, deep in her thoughts. Ming squatted down gently beside her and gave her a kiss on her luscious lips, intending it to be just a simple peck. Unsurprisingly, Beth kissed him back hungrily. Did she just have a dopamine rush? Did she possess the gene variant? Was she now totally spent and vulnerable to her natural impulses? Beth was not asking, she was not thinking anymore.

To hell with self-control—Beth's brain had given up already!

In the background, '*Hold On*' by Michael Buble was playing from a CD in the Meridian. Beth had put it on when she started earlier in the day. The CD was a collection of their favourite songs that Ming had specially curated and pressed for her. It had been replaying non-stop the whole day like a broken record.

Beth got up and led them both to the bedroom. Ming followed her with glee, picking up her glass of red wine on the coffee table and emptied what remained of it along the way. She drew the curtains slightly to thwart the glare of the afternoon sunlight and proceeded to undress herself. It was clear what Beth wanted. He wanted her too. He just was not expecting it to be before dinner.

Soon after, the heavens unleashed its brilliance as the sun settled down for the evening. Lovemaking in bright daylight is lovely for sure. Making love under a vibrant and colourful sunset? Well…that is just fucking awesome!

'*Yesterday Once More*' wafted in from the living area. Karen Carpenter's melancholic voice and the nostalgic lyrics interspersed with their thoughts as they laid in a loose cuddle on his side of the capacious bed. His temperature felt perfect. Her mildly sweaty pale skin warmed his tanned skin also.

Will I ever have enough of her wonderful and unique after-sex aura, Ming pondered.

Is anything more intimate and vulnerable than this, Beth was also wondering.

They talked sparingly about some things and nothing. Slowly, each drifted away into a world of their own. So near, yet so far.

Outside, the day surrendered itself to the creeping night as the accompanying darkness overran their space, filling the room with an indeterminate blend of intimacy, mystery and suspense.

No longer bothered with dinner, they held each other's embrace until sleep overpowered them. Then, they slipped further away into their own labyrinth but their favourite songs, still flowing from the Meridian, seemed to harmonise their dreamscape somehow.

Just Played an Excellent Hand

"Beth, this is brilliant. I must say I'm impressed with what I've seen and heard. For progress, you seem to have made a quantum leap from our last lunch," Beth's publisher was exceedingly pleased with the presentation of her work so far. His grin was so broad that any broader he would have needed a broader face, and he already had a broad face. One could only imagine the tremendous relief on his part as if an unmeasurable weight had suddenly disappeared from his also broad shoulders. Moreover, they are back at the same Japanese restaurant.

It's a good thing I don't lunch with him every week, Beth had thought to herself yesterday when he suggested the location for their lunch today. "Sure. C ya" was her crisp reply to him then. It's also a good thing they serve very fresh sashimi and sushi, and great chawanmushi too, she had thought also. Beth loved fish, all kinds; she could have it every day and would not be sick of it at all. Eggs and broccoli also.

Back to lunch today. "I'm glad you are happy with my update. I was so concerned with your voicemail last week. I thought you had cold feet regarding my essay and had called to deliver the bad news,"

Beth disclosed truthfully. At the same time, she watched his reaction carefully, the polite kind without the discomfort of a stare.

"C'mon Beth, why will I do that? It's not ethical, is it? You've known me long enough," he gave a gawky laugh to cover up his own discomfort. Indeed, his own body could not hide his lie: he had called that night because there was exactly a possibility of a substitute for Beth's essay. It had come in just a couple of hours earlier from one of his other favourite columnists. After evaluating the idea and reviewing whatever work-in-progress that was available, he was tempted to *really* switch Beth out, though not completely certain nor settled with his inclination.

He decided to use a phone call as a toss-up, unconsciously looking to chance to help untie his predicament. If Beth answered his call, which he could not be sure as he rarely phoned her and never at such a late hour, he would take that as a *yes* and deliver Beth the bad news accordingly. If she did not, the status quo would stay. He deftly left a neutral message on her voicemail also, which he thought would not betray the real intention of his call. Furthermore, through the message he left on her telco's voicemail system, he had embedded a second chance for the toss-up just to be doubly sure, in case the universe was unsupportive of his ploy. If Beth had returned his phone call, he would also proceed with his half-hearted inclination to switch her out.

Beth's sensing was right on the mark—he had cold feet on the night when he called. Alas, for all that turned out, Lady Luck was on Beth's side. Did he not decide to stick it out with her after their first review? How untrustworthy was that? A common experience actually in the ruthless dog-eat-dog world of business, where personal survival is paramount.

"It's precisely because I've known you long enough, you old bumptious fox!" No words, just thoughts and quiet satisfaction. Beth's sparkling eyes smiled sweetly back at him, which mixed with her kind of peevish smugness made her especially attractive. Beth had caught his lie. However, this was going to be her final project with him and the industry, there was no need to burn any bridge by calling him out.

Instinctively, her publisher knew Beth had caught his lie. "I should have known better than to lie to Beth, what am I thinking of?" He chided himself, in his mind of course. He was also grateful that Beth was kind enough to let his self-centred ruse slide, completely ignorant that he had misread her intention totally.

In a moment of wistful glance, Beth's attractiveness seized him out of the blue. "I have never seen this attractive side of Beth before," his inner voice buzzed with a little instinctive lust. He fleetingly considered checking themselves into a hotel room there and then (after all, the restaurant was in an exquisite downtown hotel, its rooms would have been most appropriate and agreeable). Fortunately, he banished the uninvited thought almost instantly. Did he just experience a rush of dopamine? Did he possess the gene variant? Was he being a bit too presumptuous (did Beth's social sensibilities not matter?) and egotistical (had he considered if Beth found him attractive enough to jump into bed with him just like that?) to even think it?

"Good thing he sent that despicable thought packing as soon as it entered his consciousness—this probably helped to redeem his own self-respect." Someone scorned.

Beth sensed his lascivious glance. If she was much younger, she would have felt vulnerable (she was very attractive indeed) and frozen with insecurity. Now that she was more mature and confident, she would just dismiss such furtive stares as crass and unworthy of her agitation.

"Why waste time and energy on people that don't matter. Besides, my dealings with him would be ending soon—why bother?" Someone-New echoed Beth's dismissive thought.

Moving on, she enquired deferentially, "You ok with the title? You didn't think I was going forward with Genetics and Infidelity, did you?" and prepared herself to defend her choice.

A Free Pass at Infidelity—the image of a board game, the game of life, and the hint of chance and randomness. Take you own pick, everyone likes to play games. This will definitely resonate with people. Intelligent readers will get it. Beth glowed with confidence at this thought.

What Science Tells Us about Human Promiscuity—genetics deal us the hand at the start, continuing with the board game idea. We play the best game we can with every throw of the dice, at every turn. Along the way, if we meet with *Infidelity* or *Promiscuity* situations and follow some instructions predetermined by the gameplay (like instructions encoded in our DNA), shall we not get a free pass after executing the instructions *faithfully* (as predisposed conditions expressed themselves)? Why punish us because of our *unlucky* draw of the card or throw of the dice? Blame our genes for the immutable hand dealt to us originally!

Beth was certain that this was *the* title absolutely, but she wanted to close off this important item to avoid any misunderstanding later on. Marketing and promotional collaterals would follow this decision; it would be prudent to ensure no wastage of resources. In addition, she acknowledged (to herself) that she might potentially have played with sophistry regarding such a title. However, that was all right by her, she was at home with her own sophistry. Interestingly, she was not alone.

"Of course not. A Free Pass…at…Infidelity…What…Science Tells Us …about…Human Promiscuity?" He articulated the words slowly, mouthing the words deliberately, just audible to himself above the din of the restaurant, to get a feel of how they sounded to his ears. His forehead furrowed slightly, and the black of his eyes were looking up, as if asking his prefrontal cortex for feedback.

"I think it's an excellent title. Sounds like a winner. I like the implicit idea of a game of chance and the imagery of a dice toss." He answered finally, sensing what Beth was getting at. An intelligent man after all—the kind of reader Beth would like and the kind his publication would want.

"Will definitely attract attention and arouse everyone's curiosity. *A Free Pass at Infidelity* will also be a superb blurb for the billboards and magazine stands. Online banners too. *I love it.*"

So transparent: Beth could really read him like an open book. Probably more like Beth's proclivity towards safety and self-preservation ("better to be safe"—remember?) and her worrier nature (overthinking?) had sharpened her social sensibilities and character judgement. After a couple more toing and froing on the administrative details of the project, he settled the bill to signal the closure of their working lunch.

"Great work again, Beth. Thanks." He effused his gladness as he moved towards the elevator lobby while Beth made her way to the toilet.

"You are most welcomed. Just remember to pay me my dues when your sales shoot through the roof, yea." Beth's rejoinder betrayed her utter self-confidence, further accentuating her attractiveness.

In the elevator on the way to the basement carpark, the publisher felt vindicated for keeping his faith in Beth.

"*Really?* Probably more like faith in your own dare with chance, you egotistical prick." Someone mocked sharply.

"Indeed! He nearly switched Beth out if not for Lady Luck's intervention. What a piece of shit!" Someone-Else piled on the condemnation.

Maybe he was certain that Beth would come through for him finally. His confidence had just jumped a significant notch after reviewing Beth's progress. The spontaneous grin returned to his face, visible to everyone but himself. Anyone who saw his silly grin would consider his mental fitness. Luckily, he was alone.

Beth was justified to feel confident. For now, she had played an excellent hand with a providential draw of the card, and a lucky roll of the dice. She had taken her chances very well, extracting every mileage she could get out of the situation for herself.

Two months later, the sales of the 2011 special year-end edition would shoot through the roof and quite a number of other roofs also. Reprint requests for her essay from local and overseas publications would rush in like a tsunami, way beyond anyone's imagination, overwhelming her publisher thoroughly.

Just as her publisher had wanted it, her essay was the talk of the town at Christmas and New Year's parties. Just as Beth had wanted it, she exited the industry with the essay of her life. It was a crowning achievement for her and a memorable parting gift to the industry. All the same, she would part ways with her publisher at a high point, in the process engendering a kind-of tearful regret, entirely on her publisher's part. On her part, she would make a no-regret move on the board game of her own life.

Despite the inconclusive ending in Beth's essay, its reception seemed to point to one plausible conclusion: humankind world over was hoping for a free pass at infidelity. Probably safe to conclude that this was a universal one (want?). Everyone seemed to hope that science might give him or her a cop-out. Alas, there was no such option on the board, so no combination of dice throw could open up such an escape path.

"Can one not cop-out by opting-out—just quit this game?" Someone suggested.

"Is anyone ready to do that?" Someone-Else seemed sceptical.

"How about giving chance some time to work things out—wait-and-see what science would reveal next on this matter." Someone-New submitted for everyone's consideration instead.

No Way of Knowing

It had taken a remarkably short time for Beth to withdraw from the world, their world to be exact.

Is it a couple of days, perhaps more? Ming thought so but he had no way to find out. Beth's subsequent disappearance after her no-show at the rendezvous had come as a devastating blow to Ming. It was such an unbelievably clean break that he would marvel at her cleverness and discipline years after. From his vantage point, what took place that fateful afternoon seemed so meticulously planned and flawlessly executed.

He had missed some cues—life-changing ones—after all.

…

"Hey baby, r u on the way?"

Ming texted Beth after waiting for about half an hour.

By then, a few other people, at different times, had come by the bench ten to twelve metres away from where he sat, and had departed after some other parties, supposedly their friends, married up with them.

By then, Ming was also sweating profusely under his shirt, greyish-looking damp patches appeared on parts of his cream-white shirt under the armpits, and they were slowly spreading outwards like an invading army of tiny insects.

By then, the windless air had become more humid, the afternoon sun had descended towards the horizon, moved him out from under the shade of the Tembusu tree, and shot shafts of hot sunlight onto his bench and the one ten to twelve metres away.

By then, his mind had worked itself up into some sort of a frenzy, bombarded him with questions, and cast an uneasy shadow upon him, ever more foreboding by the minute.

Beth had been late before but never this late. Usually, she would text if she was going to be late but their chat-line had been unusually silent so far.

Did something happen? Was she in some kind of trouble? He had no way to ascertain this. He was resisting the urge to call her on her mobile phone all this while.

How long now since Ming texted Beth? A minute most probably but it sure felt like forever. He waited but no reply still, his patience wearing thin now. Ming contemplated sending another text.

Just then, a WhatsApp exit notification from Beth appeared on his phone. Was his text the cue for her next move? Regardless, Beth had deleted her WhatsApp account, her number no longer in the app's directory.

Immediately, he called her on the mobile, not bothered with their made-up rules anymore. It went straight to her telco's voicemail—she was unreachable at the only number he knew! Automatically, he checked her Instagram account there and then. Impossible, his access now permanently blocked also! Beth had just vanished totally as if magically teleported out of extant reality. She had become completely inaccessible to him now.

A vertigo-like giddiness seized Ming after what seemed like a lifetime. Time stood still as he felt himself swirling on the spot. Now, he felt completely out of place with his recollection of the happy times when they were last at this place.

"What a way to burn and crash! Not even a goodbye." The channel connecting them had gone dark completely. Beth had pulled the plug first, reducing him into a formless heap of mushy mess in the process.

"Why did she do that?"

"Did Beth guess what I was intending to tell her?"

"Were we destined to be star-crossed lovers right from the start?"

The questions percolating in Ming's restless mind kept him awake that night. For days after, they churned endlessly in his brain like a washing machine that could not stop or would not stop even if it could. There was an enigma about Beth when they were together. With no answers and no closure, the mystery about her lingered long after their traumatic separation. For Ming surely, but there was no way to tell for Beth.

Ming would be in limbo as long as closure eluded him, the suspense embedded deep in the recesses of his mind mostly. Sometimes, the memories would coalesce unexpectedly and plunge him into depression. His autonomic system would seize up as if giving him a heart attack when past events flashed unconsciously in his mind. Then, the open questions would dredge up each time, fogging up his brain every time. Ming could not help himself. He would fall until he hit rock bottom, staying there for hours sometimes, days or weeks even at other times.

"Will a time come when he can feel no bottom at all?" Someone asked anxiously during one of those mental freefalls.

"Hard to tell if Ming's resilience will ever fail him, we do not know yet where his break point is really, assuming there is one." Someone-Else replied warily, finger crossing at the same time.

Thoughts of suicide crept into his mind on several occasions, holding everyone in prayerful suspense each time. Fortunately, he did pull himself back from the edge of the abyss and crossed these dark moments to the other side every time. Thankfully, Ming's ability to handle such fitful panic attacks and manic-depressive episodes improved as time passed. However, they would never go away altogether. Time heals all wounds, someone said. For Ming, time just numbed the pain gradually and buried them deeper little by little.

Apparently, shortly after the publication of her exceedingly well-received essay—*A Free Pass at Infidelity? What Science Tells Us about Human Promiscuity*—Beth started to wind down her engagements with the various media publications. By then, she had put her writing on hold for about two years, after the release of her eighth novel—*The Debauched Sepulchre in Wat Khemathaya*. Notwithstanding, her fan club remained as strong as ever, if not stronger as later generations of the target reader group for her novels would continue to lap up the stories of *Therasudorsa*. Furthermore, her disappearance seemed to cement her cult status among her loyal readers. About the same time, they started calling her creation *BTU—Beth's Therasudorsa Universe*.

Beth's timeline and build-up of *BTU* was such that her readers could begin with any of her first three books and still obtain quite a good understanding of the story and enjoyment of the series. Her storytelling style—lyrical, vividly descriptive and highly imaginative with easy flowing prose and narrative momentum—would surely draw her readers into a fantastical escape. They would be lost in the magical universe of *Therasudorsa* in no time. Thereafter, they could go back and forth, as they wished. Almost everyone would eventually read all eight of them in the series though not all in the same order.

"Think I need a break from *Therasudorsa*."

"The stories and the universe are at a logical holding pattern with the completion of book eight. They can rest here as-is forever. I am okay for everyone to imagine what he or she wants regarding what can come after, or before even."

"I can always resume if a second wind returns, after all I own all the intellectual property rights…Maybe I can franchise the whole thing off to writers who are interested, like *Star Wars*."

"Let's see what happens."

Beth contemplated shortly after the publication of her eighth novel. Intuitively, she needed to rejuvenate somehow.

Beth branched into media work not long after but her experimentation with this was short-lived. Ming knew all these as they were together already. He was by her when she evaluated a career switch to media publication and advertising. Typically, Beth knew what she wanted for her own career; she would come to the decisions mostly on her own. Ming would be a sounding board to her—to help flush out any blind spots she might have missed in her consideration. However, she had kept her exit plan from the media industry locked up in her innermost sanctum right from the start. Consequently, Ming was completely in the dark that her special project was also her parting gift to the industry.

As part of her disappearing act, Beth had cared off the maintenance of *BTU* and her fan club to Megan Chan, her editor for the *Therasudorsa* oeuvre. To everyone else, it appeared that Beth had informed Megan on her whereabouts and sworn her to secrecy (duh!). To Megan, she only had a Hong Kong postal box address for business and fan mail forwarding purposes, plus an email address: *7hera5ud0r5a@gmail.com*. (Some things are just so intuitively obvious after the fact.)

"It's strictly for the business between us and for emergency only." The second part of the general perception was true; Beth had gotten Megan to sign in blood, figuratively speaking of course, never to divulge this information to anyone, not even someone claiming familial ties.

"When in doubt, always email me first to check before you do anything." Beth had instructed strictly. She was not completely certain if Megan would be trustworthy. However, her working relationship with Megan had assured Beth somewhat. Besides, there was no one else really. This was one of those times she would have to take her chance and trust her gut, like *leap before she look*.

How did Ming know this? He had called Megan using a pseudonym and posing as a *BTU* fan, half his real age (he had thought—our voice do not change very much once past a certain age). He figured that concealing his real identity would be crucial to his effort to get in touch with Beth. Ming was credible as he had used everything he had gathered from Beth's novels and the *BTU* fan club to beguile the initially clueless editor. As they talked, Megan had considered Ming to be such a devoted reader. She was thoroughly impressed with his deep exegesis of *BTU* and Beth's oeuvre. Admittedly, she felt as if they were cult believers, earnestly converted to the religion of *BTU*, and ardently exchanging Easter eggs each of them had discovered or imagined.

However, Megan developed a nagging discomfort that something was not right after a while. An indistinct hum was droning at the back of her mind. A woman's hunch? Only after they had hung up did it dawn on Megan that the caller could possibly be a compulsive-obsessive fan-cum-stalker: he was so intent on finding out Beth's whereabouts and avenues to reach her. Immediately, the association clicked in her brain and a sudden wariness gripped her like an icy cold shower, instantly giving her the creeps.

"Good thing I held my ground and kept up with my feigned ignorance." Megan recalled with self-redemptive consolation. "But I really didn't know Beth's current residence. Will I give in to his persistent entreaty if I really know?" Self-doubt overcame Megan at this thought. Nevertheless, she was right to have trusted her intuition: established through years of experience and skills from dealing with people.

Ming had considered Megan utterly trustworthy throughout. He would like her as his gatekeeper and protector, if ever he needed one. She was like *Adris*—the gatekeeper of the *Heiluwak* realm in *BTU*— a two-faced character, one side facing outside of *Heiluwak*, the other looking in. Courageously, vigilantly and tirelessly on guard at the only mammoth gate into and out of *Heiluwak*. Did Beth fashion *Adris* after Janus, the god of gates, doorways and pathways (among other things) in the Roman mythology? Ming had wondered when he first came across the character in *The Deadly Mace of Barabudur*, which also featured the *Heiluwak* realm for the first time. Strangely, he had not asked Beth before. Now, he had no way of validating his conjecture.

Surprisingly, Ming managed to extract from Megan's ironclad vaulted mind some pieces of information—Beth had separated from her husband, she had shifted from her old address to another, and all these before her incognita. Her change of address was news to him even though the information was inconsequential now.

Beth had informed Megan of her new address and her separation at the same time after securing her silence. Then, Megan was apathetic to the news: the writers' community and her fan base had accepted Beth's reticence about her private life for as long as she had known Beth.

"No big deal! Her husband did not figure anywhere in everybody's consciousness anyway. Moreover, she doesn't seem affected the least bit. Her writing remains superb still." Megan thought with indifference then.

Beth's old address was obsolete now. Even then, Ming was not able to extract Beth's new address from Megan. "Do you not hear me? It doesn't matter whether I tell you or not, Beth isn't there anymore!" Ming's unwavering persistence was starting to annoy Megan. Deftly, she devised a courteous way to end the call almost immediately after. Ming got her drift as well that there would be nothing more to talk about until perhaps the release of Beth's next book in *BTU*, if ever.

"A new address and separation—are these one conjoined event or two separate items?" …

"The timing seems uncanny. Did she shift out of her home before or after I did?"

With Ming's discovery, his closet of unanswered questions had only grown in size. Nevertheless, one thing became clear: Beth had withheld a lot of stuff from him. This was his key now to her sanctuary that hid the closet of secrets.

"Keeping secrets injects doubts into two hearts that love each other."

"The deliberate act of concealment breaks the charm and gnaws at the happiness between them insidiously."

"We can resolve anger, right an injustice, and even forgive the other's forgetfulness. However, hiding something from the other or the suspicion that the other may be hiding something introduces a virus, which can ultimately kill the very thing that lovers work so hard to keep."

"Huh? Is Someone-New trying to inject its thoughts again? Albeit with stealth this time," Someone asked abruptly.

Right about the time when Beth was working on her special project, things were becoming untenable for her: the secrets she was keeping, first from her husband and then from Ming, were weighing on her more and more. Ming was not attentive enough to her words and the subtle cues. The duplicity was exacting a heavy toll on her, psychologically and physically. Did this affect her writing consequently?

Did the situation come to a head for Beth eventually? Did she just decide to crash out completely and restart anew? Answers to these questions and more were all in her sanctuary. Ming had discovered the key but the sanctuary with the keyhole was missing. He had no way of knowing now.

Back to Normal Again

Perhaps the only misfortune to have befallen Kim so far was what happened between her parents some while ago. Even then, they were careful to minimise its impact on her. Indeed, she was fortunate to have parents who loved her dearly and cared deeply for her well-being.

"But it's all good now; mom and dad are back together again." Kim found this out only after her father moved back to the one home she knew, with her mom's blessings of course.

"Let's tell her only after you have actually shifted back here if you don't mind," Mei said to Keat during one of their lunches. They had started to eat together again over the past year. Keat initiated the first lunch and others followed occasionally after, becoming more frequent over the last couple of months.

"Better to be safe, you never know, things can still change," Mei thought aloud, intending to coerce Keat into agreement. While entirely fine with her proposal, his usual sombre face grimaced: unbeknownst to Mei, the familiar phrase triggered a painful reverie, delivering a sudden and sharp constriction to Keat's heart for a short while. All the same, her cautious remark had unwittingly struck him with guilt and a dour realisation that her trust in him had yet to restore fully. Mei perceived the look of his face and his quiet resignation differently: he was ashamed and miserable like a dog returning to its home with its tail between its legs.

"It's time he tastes his own medicine." Ms Edgy interrupted with zero sympathy. Was she demanding his penitence, her pound of his flesh unconsciously?

On the first Saturday after Keat moved back, Mei and he jointly held a skype call with Kim. Normally, Kim would call each of them separately at pre-arranged times. However, nothing had prepared Kim for the total surprise she received that Saturday: her dad joined her mom on the same call from the only home she knew. She wept quite a bit before they even began to chat actually. Crying, like laughing and yawning, can be contagious. Her parents wept too. A bit more for Mei than for Keat, and for slightly different reasons.

Kim was in her junior year when her father actually relocated himself back home. The impact on her was immediate: she seemed visibly settled, her studies improved noticeably that caused her tutors and mentor to wonder what contributed to the marked change and academic progress. They did not know about her parent's separation, Kim had withheld that detail from them and the school.

"It's none of their business," Someone informed Kim when she first submitted her university application. When she matriculated in the fall of 2012 as a freshman, she continued to indicate her parents as married. This was accurate, semantics wise, as her parents did not file for separation officially. What happened was a tacit arrangement between themselves only.

Apart from this, Kim mostly avoided conversations concerning her parents and family. When musings with her friends or study group mates veered toward such matters, she would deftly change the subject. Yet, her relationships in school stifled unconsciously: she became less trusting of people and more wary of her environment. Kim was naturally gregarious until the misfortune exploded around her like a bomb, which then handicapped her spontaneity somewhat. Keeping her parents' separation as a secret led to more isolation in her social life, which somehow affected her undergraduate studies as well.

"Parents overestimate their children's resilience and underestimate the anxiety and trauma their negative actions (like perennial squabbles, separation or divorce) can cause them." Someone cautioned. While Kim had bounced back from adversities before, her struggle was different this time.

In the initial throes of it all, her life became topsy-turvy and unpredictable, especially in her first year. Some days were amazing as if nothing had happened, and all was hunky-dory. Other days were just very hard where she had only isolation and loneliness for company. Without close and supportive friends, going it alone in a foreign place was tough on Kim *really*. With her secret, there was no one to unburden with actually. It was unfair of her to unburden on her mom then. How could she, her mom was still trying to get back on her own? Kim could see this clearly in her mom's eyes whenever they skyped during that period.

How does one measure the suffering each one involved is going through? Certainly, everyone suffers to the fullest that he or she can feel pain and bear with the burden, even though one may appear relatively less scathed than another may. There is just no universal scale for emotions. There can be no accounting or comparison either. We feel fully what we feel; we experience distinctly what we experience.

Occasionally, Kim would feel a transient hatred for her father. "How can he abandon me just like that?" She would ask woefully with complete disregard for what he had done for her.

Sometimes when in a funk, she would charge her mom dolefully, "You promised me this would not happen to me, did you not?" Feelings of betrayal held her hostage as their poignant conversation replayed non-stop in her brain. Then, just as quickly, she would banish those accusatory thoughts of her poor mom and exculpatory ones would take over, as her mom was most certainly the aggrieved party.

Other times, she would blame herself when self-doubt crept in, as if she was the cause of her parents' relationship breakdown despite their assurances to the contrary.

Most distressing of all was when Kim felt compelled to choose a side. Then, as in RaeLynn's country song, she felt caught in a *'Love Triangle'* between her mom and her dad. Kim would break down uncontrollably when faced with such powerlessness. She would dissolve in her own misery for a time, unable to attend to anything at all. Fortunately, she would recover when her desire not to disappoint her parents got the better of her.

"Apply yourself fully and give your utmost to your studies. This is the best thing you can do for yourself right now," her parents' refrain (said to her separately) would ring in her ears at such times, and picked her up every time. Undoubtedly, such trauma could haunt any child for a long time. Against this, Kim's resilience was remarkable indeed.

Kim wanted so much to feel normal in her highly conservative society. "Which teen or young adult doesn't want to fit in?" Someone echoed her sentiment one day while she was alone.

"A complete family comprising parents and children living happily together under one roof is her norm. Parents that separated are not." Someone-Else explained further even though this was already obvious to everyone. Moreover, the thought of her mom being a single parent frightened Kim terribly. Already, her relationship with her dad who loved her very much and had doted on her all her life, and whom she loved as much had morphed awkwardly under new co-parenting arrangements. Some things changed and remained so forever, no matter what!

Unimaginable: the tremendous relief Kim felt that momentous Saturday morning when she saw her parents together for the first time after being apart for what seemed like forever to her. No words needed, the wonderful visual overwhelmed her totally, which shocked her tear glands into reflexive action. The reservoir holding her tears burst the dam completely causing a mini deluge of sorts until Kim reclaimed her self-control. Despite her vulnerable state, she felt utterly safe at that moment, a feeling she had not had for quite some time already. Marvellous to feel so secure in her parent's love.

"Poor girl, the weight of the secret on her is simply unfathomable." Someone commiserated.

"Keeping secrets can be so demanding on her young brain and body." Someone-Else acknowledged further. "Fantastic that Kim did not bear the burden of her secret in vain, you agree?"

Everyone yelled with one voice: *Hallelujah!*

"So glad to have kept my parents' separation a secret," Kim let out after the skype call, her exuberance clearly visible on her face.

"No more secrets, I am totally free now. So wonderful to feel so triumphant!" She exhaled aloud, expelling the unfathomable weight out of her system once and for all. Breathing became easy again. She felt contented being alone, no hint of loneliness this time. Instead, a light, celebratory kind of solitude descended upon her. Concurrently, her body felt so completely relaxed with all the stress bled out of her that she felt sleepy all of a sudden. Perhaps catching up on needful sleep was best for her right now.

Kim then fell into a sweet blissful dream. She awoke after to light-heartedness and a full assurance that her parents' reunion was not a dream at all. *Really*, everything was back to normal again.

YJ Chin

Marriage is Hard Work

4 Nov 2020
Trump lost his re-election bid. hurray! long time coming
sure hope things can get back to normal as before

Faye wrote in her journal late that night. Suddenly, she exclaimed aloud, "There's some fucking sensibility in the universe after all!" She was in the guest room with its door shut. Good thing her mum was in her room already with her door shut also and probably asleep by now.

"She obviously needs to alleviate some sort of pain," Someone said. "She seems to be swearing about the US election but actually it is just a cover for the real cause of her angst," Someone-New said knowingly. Unconsciously, Faye was still processing everything her mum had revealed to her so far. Automatically, she flipped the pages of her journal back to read last night's entry again.

3 Nov 2020
Mum called out of the blue
    she and dad getting a divorce
    assets split done…just legal procedures and paperwork left
    should take no more than a month
    no going back…FINAL! as good as DEAD!

Mum insisted she's fine, refused to let me visit
she sounded composed…is she?
almost forty years of marriage…what happened???

Dad didn't even have the decency to call me…do I even matter at all?!!
…

The night before, Faye was watching the live proceedings of the US Presidential election when her mum called unexpectedly. Every state was still busy counting and tallying the votes but the exit polls seemed to indicate an extremely tight race between Biden and Trump. Up to this point, it looked like a toss-up still, keeping everyone on edge, Faye included. Given her pragmatism, she could not understand her sentiments. After all, USA was not even her own country. Still, she seemed invested enough to want to watch the whole proceedings all the way until the eventual winner was declared. In fact, she had ask Sue, a month ago, to keep her day free tomorrow so that she could recover, and hopefully celebrate, after the whole saga.

"Shit! Thank goodness he's not my president." Faye recalled her disgusted resignation when Trump won the presidency back in November 2016.

"What the fuck! I'll most probably un-American myself if it's my country." She had thought definitively and defiantly then. On hindsight, Faye's reaction then was very understandable. The disruption to normalcy was unprecedented. So too the sensory overload. Unbelievable! Everybody who was anybody then would surely remember. Since then, it was a constant struggle: this must not become the new normal in everyone's psyche.

Back to the 2020 election, Faye just hung up on her call with her mum. She was still trying to wrap her head around the news of her parents' divorce. Her parents had separated for almost two years now but the terrible news shocked her nonetheless. She was not ready for this actually. Had Faye been struggling all this while? Was she hoping her parents would somehow get back together again? Perhaps her parents had not adequately prepared her, having avoided talk of their failing relationship with her mostly.

"Why burden you with problems you have no part in creating nor solving?" Her mum would say on those occasions when Faye asked.

Faye wanted to talk some more but her mum wanted a brief call only.

"I'm tired. Let's talk another time, if it's alright with you," her mum concluded. Faye knew very well that her mum was not asking.

Faye offered to drive over but her mum insisted she was fine and that it was very late already. When Faye persisted, agitation seeped into her mum's voice, at which Faye then dropped the idea altogether.

The call killed Faye's interest in the US election entirely. After they hung up, Faye quickly acquired a brain fog, which she tried to clear by journaling. However, the questions like a swarm of locusts invaded her mind so quickly that she became extremely wound up in no time. Stoicism, her usual approach, was easily defeated. Faye was human after all. Her parents' situation was just too close and personal—how to be dispassionate and detached.

Unable to snap out of the blues, she decided to self-prescribed a couple of sleeping pills, which blurred her vision and dulled her thoughts shortly before knocking her out completely. Wise move. She was teetering on the brink of a depressive spiral. That much she was self-aware.

"Finally, some good news." Faye reacted when she saw the *Bloomberg* notification the next day. She floated light-heartedly with a tinge of disbelief at first.

"Did Donald Trump contest the result?" She heard Someone asking. It was immaterial; Faye wanted to believe that Biden had won, fairly and squarely. Her belief held true finally.

However, it did not take long for her parents' situation to creep back and take centre stage in her brain again. Her head was light now unlike last night; she was compos mentis as well.

"Luckily I'm off today. Don't think I can work in this state." This was probably the second or third time Faye had taken sleeping pills to douse an emerging mind storm. As far as she could recall, those other times, she woke with a low intensity throbbing headache the day after. Like before, it happened again this time. Unlike previously, the headache accompanied her for most of the day today. The restless insects from last night had returned to hog her brain.

"Think I'll just drop in to see how mum's doing later. No need to ask or tell." Faye informed everyone.

She's doing this for herself as well and not just for her mum, you think? Someone quizzed.

Is she looking for some closure herself? Someone-Else wondered too.

As Faye prepared a light brunch of bacon and eggs with multigrain toasts, bits and pieces of an essay started to coalesce in her brain. At once, she left her partially prepared meal behind and went in search of the journalistic magazine that contained the essay. It did not take her a long time. Faye had a meticulous filing system, both physical and digital, and it was either at home or in her office. Scanning through the section of her bookshelves where she stored her collection of selected old magazines, she found the one she was looking for. It contained the essay: *"A Free Pass at Infidelity? What Science Tells Us about Human Promiscuity"* by Beth Neo.

Just then, her toaster *dinged* as if a timer was telling her the search time was up. The unexpected *ding* jerked her back to the present as if her earlier quest had transported her almost a decade back in time.

Concurrently, the slightly burnt aroma of the freshly toasted multigrain bread wafting in the air lured her back to the kitchen. Feeling a sudden hunger pang, she decided to abandon the bacon and eggs for something simpler—peanut butter, wild-berries jam and a huge wedge of her favourite runny Camembert. Too early for wine? It was tempting but Faye finally committed to a cup of flat white after some back and forth. She automatically slotted the magazine into her Baobao crystal shoulder bag, which was slouching at one corner of the kitchen counter.

"Was she thinking of sharing the essay with her mum later?" An inner voice asked quietly.

...
4 Nov 2020
Trump lost his re-election bid. hurray! long time coming
sure hope things can get back to normal as before

Mum's all right. she seems prepared for this. matter of time, she said

With her psychological valve just released, Faye continued with her journal as soft music played in the background. It was too late to drive back now. Regardless, she had decided to stay over. Her mum kept a guest room that she occupied mostly anyway. Some of her casual clothes and nightwear were perpetually hanging in the wardrobe also. After her stay each time, her mum would launder or dry clean and restore them without fail. She might stay until the weekend; she had not firmed up yet. Nonetheless, she texted Sue just after dinner earlier to instruct her to reschedule all her appointments for the rest of the week, and send her apologies to those affected.

"Something urgent came up at the home front. Can't wait." Faye left it at that. She was reticent with Sue regarding her private life; Sue was sensible to contain her curiosity as well. All the same, she was happy to have a couple more days off work.

...
4 Nov 2020
Trump lost his re-election bid. hurray! long time coming
sure hope things can get back to normal as before

Mum's all right. she seems prepared for this. matter of time, she said

something must have happened much earlier in their marriage…what???
think she'd given up even before the separation happened

discovered something strange about mum today
  she thinks aloud on this matter
  she seems ok for me to eavesdrop on her thoughts
  may be her way of conversing and unburdening
  after that it seems ok to ask questions but only at her pace
am I her therapist now? …w/o the couch!

Dad's strange too
he's broken up with the woman he had an affair with, the one mum discovered
he's now sleeping with a nurse almost half his age! WTF!!!
all these serial affairs: is he a die-hard romantic? at 67?!!
were there earlier affairs before these???

Mum initiated the divorce. no love lost, quite stoic – it seems
she said dad can do whatever he wants after that
no bother anymore; clean-cut; unencumbered
she's independent and self-sufficient anyway
she loves her practice…the little ones give her joy
think she's happy I came over
  …so happy I did!

anyway, dad texted to meet up next week.
happy he did. will never forgive him otherwise

Faye paused and put her Mont Blanc pen on the desk. Her journal seemed more detailed than usual. Then she removed the magazine from her shoulder bag. For some reason, she did not share the essay with her mum even though she had not forgotten. Meditatively, she proceeded to read the essay again.

"Did dad experience a rush of dopamine when the affairs happened? Does he possess the gene variant?" Faye murmured under her breath as she looked out the window.

The waning moon was bright yellow tonight. The night sky, fully visible through the wide window in front of her desk, seemed very much clear of everything else except for a long wispy cloud cluster across the bottom half of the moon that seemed to paint it with a broad creamy moustache and a happy smile. She lost herself in all its beauty and wonder. Ironically, she felt light and airy. If Faye were expecting some answers from the moon, she would have to wait forever. No answer from the stars as well, none seemed to have hung around.

'*The Sound of Silence*' exuded from the compact radio just now— the universe was advising her nonetheless. Simon and Garfunkel sang with poignant acoustics and in perfect harmony—maybe to every alienated heart that cared to listen, Faye thought absently. Sadly, her parents were alienated from each other now.

"And if it's genetically linked, does it mean I may have it too?" Faye could not help but asked the obvious, her mind now back to what she had just read.

"But I've never been promiscuous. Surely, what happened with Mok at medical school didn't count. Definitely not promiscuous, pre-marital maybe. It's not as if I was sleeping around. It's only him and there hasn't been another since." Faye felt defensive and unsure.

"If at all, Mok was two-timing me (and Faye initiated their break-up soon after she discovered this, she did not like the idea of sharing in such relationships). He was the one with the dopamine and gene problem actually. Regardless, inexcusable! The science is inconclusive and it seems there haven't been new findings since this publication." Faye felt redeemed now. She could definitely pin the blame on Mok for everything that happened then; she was undeniably the aggrieved party. However, Mok was not in the room to defend himself; those around were all on Faye's side.

"But why am I so bothered?" Faye asked with a frown.

"Yea huh, why?" Someone asked also.

"Maybe she might have forgotten. She came across some published studies casually that linked promiscuity with some variants in the oxytocin and vasopressin receptor genes." Someone-New recalled.

"More genes are associated now. Genetic predisposition to promiscuity will require more cognitive effort to exercise self-control over one's vulnerability in compromising situations. Same-old, same-old conclusions essentially. So, the fault is not *entirely* in our genes." Someone-New summarised for everyone's benefit.

Faye then wandered to her conversation with her mum earlier. They were chatting after dinner, sharing a newly opened bottle of her mum's favourite white wine.

"Is dad thinking of re-marrying?" Faye asked her mum dreadfully. She could not imagine herself acquiring a stepmother that seemed more like a younger sister to her though she would love to have a sister she never had. Inconceivable! At this thought, she wondered why her parents had stopped after giving birth to herself. However, she did not ask her mum that, it was inconsequential now. She was mindful to avoid matters that might cause her mum more pain than necessary; Faye killed this curiosity in her mind.

"Marriage is hard work after the romance has evaporated. It's a battle—episodes of hell and short periods of blissful coexistence. The geniality interrupted every now and then by disagreements or pent-up irritations. Most try to hold together for the kids. It gets harder after the kids have grown up, especially if there isn't a strong enough friendship to underpin the bond."

"Your father knows this very well. Does he want to get out of one and get into another so quickly?"

Her mum ruminated woefully, as if Faye had provoked her gloom. Faye reached out to give her mum a hug; she regretted asking.

Her mum hugged her back tightly.

"No tears and no red eyes. Think mum has really moved on." Faye concluded quietly, breathing easier also. Her therapist instincts had kicked-in naturally.

They left the question hanging in limbo, or perhaps the answer was self-evident.

"Maybe I'll ask him when I see him next week." Faye thought after her mum's rhetorical non-answer.

Are our decisions ever completely rational, especially after the hormonal flush in our brain, our mind a little mixed up after the chemical overdrive?

Her mum's despondency about marriage surprised Faye, considering her mum's past nudges at her, especially those times after her parents had already separated.

For her mum, this final experience would eclipse everything else before it. Whether the marriage lasted twenty years or forty years, the duration did not seem to matter. Her mum would remember primarily the end of this relationship as long as her memory stayed intact.

YJ Chin

A Stranger in the House

The throngs along the walkway seemed like an odd admixture of light strolling and hassled rushing. The swirling air of thoughtful giving and whimsy indulgence seemed almost schizophrenic. Stifling weariness for Keat. For Mei, it was impassively interesting since she had not seen such a gregarious crowd for quite a while.

They were sitting on a wooden-metallic bench by the wide pedestrian walkway that afforded them an unobstructed view of the people spilling out from the shopping malls, watching out for Kim from their vantage point also. She should be almost done with her shopping by now. Loud Christmas carols were also escaping the overcrowded malls as the doors open (mostly) and shut (only occasionally). Hordes of people of all colours, shapes and sizes were trying to get ahead of everyone else onto the walkway and streets.

It was the season to be jolly; everywhere was a riot of decorations mainly in iridescent red, green and white colours, with sporadic splashes of gold, silver and blue here and there.

The festivity and boisterous mob did not rhyme with Keat at all; he disliked crowds mostly. He would much prefer to hold out at home, hunkered down with a business magazine or a good novel for company. Nowadays, it was altogether likely to be Netflix or HBO, if *GoT*, *Westworld* or *Stranger Things* were in season also.

"It's an excuse for the retailers to recover from their loss position more than anything else. But if you really want to shop there or just to take in the Christmas spirit, we'll be happy to go with you," Keat held out this possibility when Kim suggested to go downtown shopping after breakfast that morning.

"Onz, dad. Let's make it a Saturday night out in town as we used to do when I was in primary and secondary school. Besides, Fred's here for the first time, let's bring him to see the Christmas light-up yea." Kim was exuberant with anticipation.

"You sure he hasn't seen enough in SF or NYC?" her dad asked, giving her a teasing smile.

"Oh, c'mon, it's not the same and you know *that*. All the same, it'll be fun." Kim tossed back a playful grin. It felt wonderful to be among loved ones. She was so happy to be home.

As usual, Kim was back for the Christmas holidays—typically for the whole month of December, and leaving only after the New Year. This year, she had brought someone special along. They had met about eight months ago shortly after she started her doctoral program in applied mathematics at a prestigious university in California. Fred was a senior at the same university almost finishing his program in computer science, specifically artificial intelligence. Even more specific: machine learning in healthcare.

Despite Kim first sharing their relationship with her parents a couple of months back during a skype call, her dad was still fuzzy with Fred Connery. Keat was still trying to wrap his mind around it (him) as if Fred was an idea that had yet to form fully in his head.

Keat still did not know what to do with him (it) now that he had presented himself at his house fully formed: all 6.28 feet (or slightly more than 1.9 metres) and 202 pounds (or almost 92 kilograms) of him. (Why are Americans so bothersome? Why they cannot just go along with the rest of the world? Keat, clearly irritated, asked no one in particular.) Perhaps there was nothing for Keat to do; it was her daughter's life after all. Was his intuition in overdrive?

For Mei, things were more challenging: Fred Connery was nowhere in her brain's registry, even though Kim had introduced him to her a couple of times over skype when Fred joined Kim in those calls. Fred as Kim's boyfriend, and potentially part of the family: these concepts just did not associate in Mei's cognition and memory bank. Even now, with Kim and Fred together right in front of her in flesh and blood since she was back home.

Initially, Mei just looked pass Fred and asked Keat why he had let a stranger into their house, and insisted that Fred be sent away immediately for her safety. Over the last week, it got a little better with Mei ignoring Fred at the occasional dinners or asking Keat why was the stranger eating with them, talking rudely at times and so loudly most times.

Was Mei starting to recognise Fred as the same stranger though still a stranger? Keat was hopeful for Mei's short-term memory to improve when he considered these minor episodes. Another hopeful sign: she seemed able to tie unfamiliarity or changes in her environment with potential danger.

Mei's condition: early-onset Alzheimer's disease at its earliest stage (she was only fifty-five). This official diagnosis was slightly less than a year ago now. Most evidently, her ability to form new memories became impaired, affecting her facial recognition and name recall faculties. Fortunately, she could still remember Kim whenever she appeared during their skype calls or like this month when she was home for Christmas and New Year. However, in between calls, the memory of her daughter got lost in her brain sometimes. This was worrisome.

Consequently, Kim took to video calling her mom more frequently, albeit for shorter duration when she was just talking with her mum only. "Better to be safe." Kim said when she informed her dad of this plan (which remark unknowingly triggered a mild depression in her father after that; luckily, it lasted only a couple of hours this time; lucky for Keat too that his daughter was not around to witness his meltdown).

All the same, Keat would frequently be in Mei's face to ensure he was not lost on her at all. About his intuition with Fred, had he also taken on the mother's role unconsciously, given Mei's condition?

Keat was diligent in educating himself on Alzheimer's disease— its nature, what to look out for in Mei and how to care for her. From the current literature on the condition, he realised that there was no cure for the disease right now. It was quite clear that once Mei started showing signs of the disease, it would be down to managing the condition for ease of quotidian activities and her quality of life. This might include medication to slow down its progress only, there was still no treatment to stop or reverse the condition. Equally noteworthy: the stress put on the caregiver was most often underestimated and under-appreciated. This led Keat to temper his own expectation for Mei's improvement, and impressed on him the need to take care of himself at the same time.

Upon understanding the condition a little deeper, Keat wondered if he had contributed to the development of Mei's condition in some ways. After all, Mei became highly stressed and mildly depressive for some years after the trauma of his affair and their subsequent separation. Studies had shown some correlation between stress and depression with dementia, and depression being a risk factor for dementia. While he knew that correlation did not imply causation, he still struggled, feeling somewhat responsible for Mei's current condition sometimes.

"Perhaps his guilt is coming home to roost now," Someone whispered gently.

"*Please*…it's so long already, really time to let go," Someone-New replied, clearly on Keat's side, "he needs to find closure for himself somehow."

Someone-New was wise here: apportioning blame, if possible at all, achieves nothing; it cannot undo or improve Mei's condition or contribute to Keat's mental state to care for her.

Anyway, Keat decided to scale back his career commitments with a view to retire in the next two to three years. They were very comfortable socio-economic wise, and had been so for quite some time already. They were adequately sufficient to take care of Mei's chronic condition as well.

What is money for, if not to deploy it towards what is important and where it matters? At this stage of his life, what could be more important? After all, Mei and Kim were all the family he had left.

At this stage of his career, he enjoyed coaching and mentoring his people and the younger staff much more than the thrill of the business. Perhaps Kim could do with some of his experience and guidance as well, particularly as she was navigating the final phase of her studies and thinking strategically about what she wanted to do after that.

While Kim was still feeling herself and finding her ground regarding her mom's condition, she was forever grateful that her parents were back together again.

"Good thing dad is around to help and care for mom," Someone voiced her thought. Then Kim digressed…

A TED talk Kim listened to a couple of years ago trickled into her consciousness: it is on Alzheimer's. The speaker said then—by some year (was it 2050? she could not recall exactly), if we live beyond a certain age (was it 65 or 85? she could not remember exactly either), one in two of us would suffer from Alzheimer's disease. The speaker gave a mental picture of this statistic that lodged in Kim's mind firmly: one would become a sufferer and the other would know a sufferer and perhaps be a caregiver (in some form). What an uncanny impulse from her memory system? She had brushed off the talk when she first heard it.

"Just another general statistic that seems irrelevant to me," Kim had told herself then.

Now, her parents were part of the statistic.

"The general included me, it happened to specific people I know." Kim realised when her dad informed her of her mom's condition.

"Amazing how our appreciation of statistics sharpens with personal experience," Someone-New annotated quietly.

"It's tragic actually. Her mom is so young. Not even 65, or is it 85?" Someone said in a matter-of-fact tone without any malice.

After a minute or less, Kim's mind returned to her earlier train of thought, as abruptly as her mind had jumped tracks earlier. The other positive aspect of her parents' reunion that comforted her: dad would be around to help me think through stuff.

His illustrious career and experience in tech will be good insights since I'm thinking of getting into this sector myself. Kim thought.

"Tech will need lots of mathematics to spearhead its breakthroughs and tackle its challenges; applied math no less." Kim whispered unconsciously. Just as well, she smiled smugly as she considered her choice of study and the increasingly crucial and indispensable role of mathematics in science, technology and engineering.

All the same, Keat remained his daughter's hero. This despite his lapse in judgement and daft decision that inflicted unnecessary pain on everyone at one time. Nonetheless, his wife and daughter had forgiven him already.

Kim was in a good place now, her mom's struggle notwithstanding.

Artificial Intelligence

"Dad, what do you think?" Kim asked her father impatiently the day after Christmas. They had settled down for a chat after brunch in Keat's study.

With Christmas over, everyone seemed more relaxed now. While they were not particularly religious, Christmas somehow held a special place in their familial rituals amongst the holidays and festivities in their society, other than the Lunar New Year of course, which was not religious in nature at all.

When Kim was younger, they tended to be on vacation during this period, dovetailing the Christmas cheer with the locals wherever they were, if Christmas was indeed a celebrated holiday there. Otherwise, they simply indulged in a sumptuous meal at the best restaurant in that area.

Kim had been waiting to have a substantial discussion on the focus of her doctoral program with her father since the whole of last week. She had scheduled a discussion with her mentor to close on the theme of her research when she resumed school after the New Year. It was pertinent to her that she consulted her father prior.

"Technology is the future, yes? Across the broad spectrum of technology, AI (artificial intelligence) is going to be crucial and life changing. In fact, human species-impacting, I think." Keat thought aloud.

"I've seen the evolution of IT (information technology) in cycles from its most fundamental at the infrastructural layer: computing, communications and connectivity, data storage. While its inception pre-dated me, I was fortunate to have experienced its mainstream adoption, first among businesses and then the consumer with the advent of the PC."

"They are like our skeletal-musculature system and maybe our internal organs, which we do not think about very much but nonetheless, enable the vital functions for our life." "We know it's there, we feel their presence sometimes, especially when things break down, but most times we take them for granted mainly," Keat was in an expansive mood now.

"Come to think of it, this is so true. If not for the fact that I am a STEM student, I would have paid little or no attention to machines like computers, much less the networking stuff that amorphously connect us all together," Kim interjected as if she had just received an epiphany of sorts.

Keat acknowledged Kim's remarks positively and continued his rumination, "With internet, a whole realm developed at the experiential layers—community, contextual and social, convenience and mobility—touching every aspect of our lives as social human beings."

"We are interacting with this tech every day and most conscious of these presently."

"Now, everything seems to be coalescing together to impact humanity at its very core—our cognition and consciousness, our identity," he surmised with climatic expression as if he had reached the crescendo of his presentation.

"Why so showy, he is not in a business meeting anymore," Someone pointed out in a timid voice.

Then Keat paused for all these to sink in for his daughter. He watched Kim for her reaction at the same time.

"And AI is really the core and all-encompassing technology area to target cognition and consciousness, is this the way to think about it, dad?" Kim rejoined deferentially, vocalising what she considered as the logical conclusion to her dad's animated exposition of the evolution of IT. Keat was pleased with what he heard. Nevertheless, he knew his daughter to be intelligent already.

She would surely get it. She already did when she chose her undergraduate major and area of focus for her masters and doctoral programs, Keat thought quietly.

Just some affirmation and assurance will do for her next phase, he had concluded also when Kim shared her thoughts over the past week, every now and then while they were going through stuff here and there around the house.

"If you think so," Keat smiled fondly.

"Certainly not an everyday occurrence: to be smack right at the centre and in the early throes of a completely new revolution in science and technology. I am so excited for you even thinking about it. A no-brainer-no-regret decision for you, don't you think?" Keat asked rhetorically. His cataract-corrected eyes also beamed at Kim approvingly.

"The virtuous circle of AI is evidently building up: consumer and business are becoming more accepting of AI-embedded solutions, some even consider such deployments to be inevitable. There'll be lots to do and lots to choose from as the field flourishes," Keat advised confidently.

Kim's eyes sparkled in agreement. She became animated herself, clearly overwhelmed with eager anticipation, as they dived deeper in their exchange. Kim liked mental challenges, the more complex the better, and the more seemingly insurmountable, well…the more it would excite her. All the same, her chat with her father had settled her finally; felt like old times indeed.

Unexpectedly, Kim turned pensive: it would have been so good if mom could also join in our discussion. However, she did not give voice to her thought immediately.

"What's wrong, Kimmy?" Keat sensed a dark cloud descending on his daughter that changed her mood instantly.

"Dad, you think AI can be of any help in mom's case?" At this, Kim automatically injected her thought bubble into their topical discussion.

Keat paused, taking in the delicacy of her sentiment and thinking of the ripples created by her question. He knew intimately that Kim was still grappling with the reality of her mom's condition (especially affecting now that she had gotten to observe her mom up close and personal) but had yet to articulate her emotional turmoil fully. Father and daughter had not found the time and place to talk about this really. Maybe now was the time and this was the place: his study, his private sanctum where he had wrestled his past demons and confronted the most difficult problems in his life.

After a while, Keat broke the silence and replied cautiously with a non-answer initially, "It is a difficult question to answer, and I may not be across all the fields of development in AI generally, and AI in healthcare specifically."

Sensing Kim's receptiveness, he continued, "I believe in the long run, AI and tech will be able to solve life debilitating diseases like dementia. Did we not talk about technology tackling cognition and consciousness as the current challenge earlier?"

"Already, the developments in AI, robotics, brain-machine interfaces and material sciences are converging to tackle problems involving the human condition…however (and there is always a however with difficult questions), my guess is that it may not be in time for your mom. There's still some ways to go, Kimmy."

Seeing Kim's weepy eyes, Keat reached out concurrently to give his daughter a gentle hug.

"I'm afraid we'll have to count on the scientists and doctors to do what they must, and the best they can," Keat added, hoping to dial back the apparent disappointment and inject some needful optimism into his earlier reply. However, he felt helpless, as his last rejoinder was vague at best.

Then a light-bulb moment: a certain image of Fred Connery formed in Keat's mind. "Maybe Fred can provide more perspective and insight since AI in healthcare is his thing," he suggested.

Keat's suggestion was lost on Kim. More likely, she ignored it; Fred did not seem to figure in her mind right now. Instead, she asked in a soft and subdued voice, still holding on to her father for comfort, "We talked about *Black Mirror*, remember?"

"Yes, Kimmy. I remember our lively chats on the various episodes. Some intense arguments too. But what about it, baby?" Keat asked trying to feel her emotional pulse somehow as her eyes were facing away from him now.

"*San Junipero* came to my mind as you were talking about the converging fields of development. It will be nice if the technology is here today already and we can capture mom's consciousness—her memories, her identity, her personality—and upload her to some cloud somewhere before all of her disappears with her condition. With a slight twist, perhaps mom can be accessible while we are still here, with mom in a so-called alternate reality." Kim shared her idea dreamily.

Keat paused briefly to consider Kim's loaded notion.

"I can appreciate why you will want this, Kimmy. However, we have to ask ourselves to what end and for whose benefit if the technology becomes real. You and I may want it surely. Nevertheless, we need to ask if mom wants it. Are we being selfish to impose this on her? Mom must have the final say since it's her consciousness, like Kelly or Yorkie in *San Junipero*. Agree?" In posing the ethical questions to his daughter, Keat was also wondering himself.

Looking into his daughter's glassy eyes, Keat saw her sentiment morphed into an impassive display of ambivalence then.

("Why the seeming detachment in Kim? Does her mom not matter?" Someone asked with deep concern.

"There's so much for her mind to unpack," Someone-Else said.

"It's a difficult conundrum actually, so full of unknowns, conflict and contradiction. Sometimes technology is the easier part," Someone-New suggested, conscious of the moral dilemma and cultural norms involved.)

"I cannot bear to see the black hole in mom's eyes when I am eventually deleted from the memory repository of her fragile brain." Kim confessed after a while, her ambivalence replaced by a painful struggle to hold back her tears now. Was she afraid of losing her mom completely? Fearful that the one she loved would forget her, who once loved her also?

Kim's words entered Keat's innermost sanctum there and then, without knocking, without asking. An eerie déjà vu fell on Keat: was Mei going to do a disappearing act on him as well—gradually initially, then suddenly and absolutely—albeit unwanted and unplanned this time?

Missing Persons

2 Jan 2020
I think it's her

Keat wrote in his journal, a couple of hours after he had returned from sending Kim and Fred off at the airport. He felt certain though he could not be sure absolutely.

…

2 Jan 2020
I think it's her
Beyond the immigration checkpoint machines, maybe 5m?

Keat continued journaling in his study. He felt compelled to jot down this detail about the location where he had spotted Beth earlier. Why, to ensure this impression would never be lost?

Keat had just said his goodbyes to Kim (mainly), with his fatherly hugs and kisses, and to Fred. (Mei had done so similarly shortly after dinner and they had put her to bed before leaving for the airport.) All of a sudden, Kim became blur in his vision as he watched her procession through the immigration checkpoint.

…

2 Jan 2020
I think it's her
Beyond the immigration checkpoint machines, maybe 5m?
Kim passed behind Beth! They don't know each other anyway

Keat assumed his daughter and Beth were strangers. If only he knew—he had been so wrong all this while and he had missed so much. After all, Beth's novels had a wide appeal among Kim's age group when she was younger, even now actually. Most of her fan base started getting interested in her novels when they were in their mid to late teens, some as young as twelve years old. Keat did not know that Kim had in her possession the entire *Therasudorsa* series of books. Perhaps he should have paid more attention to Kim's fictional collection instead of just focusing on her non-fiction catalogue. Kim had the habit of rereading novels that she liked very much also. Subsequently, she brought along all eight books of her *Therasudorsa* series when she left for California for her undergraduate studies.

Nevertheless, the fantasy genre was not something up Keat's alley actually. He could never understand the fascination that people had with *Harry Potter* and all the witchcraft and wizardry make-believe.

"Highly imaginative and magical, I must give it but I find it utterly childish." He had commented to Mei soon after JK Rowling released *Harry Potter and the Philosopher's Stone*. Mei just took this in patiently, as one of Keat's many opinions about stuff, from important issues to the mundane minutiae.

"Maybe he needs to give more time and thought to these things before jumping to conclusions so quickly. He may miss some stuff, nuggets of gold even, in his haste." It would be sound advice for Keat if only Mei had given voice to her thoughts. However, she wisely decided that this was not a button worth pressing at that point and so held her tongue.

Then Beth came along, and some people changed. Quietly, Beth would revel whenever she found Ming reading her books. However, she became upset when he foolishly categorised her works as fantasy at one time. "There exist no neat, ready-made pigeon holes to hold my books. Wiser to avoid labels," Beth had told Ming off angrily then. So humbled, he felt like an ignoramus in her craft and would be extremely careful with his opinions when discussing any work of fiction with her thereafter.

Incidentally, Mei had bought Kim her first novel in the *Therasudorsa* series—*The Fiery Sabre of KangoWatu*—when she was thirteen. There was no particular reason for the gift other than Mei wanting to broaden her daughter's interests and perspectives with different genres of fiction.

Kim was so enthralled with the *Therasudorsa* universe that she bought the rest of the entire series herself: after she had saved sufficiently from her own monthly allowance to afford one at a time.

On top of this, Kim had actually attended a couple of Beth's reading sessions and even got Beth to autograph her first novel (given by her mom) which she showed Mei afterwards. Kim shared her fiction-related stuff with her mom only.

Keat was completely in the dark regarding all these. It was never Mei's intention to withhold any of these from Keat; it just did not cross her mind to inform him. Instinctively, she might have assumed that such fiction would not interest him at all; his opinion, more than a decade old now, might have informed her subconsciously. Would there be any difference if Keat knew any of these?

At such a young age, where did Kim learn to compartmentalise what she shared with her parents—some stuff with mom only, other things with dad only, yet some others with both and the rest with none at all? Is this how children start to keep secrets? An instinctive behaviour?

Back to Beth-spotting: Kim had missed Beth probably; otherwise, she would have recognised one of her favourite writers whom she had met in person before.

Altogether likely: Kim, as usual, felt harried with noisy crowds at busy airports, and preoccupied with locating the departure gate for her flight. She liked to give herself ample time at the gate just in case. ("Better to be safe", she would say to whoever she was travelling with). Keat should know this about his daughter by now. However, this did not occur to him though he did notice that Fred was not particularly attentive to Kim at the airport.

Another most likely possibility: Keat was simply mistaken; there was no Beth at all.

If not for Keat's constant gaze on his daughter as she passed the sliding doors to the immigration checkpoints, he would not have paid any attention to a woman wearing an elegant cream-white straw floppy hat. Immediately, the extremely familiar hat consumed his mind completely. Kim faded like a mist as the woman came into focus simultaneously; the woman seemed to be in conversation with another woman and a man. The hat had a navy blue ribbon on it, one of Beth's favourite which she used frequently while travelling.

Instinctively, he strained his eyes to catch a better glimpse of the woman with the hat. Ming noticed too the familiar semi-formal semi-casual tank jumpsuit that Beth liked. She would wear them sometimes for the reading sessions, mostly in conjunction with her book launches, for her fans at selected libraries and bookshops. It was not just the familiarity of the style of the tank jumpsuits (and Beth had a few pieces of such), it was also the particular colour that was her favourite—spruce-like, that unique combination of blue, green and grey hues. Normally, the sartorial tastes of random people did not interest Ming at all but this one was different: the mental associations in his brain triggered by familiar styles, colours and shapes were just too intense to ignore.

Ming struggled to make out her face, partially hidden by the hat and partially hidden from sight. The woman with the hat was facing slightly away from him. Occasionally, passing travellers blocked his line of sight also. Part of her fair-skinned nape was exposed. Was her hair neatly coiffed into her hat or was she wearing a pixie hairstyle? He could not really tell because of the distance. However, the sight of her nape brought back memories of distinctive smells—a clean-and-sweet-smelling Beth scent and one accentuated with a rose-and-woody fragrance, and then there was her unmistakable after-sex sweaty aura. *Of course*. Without a proper reference, it was hard to tell her height though he was inclined to believe that the woman with the hat was as tall as Beth.

"Was she travelling alone?" Ming took to thinking instead of writing as he put his Mont Blanc fountain pen on the table. Unconsciously, he was trying to reconstruct the scene as he had seen it two hours ago, probably three hours by now. It should be fresh in his mind, especially for a person that remained deeply embedded in his heart still. He imagined an outline of some sort around her but nothing seemed to fill in, no other image formed in his mind besides the woman with the hat.

Was he imagining stuff? Was it a chimera? Like the mirage of an oasis to a tired and thirsty soul in the desert: his mind bent to the needs of the flesh, and succumbed to the vagaries of human nature and the environment. A state of the mind and a longing of the heart perfectly juxtaposed by the surrounding condition to create a fictional illusion—nothing more.

"It must be her! *Really!*" Ming felt quite certain now.

As his memory system took control, he fell into reminiscence automatically, just as the longing melodious voice of Freddie Mercury from his Meridian suffused the ambiance of his study. It was a quarter to midnight now; the lyrics of *'Love of My Life'* sounded all the more nostalgic and obsessive in the stillness of the night. His memory ebbed and flowed with the song: how he longed to own her still.

"Did she travel until she arrived at a life of her own?"

"Where would that be?"

"How long did she take before she finally settled down?"

"More unhelpful questions..." Someone-Else lamented. As time passed, Ming wondered if the need to acquire the answers however plausible was even necessary. If he had known any of these, would it change anything?

Unwittingly, Beth had transformed Ming: subconsciously, he was like a detective with the Missing Persons division of the police department, albeit an untrained and uninitiated one.

Alas, the questions would be unanswered, if only Ming was prepared to accept this; he could not even grasp fully what he already knew. He would need to live with the unknowable as his base-case closure, for there would be no closure of any other kind. Many Missing Persons cases remained unsolved for a long time, and some remained in cold storage forever.

However, to have any chance of finding a missing person at all, someone must report the missing person and a case file opened as a start. Ironically, there would never be a case file on Beth: no one reported; no one ever would. Moreover, Ming could never be the one to file the report, no matter how earnestly he wished to do so.

He could never overcome this one struggle.

Something Special

8 December 2022

Dear Beth,

I have just sent another package of fan mail to HK that will deposit at your postal office address by tomorrow. Please retrieve them in your good time.

As you already know, I sift through all the mail that are addressed to your BTU fan club and those sent to my publishing firm attention to your name or anything relating to your works. I also maintain a record of the post-marks and details of the senders wherever available, in case something crops up where historical records may be helpful. Interestingly, I have found some use for these now.

There is something new and not so new at the same time. Remember the one particular fan I mentioned to you many years ago (sorry, I can't be more specific, my memory seems to fail me here) who called me a few times trying to pry your contact information out of me? He subsequently sent you a letter post-marked on a particular date: 18th November. From my records, he sent a letter each in 2012, 2013, and 2014 on the same post-marked date. He stopped after that which is also the end of the not so new part.

What is new? He has sent you another letter this year. Given this lapse of time, we decided to inspect the letter a little closer. We think there is unlikely to be any malicious content in the letter after doing so. Better to be safe, as you had often advised us in the past. Incidentally, he happens to be one of the few fans who sent letters to my publishing firm instead of the fan club. He is one that includes the sender's details also. Uncannily, his letter arrived on the day just as I was about to seal off your package for delivery. He seems special and he has top of mind recall for me among your fan base: partly because of the confluence of the aforementioned points, partly because of my initial impression of his earnest interest and deep knowledge of your oeuvre. He seems genuinely serious about getting in touch with you. To what end and for what purpose? My guess is that you may have the answers. Again, his name is simply: Ming. His letter is probably still at the top of the package since it was among the last few items in my packing. Otherwise, please take note when you work through this batch of fan mail. I think this would be of interest to you. If not, please forgive me for being so presumptuous.

Coming back to our usual topics, a quick report on the sales of your novels. Each of the books in your series continues to sell well. You may be interested to know that up until the end of November, sales of the first two books are about 10-15% higher than the rest. We suspect we may be acquiring a new segment of readers, perhaps even younger ones too. Once we have closed out the financial year, we will give you a full report as usual and forward to you your share of the sales proceeds. If there's any change in your payment arrangement, please inform us as soon as possible.

Lastly, I have attached the invoice for the quarterly admin charges of our services with this email also. We look forward to receiving your prompt payment. Short of sounding like a broken record, if you ever decide to publish again, I will be more than glad to have that conversation with you. Meanwhile, please keep well and stay safe.

Yours faithfully,
Megan Chan

"Why does Megan still write so formally to me after all these years? Only in the last para did she allow herself some informality." Beth drew a deep sigh as she closed her Gmail and shut down her computer.

Automatically, Beth called up her usual logistics company to activate the process to retrieve her stuff as soon as possible in anticipation of the Christmas holiday frenzy. Parcels and gifts would be flying everywhere and all over the planet. She definitely would not want her stuff to be stuck in the system, or go missing in some customs warehouse. Especially not this time.

Over the years, Beth had come to expect this as her Christmas present. She would spend Christmas and Boxing Day or longer reading her fan mails selectively depending on what visually triggered her fancy. With pleasure too as if this was her main connection with the world now.

Surprisingly, Beth had progress towards friendship with a small number of fans. She had selected the group members based on her gut feel. There would be about fifteen of them at any one time, all in their late teens and early twenties when Beth started including them. They were all girls except for three to five boys, collected over the first few years after she settled down at where she was now. She created a separate channel for them to connect with her directly and more frequently but still remotely and virtually only.

"Sounds weirdly like some cult leader and his apostles, you think?" Someone said suspiciously at the start of this exclusive grouping.

Interestingly, she became Aunt Agony for some of these girls and even one boy, as trust and familiarity built along with the frequency of their interactions. They shared with her their life challenges, especially their relationship ins and outs and ups and downs, and sought her advice on specific problems in specific situations. For Beth, they were like the children she never had.

"Always about relationships, nothing about studies or careers, why? Isn't she bored with the same-old, same-old? So unlike her!" Someone-Else seemed genuinely puzzled at some point.

"Plus a small clique within a group…you recall the cult leader you mentioned at the start? So uncanny, like some transfiguration, you think?" Someone-Else added.

At one time, Beth even toyed with the idea of a meet-up with this special group (conscious exertion of her natural need for *real* social interactions finally?) but decided against it after some careful thought ("better to be safe" was the stronger impulse?). Nonetheless, she encouraged the group to meet among themselves (sans herself). This initiative was instrumental to the boy starting a relationship with one of the girls, three years younger than he was. Conveniently, they lived within an hour's drive from each other. Incidentally, they shared similar socio-economic backgrounds.

Cheng stopped writing to Beth shortly after he and Sarah got married, almost two years ago now. The gist of his final email: Sarah and he clicked so naturally because they were compatible but he believed the chance of their union would be near zero if not for Beth. She brought them together through a group setting, and their deep-shared interest in *BTU* underpinned the strong bond between them now. However, Sarah continued to write to Beth though not as frequently as before. Now, both were busy building their careers and preparing for little junior due anytime soon—that was Sarah's last update a couple of weeks ago.

"They seem to be in such a good place," Beth smiled approvingly as she daydreamt about this special group. It never occurred to her that she would have a front row seat with an intimate view of the significant happenings in the lives of some fans. The positive contributions she made to their lives were pleasant surprises, which gave her much contentment as well. She felt extremely happy for her young charges at the same time. Unconsciously, she seemed to have taken on a self-imposed responsibility for some of them, and quietly enjoyed that too, even felt protective of them sometimes.

For the usual fan mail from Megan, she would set aside those she decided to respond to and would spend a good part of January writing to her fan base if she was not travelling, otherwise she would push this out to February or even March. Her fans would be glad to receive a reply from her, the timing of such should not really matter at all, or so she thought. Now and then, she would add to, more like replenish, the group of fifteen with new members as life drew the older members away naturally.

Of course, Ming's letters received no action whatsoever. Still, it was a painstaking decision each time as Beth would struggle with herself on what to do. Even after she had decided (again), a soft voice in her head would drone on, accusing her of this and that, giving her a migraine now and then. It took a while for her to finally box things up and lock them away completely after Ming stopped writing to her. And with this, her migraines too.

Now, another letter from Ming was finding its way to her. What does he want this time? Will this unbox old stuff? What about the incapacitating headaches? Questions abounded as Beth awaited the arrival of her package.

Regardless, there was something special to look forward to this year. Beth's heart fluttered whenever this anticipatory thought flitted into her head. Megan had successfully lodged the highlight of her letter in Beth's mind as intended. Unintentionally, Megan had provoked what was inside Beth's innermost sanctum, resting quietly since locked away. Until now.

Hangataun, the banished prince of the *Heiluwak* realm in the *Therasudorsa* universe, did return finally to awake his loyal dragon *Komodaroah* from its prolonged hibernation in its snow-encrusted dungeon. Even before the prince's actual return, the snow had begun to melt already, rousing the dragon ever so slightly.

Could *BTU* fill some blanks? Easter eggs in plain sight, missed entirely?

YJ Chin

.

Fireworks

"Here, let's toast to a New Year?" Faye's mum brought out a pair of flutes and a bottle of champagne to the balcony after a quick cleaned-up of her kitchen and the dinner table. Her mum's gaily smile lightened Faye's cloudy mood and lifted somewhat the enervating heaviness that had been weighing on her for the past month or so. The dinner with her mum earlier was very good actually but Faye quickly descended into a funk when she relocated herself to the balcony after dinner. The dark gloomy night sky hiding the twinkling little stars was not helpful at all.

"It looks like a storm is building up somewhere despite the 4-hour weather report forecasting no rain at all," Faye grumbled softly at this thought.

"Well, it did not say no clouds and no wind. Maybe there is an updated report?" A timid voice replied still hopeful of no rain.

Regardless, it was about two hours to midnight and they were planning to watch the fireworks by the bay, which would be visible from the balcony. Fireworks used to be a special affair annually during National Day only. However, New Year's Day was included in the national fireworks calendar since 2021, two years ago now. Perhaps it was a bid to lift the national mood out of its economic doldrums then, and distract everyone with something to celebrate. However, that something was not immediately obvious then though everyone seemed to like the idea of having something-to-celebrate very much. So, would the real weather turn up unexpectedly to rain on the nation's parade later?

"It's still early," Faye returned a puzzled half-smile as she was expecting the champagne to be brought out closer to midnight and drunk only after the singing of *Auld Lang Syne* past midnight. After the fireworks, of course. Nonetheless, she gladly accepted the flute handed to her.

Time to drown my sorrows with some poison.

"Did Faye just think that?" Someone alerted everyone.

"Why not? Let us enjoy ourselves while we still can. Who knows what will happen next? An alien ship may just fly by and beam us away. And we may never get to drink our hearts out like this ever again." Her mum's jocular response and teasing eyes aroused Faye's suspicion.

"Mum seems to be in a jolly good place, her cheerfulness certainly lifted my moodiness during dinner. She is her merry self again—is something going on that mum is not telling me?"

Faye then fell into a reverie, unconsciously.

...

"Sean, think I will have to refer you to another psychotherapist to continue with your treatment." Faye informed him towards the end of their seventh session that had overrun its usual hour by almost another hour. She had determined unilaterally and painstakingly the night before that this had to be her final session with Sean.

"Why Faye? What's wrong?" Sean's earnest eyes flashed across her mind when she recalled him asking that.

Sean's reasonable question nonetheless put Faye into a trance of sorts and threw her reverie one level deeper, to the fateful night *before* her seventh session with him.

"This will be the best for everyone, agree?" Faye was not aware she was asking anyone for permission.

"Agree. Your professionalism is threatened. You risk crossing into the inappropriate territory—not physically yet but psychologically already. That is definitely a *red* flag." Someone replied immediately, clearly protective of Faye.

"What do you mean? I'm always careful with my decorum," Faye asked innocently.

"Perhaps she really has no idea what went on in her head that night?" Someone-Else whispered to Someone. Everyone else looked everywhere and nowhere, feigning ignorance with its silence.

"But I would surely miss my sessions with him very much." Faye followed shortly, with a tinge of despair in her voice, when no answer to her question was forthcoming.

"Well, look at the bright side: if you still feel the same for Sean, and you know what I mean, maybe it is better you let another specialist handle his case. Then no worries about professional ethics anymore. This can end your immediate struggle. You can follow your heart and do whatever you want after that." Someone-New urged plainly.

Faye allowed herself a weak smile at this thought. She had fallen for Sean round about the fifth session (maybe a session earlier) but she had not allowed herself to admit it. Her heart had been on a roller coaster ride ever since.

"Her intelligence should see her through this upheaval, agree?" Everyone nodded, seemingly confident and united regarding this.

"Let's hope it's not some transient counter-transference." Faye concluded lucidly. Intelligence aside, Faye had allowed herself some honesty finally.

...

"Hey baby, c'mon, let's not wait anymore." Faye's mum gently *clinked* their crystal glasses, which knocked Faye out of her reverie. Her mum had already filled the pair of flutes with what looked like a gold-tinted effervescent liquid reflecting a now cloudier night sky.

"What's up, honey? You seemed to be in some kind of an *Inception*." Her mum asked after taking a greedy gulp of the sparkling alcohol, trying to sound insouciant.

"Wow! This mother reads her daughter like an open book. Wonder if she knows how many levels deep Faye's reverie transcended to?" Everyone exclaimed, totally impressed.

Her mum knew when to be patient also. She settled down and waited to hear what was bothering her only child. Fireworks aside, she was prepared to wait as long as it was necessary. Anyhow, Faye was in no hurry to go anywhere. They would have the night and the whole of New Year's Day to talk things over.

She was also involved somewhat when Faye initiated her relationship with Sean not long after he stopped being her client. Mother and daughter had discussed the matter quite deeply on the weekend before Faye asked him out on their first social dinner.

Sean was tentative initially after the first date but agreed to continue seeing her over the next couple of weeks. Naturally, Faye's feelings for him grew stronger and deeper as they met more and more. Sean understood fully how she would like to take their relationship forward. He could tell also that Faye was eagerly waiting for him to break out of his ambivalence, one way or the other.

When Sean finally reciprocated, Faye was terribly thrilled as if an unmeasurable weight lifted off her. That was the start of what she thought would be a good thing for her, and for him too, or so she thought.

However, for Sean, this would be the start of the end though he would not know that for quite some while yet. Was it selfishness on his part, or was he genuinely emotionally insecure or self-deluded at that stage? Clearly, he was of two minds still despite his reciprocity.

After a lengthy pause, Faye opened up and filled her mum in on the latest happenings between Sean and herself.

"I'm so sorry to hear that darling. But this is not the end yet, is it?" Faye's mum commiserated after a while, careful to be sure that her daughter had paused for the time being before she interjected.

"Yet? Why yet? Does she know something Faye doesn't?" Someone-Else alerted everyone this time. Sadly, her mum knew that the end was imminent for Faye and her choice of words had betrayed her intuition.

Simultaneously, she was trying to be as gentle with Faye as she knew how. It hurt her very much to see her only child in such a distressing and helpless state: she is all the family I have left, what can be more important than this?

Love when done right can be heaven on earth. Love can also be fleeting. When it departs unexpectedly, hell will surely take its place. Her mum had gone through this before, now her daughter would be going through it. However, it was also different: different age, different life stage, different length of time though the last part did not seem to matter. Her mum did not count what Faye went through with Mok in medical school, it was no big deal to her mum—Faye was unsure with Mok, her recovery was very short and she came out of it much stronger and better. However, she knew this time was different: Faye is wholly into this with Sean. A mother's intuition?

Faye became very quiet again. Her mum's question had tossed her heart into turmoil and caused her mind to wander off another time.

Meanwhile, her mum was rehashing their past conversations in her mind.

"But you know what you will be in for."

"He had an affair and separated with his wife. He chose another over her daughter who has been the apple of his eye since birth." (Faye could identify with this part immensely.)

"Moreover, he still struggles, feeling somewhat responsible for his wife's descent into dementia, which seemed to have also caused her death ultimately."

(Mei's death: an untimely heart attack; did her heart forget its procedural duty to keep beating and pumping? Maybe a culmination of takotsubo cardiomyopathy, commonly called the broken heart syndrome also.)

"Sean has been mildly depressed since her death, almost two years now. Was this not his state when he became your client?"

"Are you sure he is stable enough, fully able to enter into another relationship? Does he realise that you cannot be his emotional crutch or his mid-life crisis filler?"

"This is not about you, agree?"

They talked about everything at such great length. Her mum laid out all the facts before Faye in case she had missed them.

"Love can be blind; did someone not say that before?" Someone asked flatly.

But she was clearly happy while it lasted, I must give her that. Six months can zoom by very fast when one is in love but it's not a short time either. Her mum could tell that once her daughter had allowed herself to love Sean, she would jump right into the deep end with her whole heart.

Unlike the case with Mok, there was no wavering this time, for sure. When she loved so fully and so fiercely, there could be no avoiding the ghosts and the vampires as well. Faye would have to sleep in the bed she had made, however painful it might be.

Right now, I can only do what I can to ease her pain and help her to pack up properly if it comes down to the inevitable. Her mum thought.

"Have you try talking it over with Sean, at least one last time?" Her mum asked softly, hoping to bring Faye back from wherever she was now.

"Did everyone just switch roles?" Someone asked as it appeared that her mum was now the therapist and Faye seemed to have taken up Sean's position.

"Think he's been avoiding me. He has busied himself with a three-month consulting engagement in the US that has taken him away since the beginning of December. We were supposed to have Christmas dinner with you remember?"

How could her mum forget, Sean's last minute cancellation of his presence at the Christmas dinner was the start of her mum's suspicion.

"Maybe he didn't want to talk until he's *really* ready to talk." Faye whispered but the attentive mum heard it nonetheless.

"Giving excuses on his behalf, not a good thing," Someone informed, feeling very worried at the same time.

"But everything happened so suddenly and so quickly within a spate of just a week or two before December." Faye's voice became shrill but firm, her pain struggling behind her stolid face.

Sean and Faye last met each other around mid-November.

"He claimed to have no time. However, we make time for what is important to us, don't we all?" Her aching heart was talking now.

Then their most recent calls came to mind: they were short (less than a minute mostly) with monosyllabic answers usually. Sean was always in a rush, and his words were evasive and apologetic.

The last one before complete radio silence: I've been engaged to consult with a firm based in Austin, Texas…will be there from December till Feb or March…may be longer…depends on how this first phase consulting goes…don't call me, I'll call you.

"Sean was talking in fits and starts, like during some of his therapy sessions with me previously," Faye added. Would she be as patient with him, and wait for him to awake from his wandering state? Regardless, she felt numb now as if she had been exhausted of pain.

"He said he'll be back around Feb or March, guess I'll give a call then," Faye said under her breath. Nonetheless, her mum heard it but said nothing.

Suddenly, the ships out at sea beyond the bay sounded their horns as in a chorus.

As if this was the cue, the fireworks began, determined to put up its best show of lights for the night, with the warm and humid air to resound its thunderous blast.

The heavens played along by discharging a web of electricity in the distant horizon, flaring up the bay's background synchronously. Then the real blast thundered pass, briefly drowning out the singing of *Auld Lang Syne* all around.

The heavens were considerate: it waited for everything by the bay to return to darkness, and then it unleashed the rain, first gently then horrendously. Regardless, the jovial and resilient singing continued unabated.

Mother and daughter watched the whole spectacle in silence, thoroughly secure in each other's company and solitude.

Faye knew what her mum could give her: a love like a lighted fireplace on a frigid winter night—warm, comforting and dependable as always.

Her mum knew what her daughter wanted for herself: a love with exciting fireworks some times that could transform into a lighted fireplace on a frigid winter night—the kind with magic she could never give her.

Don't Blame the Universe

"Hey dad"…Kim texted her father and paused for his reply. She wanted to have a synchronous chat with him. With her mom's passing three years ago, her dad had backfilled most of the space she had shared with her mom previously. She wanted to share something interesting from her trip immediately, something she thought they had talked about before though she was unsure. Sometimes she was mistaken: thinking she shared some things with her dad already when actually she had previously shared with her mom only.

"If dad doesn't reply within the next five minutes, I'll tell him another time though it may not be as fun." Kim thought to herself, after getting into a Lyft cab. Then again, it might never happen since Kim could be whimsical with some matters or forget completely if it was something not that important.

"Hey Kimmy" Keat replied a couple of minutes later.

He was expecting Kim to text as he had asked her to do so whenever she got off an airplane, to be doubly sure she got off safely. She was flying back to San Francisco that day after attending an AI conference in Seattle. Microsoft and Amazon had jointly put up the biggest IT symposium on

Artificial Intelligence, Robotics and Everything in Between.
The most significant global tech event in 2023

Kim had signed up for the 'AI in Healthcare' track with a sub-track on *"Artificial Consciousness: Eternal Life for Humans Now"*.

"Sounds uncannily like *San Junipero*, u think?" Kim commented to her dad after she had signed up for the conference. She recollected this part of their conversation, about six months ago now, while she was just waiting for her dad to reply.

"Glad u landed safe"…"Conference good?" …

"Anything interesting?" Keat continued. He had kept up with his interest in science and technology ever so often even though he was retired now.

"A little bumpy on the flight, otherwise all good"…

"Gr8 conference"…"Dad, *San Junipero* really happening"…

"Amazing"…"Scary 2"…

"Next year"…"Sooner or later anyways"…Kim was still excited from what she had discovered at and learnt from the symposium. Her dad felt the transmission of her animated disposition over the internet; she felt her phone burning as she texted.

Keat just read her texts quietly. Of course, he expected her to talk about the conference she had just attended but he was wondering if there was something else also.

"But this is not the most interesting bit" Kim continued, seeming to validate Keat's gut instincts.

"Go on" Keat let out a gentle sigh at this point, unconsciously. Was it a sigh of relief?

Good thing we are not using video, he thought to himself.

"Why he thinks that?" Someone asked, clearly puzzled.

"Remember my *Therasudorsa* series?" Kim asked.

Keat went cold instantly. His vision fogged as he looked away from his screen initially. Kim's 'my *Therasudorsa* series' rang in his ears, as if a smoke grenade had just exploded in front of him. Ironically, every splintered piece just snapped precipitously back into place the next moment, as if time just reversed. The clarity and sharpness of his psychological vision gave him the creeps at the same time.

"Of course, Kim could be, and most likely would be a reader of such novels, how can I be so daft and naïve?" Someone heard Keat scolding himself and saw him pulling his hair with both hands at the same time.

"I have *missed* this for half my lifetime." Keat exclaimed aloud now. Luckily, he was alone in his study with the door shut.

Maybe it's time for complete honesty, Keat supposed, feeling suspended between two separate lives.

"What does that mean actually?" Someone-Else asked.

"Hey dad u there?" Kim texted again, wondering what was holding her dad up at his end, completely ignorant that she had just unsettled him.

"No" Keat reacted robotically to the *ping* and vibration of his phone initially.

"I mean I didn't know your series"…"U told mom?" He clarified a moment later, mindfully now.

Okay, that is a good start, Someone noted tentatively.

"Oh yes, must be mom then"…"Anyway, u familiar with *Therasudorsa*?" It did not matter to Kim now whom she shared *BTU* with previously, it would be just her dad for everything hereon.

"Yes"…"Read all 8" Keat replied with some hesitance, feeling nervous about where Kim was going with this, his stomach churning at the same time.

"Quite forthcoming indeed, he didn't have to share the last bit but he did, seems to be on the right track." Someone-Else observed, trying to convince everyone now.

Keat had ring-fenced details of his affair from his family; even Mei did not know Beth was the other woman. He had guarded Beth's identity very tightly. Why? She was a public figure? Mei might make a scene if she knew? He did not really know nor ask himself then. He just acted on his gut instincts: it *must* be so!

Unconsciously, Keat was still protective, he was not about to let Kim into his innermost sanctum—not this part, at least not yet.

"So much for honesty, eh?" Someone-New said cynically, dashing everyone's hope at the same time.

"Gr8"…
"I didn't know that"…
"Else we cud all have discussed this together"
Kim continued innocently. Keat could feel her exuberance still.

Mei would be suspicious if she knew Keat had read every book in the *Therasudorsa* series. Perhaps it was a good thing Kim did not share fictional stuff with her dad after all. *Really?*

"No point dwelling on what-if's anyway." "To what end and whose benefit?" Someone urged. Everyone seemed to agree.

"Anyways"…
"Dad, u there?"
Kim's incoming text brought Keat's drifting mind back one more time. By now, Kim was getting suspicious of her dad's seeming absent-mindedness.

"Here"…
"Wat about the series again?"
Keat's anxiety was becoming visceral: his pulse was escalating, his stomach groaning and he was perspiring in an air-con room now. Kim was taking too long (even though it had only been a minute, maximum two, and Keat was the one holding up the conversation actually). He was still looking for the light Kim might be holding out at her end of their chat tunnel.

"I bumped into Beth Neo"…"You know?" …"The author?" …

Did her dad just suffer a mild heart attack? There was no reason for Kim to suspect this. There was a reason though for her high-speed, furious and deft fingering to continue stressing her phone—to keep pace with her runaway thoughts in her bid to share this exciting news with her father.

"Inside the airport actually"…"Along the hallway"…

"I was walking out"…"She was going to her gate"…

"Such coincidence"…

"So fortunate, don't you think, dad?" Kim felt an immediate sense of release after sending her last text, completely oblivious that she had dropped a bombshell unwittingly on her helpless father just then.

At the other end, Keat was completely stunned as he read and reread every word of her texts. He did not know what to think really.

"Unbelievable! This cannot be real! *They don't know each other!*" Did he still believe his own gospel? Anyhow, he appeared not to get what his daughter had just said regarding Beth. Had he just been bombed out of his wits? Regardless, Keat's mind was all wound up, his chest tightened, and his heart was pounding quite hard in his ears by now.

"How long has it been?" Keat asked softly after a mindful while, moving pass his denial now as some other memories tethered him back to reality.

"Depends, ten, eleven maybe, her disappearance as reference point? But please, please don't hold me to this yea." Someone answered, trying to be helpful but clearly wanting no responsibility (or blame) of this at all.

Stumbling through his fogged-up brain, Keat desperately tried to unpack everything that his daughter had just dumped on him. Now, he was struggling to pull himself out of a mental quicksand of sorts, and pull himself together all at once.

"Hey Kimmy, tell u what"…Keat finally texted back seconds later but he felt like a lifetime had passed after he came around from his shell shock. For Kim, it felt like minutes but she had no idea of her dad's meltdown just.

"U get back home first"…"We chat again later"…

"Something urgent just cropped up"…"Ok?"

Now, Keat needed time away to properly take stock of another lifetime. Would anything be different, now that he knew what he just knew and what he had missed all along?

"Whatever happens, I'm not abandoning Kim ever. This much is clear." Keat whispered unconsciously but with a deep conviction. He was compos mentis also.

"That is the wisest thing he has determined so far," everyone cheered unanimously.

"Not to dull anyone's spirit…he still has to decide how honest he wants to be with his daughter. There's no free pass here." Someone-New emphasised to everyone consciously.

Kim was halfway home already by this time. Her father's last text genuinely puzzled her.

"Dad didn't sound like anything was happening when we started, then he became absent here and there, and now something so urgent all of a sudden!" Kim grumbled feeling a little peeved.

"I was just about to deliver the punchline!" Clearly, Keat's final request had dashed Kim's enthusiasm. Nonetheless, she acquiesced to her dad's request; she figured correctly that her dad was not in the right frame of mind to appreciate her punchline anyway.

What an anti-climax! The monotony of Kim's ride home further dampened her mood.

"Everything will be dead by the time she gets home; don't think it's possible to resurrect her interest again later on." Someone declared confidently.

"Well, let it be," Someone-Else shrugged with resignation, "don't blame the universe if he blows his chances to put things right when presented with the opportunities."

Everyone in the universe concurred unequivocally.

Woman without Men

A mellifluous tide
Smooths the sand below
The frizzy foam hides
Tiny crabs, in empty shallows

A feisty gust
Rustles the leaves asunder
Whistles as it thrusts
Halts suddenly, quiet surrender

A gibbous moon
Kisses the fleeting cloud
All crickets pause to swoon
The sentient stillness, now aloud

Lyrical spaces
Dot an inaudible prelude
Hypnotic, the music seduces
Wanting, the elusive solitude

A yogic
Meditates mindfully
Tunes in to the magic
Of his hushed breath only

Fades unto death
Dream's final stop
Hears then not the breath
Save the peace of silence, non-stop

"A poem, just like that. Nothing else." Beth paused to take a sip of hot camomile tea from the huge ceramic mug on the coffee table, her very cold hands cupping it for warmth. It was the same mug she had gifted Ming one Christmas while they were still together. She had devised a final visit to Ming's studio just days before their fateful rendezvous and while Ming was still away on a business trip. This was part of her meticulous escape plan to tie up the remaining loose ends.

"Ming won't miss this for a day or two. He may not even notice that it is missing," she surmised then. The mug was the only item she had reclaimed, all others were her own or gifts from Ming.

Beth was reading Ming's letter, curled up on a two-and-a-half seater sofa situated by the fireplace in the living room, her favourite spot during this time of the year. Snowfall started early this year, making the winter especially frigid and biting this time round. For now, the fully alive wood-burning fire felt warm and comforting. She had muffled herself with a thick, spruce-hued over-sized woollen shawl, complementing the emerald green merino wool pullover she was wearing, a Christmas present from Ming.

"Feels adequate for now." Beth whispered when she settled down on the sofa shortly after dinner. Just then, a car whizzed past her house, the sound of its wheels peeling off the wet road informed Beth that a gentle snowfall had started up outside already.

Fortunately, the heavens decided to take a break yesterday and today after dumping tonnes of snow on her neighbourhood over the whole of last week and the weekend just. This effectively choked off all traffic, trapping everyone indoors for the most part.

The local council was attentive to the situation and diligent with its duties. The snowploughs were out in force as soon it was safe and practical to do so. Workers were furiously labouring away a good part of yesterday to open up the town's organs and arteries, resuscitating everything back to life bit by bit. The sun was in and out of the fuzzy sky still laden with prefabricated snow, which together with the chilly air seemed to remind everyone of the capricious condition. Consequently, everyone remained swaddled up from head to toe throughout the day.

Nonetheless, people was out and about as the roads cleared—replenishing stuff, catching a chat with friends and neighbours, running to sweat their system again, or just walking their restless dogs. The shops were vigorously making hay while the sun shone. Healthcare and social workers went house visiting to ensure everyone was all right, especially the old and the feeble, as well as check on the solitary residents like Beth.

Most fortunately for Beth, her logistics company was able to deliver her package just as dusk was falling, which was getting earlier also as the winter wore on. Her heart pounded so hard the moment someone rang her doorbell, as if an electric bolt had shocked her suddenly.

"The agonising wait is over finally!" Someone let out a tremendous sigh of relief then. Beth could not recall the last time she was this excited and out of control while anticipating the arrival of a mere delivery package.

"But this is something special," Someone-Else cheered too.

Be patient, it's not going anywhere. Beth calmly informed herself after she had brought the package into the living room and placed it on the floor near the hearth of the fireplace, at the same time ensuring it was out of reach of playful sparks. After recovering from her initial excitement, Beth decided to open the package after dinner, instead of waiting a couple more days until Christmas, which was the time she would normally unpack the package.

The CD that Ming had pressed for Beth had been playing non-stop on her Meridian since she started preparing for dinner. She took the CD only, also on the same final visit and decided then that she would procure the audio player for herself after she had finally settled down at wherever she would settle down at finally.

When she realised that the specific model had gone out of production, she went hunting in specialist audio shops that also buy and sell vintage or pre-loved audio equipment and accessories.

Fortunately, she found an exact original while on a musical-drama-and-poetry vacation in London. She then got it refurbished by a master artisan there before she brought it home with her. At this stage of her life, she was determined to be good to herself, she wanted what she wanted and spared no expense to have it. The seemingly pristine Meridian now held pride of place above the mantle and fireplace, an impeccable addition to her living room indeed.

"What If" by Kate Winslet was spinning in the Meridian when Beth opened Ming's letter. At first, she read his poem silently. After some while, she read it again, a few more times, each time louder than before, and automatically with a voice increasingly more manly than womanly. Intuitively, she was mimicking Ming's baritone timbre however fuzzily her brain remembered it. She wanted to hear his words, the prose resonating in her inner ears as if concentrating all her senses at once might increase the likelihood of drawing out Ming's mind: his thoughts when he was composing the poem for her.

What is he like now? She wondered after quieting down.

After some time, Beth retrieved Ming's earlier letters from the coffee table to reread all of them slowly, and aloud. She became silent after that, and then listened intently as if wishing for an echo of his voice. Instead, she heard the same questions droning ever so softly in her head.

Why did he stop writing after 2014?

What made him write again?

What happened in the intervening years?

Is he well?

Is he resuming this letter routine from now on?

…and on and on and on.

Beth's emotions stirred again but she could not quite describe the exact experience of her inner life. Ineffable? Maybe Beth had come up against some chasm she simply could not cross also despite her attentiveness to the nuances of language.

In the still of the night, she felt the warm and comforting touch of the lively yet tamed fire. Her mind also saw the dependable fire reflected so beautifully in her own distant eyes, dancing away with abandonment while embracing her wanting heart with its raw energy.

"Woman without men, I'm fine for a while now. Do I really need any?" Beth asked softly. Her question held in limbo by Chris Martin's soulful voice flowing from the Meridian. Lingering quietly in the shadows was the gentle *'Everglow'* of a lifetime she had tried to lock away.

...

"But in the deep recesses of your innermost sanctum, there I reside still," an inner voice echoed poignantly after an indeterminate while—the very familiar sound of another lifetime.

YJ Chin

An Awesome Marvel

Faye was there early. Her hopeful anticipation at the prospect of seeing Sean again kept her awake the whole of last night. She touched up a little just to cover up her sleep-deprived eyes. It was a weekday and she had asked Sue last week to reschedule all her work commitments for the day.

As a contingency, in case Sean wants to do something else, she had thought then. After all, he could be whimsical at times though she could not imagine what that something else might be. It had been quite some while since they got together.

Faye had WhatsApped Sean two weeks ago to set up this date and was surprised with her success this time. Sean was spending more time between Texas and California now and had kept putting off her requests to meet up while he was back here.

Maybe he has run out of excuses finally, Faye supposed when Sean gave in to her persistent entreaty.

The impeccably dressed waiter led Faye to the table at a particular corner of the restaurant, which she had requested when she made the reservation. The table would afford them the privacy to talk things over. So many blanks had appeared since they stopped seeing each other. She wished very much for Sean to fill in as many of them as only he could. She hoped he would.

The corner table was Sean's favourite here: flanked by floor-to-ceiling glass windows that offered an unobstructed view of the surroundings while protecting them from the gusts outside and the hundred metres drop to the streets below. It was a familiar place. They were here a couple of times before. For lunches, and some dinners too.

"Would you like something to drink for a start? While you wait?" the well-mannered waiter asked, after he had settled Faye in at the table, and presented her with the drinks and lunch menus.

"A glass of the house red would be fine. Thank you," Faye replied. No need to waste energy on the drinks menu, she was already predisposed to his suggestion of a drink anyway. Something quick to unwind her mind and ease her anxiety. Faye felt a slight film of perspiration moistening her palms.

"Do you like this place?" Sean asked Faye after the restaurant manager had settled them in, and briefed them thoroughly on the day's lunch specials.

"Yes, very much. It's a lovely place," Faye replied with exhilaration then. Sean had chosen the location as a surprise for her birthday.

The view outside briefly held her breath as they approached the table then: the noonday sun had painted the sky with the classic sky-blue hue. A smattering of silver-lined clouds resembling fluffy white cotton wools held in place by invisible cords splashed across the otherwise clear sky. The slightly tinted windows shielded them from the glare outside. It was a beautiful day. Faraway, the expansive ocean-blue sea, sparsely dotted with dark-coloured dashes—ships stationary or crawling slothfully across the sea—rose to meet the sky at the distinct horizon. A magnificent composition of seascape art.

The thick glass windows cut out the sounds of the city a hundred metres below. One could sense the gusty howls of the wind beyond only when some sparrows flitted by, clearly challenged in their flight. The mood was surreally perfect.

Did Faye experience all of that? Or was that what she remembered? Did she touch-up the reverie with her imagination just a bit in order to heighten the allure of that moment, making it all the more extraordinary? She was being good to herself naturally; her heart needed a beautiful memory to keep her safe, and to give her hope.

Faye felt a familiar longing in her anguished heart as she recalled the first time Sean had brought her here. Today was also a beautiful day, and the view was all so familiar, albeit coloured by an aura of diffused bitter-sweetness. The music in the background was soft and gentle on her heart but heavy with foreboding altogether.

He should be here anytime now. Sean's a stickler for punctuality. She remembered this about him very well, which briefly reassured her with hope.

Sean would show up on time if he meant it to be but it was not to be. An unutterable pain would seep in to displace the hope in Faye's heart, insidiously as the minutes ticked away. He had skipped town already; she would come to realise this in the end. Then, the wine that had numbed her senses initially would become inadequate eventually.

Did Faye had any inkling regarding Sean's no-show that day? His repeated declines to meet were obvious cues. Maybe she perceived them. Most likely, she chose to ignore them. The mind looks at the world through the window of the heart sometimes, our emotions informing our beliefs and framing our vision.

There was no way to query Sean now. He did not even leave her any 'Goodbye' note. What Sean did leave with Faye, however, was a bunch of questions with no easy answers, if answers were forthcoming at all. And a closet full of memories.

Sometime later, Faye would replay these memories with an odd admixture of light-hearted fondness and mild melancholy. Despite the lack of closure and the perpetual puzzles, she would realise that her memory of the end (and its concomitant heartache) should not obscure her experience with Sean—it was the most enjoyable period of her life. He had made her happy and she had felt fully alive then. Six months might not be a long time but it was long enough for her to experience heaven on earth, and she had risked it with all her heart.

"Better to have loved and lost than never to have loved at all," Someone said in consolation but with a broken heart nonetheless.

Occasionally, doubts would arise regarding Sean's real motive for their coming together. Faye might have been his crutch during his time of grief (with Mei's passing). Their paths had surely crossed during his time of need. However, did she not show herself eager with her overtures to Sean? She was very willing to enter into the relationship despite her trying conversation with her mum. Faye knew what she was getting herself into and decided to do it anyway.

"I suppose this is not excusing Sean's responsibility, rather it's about being totally honest with herself and taking responsibility for her own actions as an adult. Agree?" Someone-New shared this rationale plainly.

"Think so, we do what we do with whom we love. This is just the way it is sometimes," Someone responded pensively.

"Regardless, Sean has been undeniably kind and attentive to her needs," Someone-New added further.

"Except towards the end when he cannot seem to find the words and courage to break off with her properly. He appears to have a problem with manning-up to things." Someone-Else pointed out, suspiciously trying to pin some blame on Sean still.

Strangely, these realisations came to her only when everything ended. Overall, they were good for each other while their relationship lasted. Such memories held Faye in abeyance sometimes. At the same time, she was conscious not to let the ending constrict her life or hem in her future. Without a doubt, such mindfulness was hard work for Faye.

"You have been fortunate most of your life. It is a great life so far. You just haven't been as lucky with love the past year. Foolish to let one setback eclipse the rest including what is to come, isn't it?" The inner voice counselled Faye.

Everyone nodded, clearly on her side.

The universe seemed to have conspired with the psychotherapist to induce an out-of-body experience in Faye. Detached from herself, she was able to see her situation dispassionately, wholly and clearly. The self-therapy had taken place at her home on a weekend.

"Faye is intelligent and determined after all. Moreover, she is still attractive, even at her age." Someone-New esteemed and everyone nodded in unison again, feeling more optimistic about Faye's future at the end of the impromptu session.

"Time for a nice hot soak and a good meal after." Faye smiled with a lightness in her heart, feeling mentally exhausted nonetheless.

"She can afford to be good to herself. She deserves nothing less." Someone gave voice to everyone's sentiment.

"She better!" At this, everyone applauded.

Meanwhile, Rachel Platten was energetically pounding on her 'Fight song', playing on the Bose system, hoping to etch its lyrics into Faye's subconscious as she made her way to the bathroom to run the tap for her bath.

The human brain is an awesome marvel: able to contain seeming contradictions and unbounded impulses in one's mind fully. Yet enable one to function effectively in a fluid reality, which has the potential to disrupt quotidian balance anytime.

"Marvellously doing all these altogether," everyone exclaimed with total admiration.

…

Unsurprisingly, questions about Sean and their split would build up in Faye's mind for a time. Fortunately, some would fade over slowly and others would fade out eventually. The need for answers too would become less pressing until the need became no more.

Over time, Faye's idea of Sean would lose its distinctiveness. No longer informed by real connections, her impressions of their time together would become more and more nostalgic as they blend in with all her past.

In time, a new hope would seep back in as Faye reclaimed control of her heart. She would feel safe to try her chance again as a new normal gained familiarity in her brain.

Lucky for Faye, her struggles and eventual triumphs would bring her to a better place ultimately.

Afterword

All the rights of creative works (music, books, movies, art, etc.) referenced or quoted in this book belong wholly to the respective original creators of those works and/or owners of the intellectual properties.

Concerning ideas, this novel borrows a fair bit from the works of Daniel Kahneman, a Nobel laureate. It seeks to bring to life the ideas and findings expounded in his bestselling book *"Thinking, Fast and Slow"*. The insights gleamed from his book and seminal work have shaped my thinking on human rationality, judgement and decision-making profoundly.

My debut novel is an attempt to share these and other ideas more widely, non-technically and in a generally accessible way—through the stories of people we may come across in our everyday lives, through their relationships and their inner struggles and triumphs.

It has been a joy for me to write this novel. I have learnt much from this interesting adventure. It is my sincere wish that you will find enjoyment reading it as well, and discover something new for yourself, perhaps about yourself too. Thank you for investing your time to do so. Please feel free to reach out to me at 7heta5ud0r5a@gmail.com to share your thoughts and feedback. I would love very much to hear from you.

Made in the USA
Monee, IL
15 November 2020

47781045R00184